06/30/2020

SWORD OF SHADOWS

SWORD OF SHADOWS

Jeri Westerson

This first world edition published 2019
in Great Britain and 2020 in the USA by
SEVERN HOUSE PUBLISHERS LTD of
Eardley House, 4 Uxbridge Street, London W8 7SY.
Trade paperback edition first published
in Great Britain and the USA 2020 by
SEVERN HOUSE PUBLISHERS LTD.

British Library Cataloguing in Publication Data
A CIP catalogue record for this title is available from the British Library.

ISBN-13: 978-0-7278-8921-8 (cased)
ISBN-13: 978-1-78029-675-3 (trade paper)
ISBN-13: 978-1-4483-0374-8 (e-book)

All Severn House titles are printed on acid-free paper.

Severn House Publishers support the Forest Stewardship Council™ [FSC™],
the leading international forest certification organisation.
All our titles that are printed on FSC certified paper carry the FSC logo.

MIX
Paper from
responsible sources
FSC
www.fsc.org   FSC® C013056

Typeset by Palimpsest Book Production Ltd.,
Falkirk, Stirlingshire, Scotland.
Printed and bound in Great Britain by
TJ International, Padstow, Cornwall.

*I dub thee Sir Craig, the knight of the
Long-Suffering Husband Guild, my patron.*

Who so pulleth this sword from this stone and anvil is the true-born King of all England.

Anonymous French poet, c. 1215

Glossary

Ale stake or **ale pole** – a rudimentary sign stuck horizontally into the wall above the door of an alehouse. If wine was served, a green garland was attached. In the medieval period, this gradually gave way to signs hanging from the stake to identify the particular house.

Anchorite – a religious who has shut themselves away in a cell built into the side of a church to live a religious life in prayer away from even those in a religious community. Their cell is called an anchorhold.

Corn – any number of cereal crops (wheat, barley, oats). Not to be confused with New World maize.

Chancel – the sanctuary of a church or chapel, where the altar is situated.

Coppice – method of woodland management, cutting down the shoots of certain species of trees to their stump for the thin sapling wood to be used for building houses, fences, and for fuel, but only cutting so much as to allow it to regrow to use again.

Demesne – usually refers to lands held by the crown or other noble, rather than a 'domain', which can describe any land.

Divide et impera – Latin for 'divide and conquer'.

Druidae, druw – the Latin and Cornish form for druids.

Emete – Middle English form of the Cornish word *emmet*, meaning ant or outsider (outsiders as annoying as ants, in other words).

Freestone – exposed bedrock, used for rough structures.

Gour – Cornish for husband.

Hackney – a riding horse.

Hærfest – Old English for 'autumn', pronounced 'harvest', a celebration of the autumnal equinox and the end of the harvest season, the beginning of autumn.

Marghek – Cornish for knight.

Mogh – Cornish for pigs, swine.

Palfrey – a riding horse with an even gait.

Petitio principii – from Aristotle, meaning, 'assume the conclusion', where a sixteenth-century translator rendered it 'begs the question', a phrase that professes the logical fallacy in which an argument assumes the very thing it's trying to prove.

Rood screen – a lattice or elaborate partition between the sanctuary where the altar is in a church, dividing the sanctuary from the choir and/or nave. It can be of simple wood, carved stone, or metal. Atop it was usually a crucifix, or rood, archaic for 'pole'.

Rouncey – an all-purpose horse used for riding as well as for carrying luggage.

Scapular – clerical garb worn over a cassock, open at the sides but covering front and back, like a long poncho.

Sowsnek – Cornish word for Saxon-born, in other words, an outsider. Similar in root to *sassanach* in Scottish and *saesneg* in Welsh.

Swyve – a medievalism for sexual intercourse.

Tintagel Castle – a castle in Cornwall, legendary birthplace of King Arthur. Pronunciation, tin-TAJ-el.

Treknow – a village in Cornwall near Tintagel. Pronunciation, tre-NO.

Wain – large open wagon for carrying heavy loads, usually drawn by draft horses or oxen.

Wattle – a way to build fences and house siding by weaving sapling boughs together. See also *coppice* above.

ONE

T all, with flaming ginger hair and beard, Jack Tucker slouched against the wall with a view of the room, much as Crispin Guest had taught him to do. He had a jug in front of him and a beaker in his face, quaffing a long gulp of ale . . . also as Crispin had taught him. His features were hangdog, no doubt partly due to the ale that had dragged down the dark circles under his eyes, and partly from his current troubles.

Walking up to the table, Crispin stood over him till the man noticed.

Jack lowered the cup, flicked a glance at Crispin, and filled the cup again. 'I suppose she sent you,' he grumbled.

He kicked at Jack's long legs. The man pulled them in so that Crispin could sit opposite him. 'I am not in the habit of doing the bidding of my own servants.'

Jack had the grace to look abashed and sat up straighter. He set the cup down and stared at his lap. 'I'm sorry, master.'

'As well you should be. Should I have to go traipsing all over London to find my own apprentice when he is wanted?'

'Oh. I *am* sorry, sir.' He moved to rise, but Crispin leaned over and shoved him back down. He picked up Jack's cup and took it for himself, sipping the fragrant beer.

'It isn't urgent,' he said, eyeing his apprentice. Jack slumped again in his seat, looking as forlorn as any mummer in a play. 'God's blood, man. It isn't the end of the world. Every man has arguments with his wife.'

'But she never seemed so angry before.' He turned anxiously toward Crispin and beseeched with his hands. 'She threw a spoon at me!'

'I've thrown worse at you.'

'It's not the same thing, sir.'

Crispin took a deep breath. Yes, she had seemed enraged. Red in the face. But she always seemed overly emotional when she was with child . . . which she was, for the fourth time running.

He shook his head at himself. Imagine *him*, dealing with the intimacies of his own servants. Well, it was another day indeed. There had been a time when his steward took care of such squabbles and Crispin would never hear about them. The steward would have slit his own throat rather than let his lord be troubled by such trivialities. But since Crispin was no longer a lord, he had to take it upon himself to settle it on his own. After all, their lodgings were far too small for any bickering to go on. He tried to appease with, 'You know how she gets when she's . . .' But was that too personal an observation?

Crispin didn't have to finish his thought out loud since Jack was nodding. 'I know, sir. And she's always with child, it seems. But this time seemed different. She was right angry with me for disagreeing with her. And she never got that angry before.'

'I think, perhaps, it was because of the nature of the argument.' Jack looked up with a puzzled expression. Crispin sighed. 'You hurt her feelings. Here she thought she was making something nice for you. And you laughed instead.'

'I wasn't laughing *at* it, sir! I was amused that she *would* make a sleeping cap for me. Isn't that for someone more like . . . well, *you*?'

'That isn't the point, is it? She took the time and trouble.'

'I got you in the middle of it. I should be beaten for it.'

'Yes, you should. So what are you going to do about it, Tucker?'

Jack slowly shook his head. 'She can't do this to you. Sending the master out of his own house! I'm going to go right home and do what I should have done in the first place.' He stood. 'I'll grovel.'

Crispin set the cup down and rose, slapping the man on the back. 'That's the spirit. But isn't there something we should be doing first?'

'What, sir?'

'Your dagger.'

Jack looked down forlornly at the dagger and took it from the sheath. There was only half a blade and Jack shook his head at it. 'I don't know how it happened, sir.'

'That will never do, Jack. Let's go.'

'Where, sir?'

'To a swordsmith, of course. I can't have my apprentice possess a faulty blade. Who'd be there to defend me should I get into a rough situation? We're getting you a new one.'

'Oh, sir, I don't deserve one . . .'

'God's blood, Tucker, I will clout you if you make one more remark.'

Jack clamped his lips shut and followed Crispin out to the street. They headed up to the Shambles and turned north near Greyfriars to the many shops of smiths. They came to a shop with swords, knives, and every form of dagger to be had, with plain scabbards as well as elaborately designed leather sheaths hanging from the rafters.

An apprentice kept the forge glowing in the background, but near the window the smith himself was polishing a blade with an oiled cloth. He looked up when Crispin approached. 'Good sir,' he said, putting down the dagger. His gaze slid to the sword at Crispin's hip before that glance climbed to his eyes.

'My apprentice is in need of a new dagger. Show him your blade, Jack.'

Jack pulled the knife and, with a miserable expression, showed it to the man.

'Oh, that's a shame,' said the swordsmith. 'Not a bad blade. Not one of mine, was it?'

'I don't think so, sir,' said Jack, placing it on the man's work-table. 'I got it long ago.'

'It's clear you need another. One with a hilt that fits your hand. You must have got that one long ago indeed, for your hands are much bigger now.' He rose and looked at his many wares. 'Now, I could try to fix that blade, but as I said, the hilt . . . well. I'd have to fabricate so much of it, you might as well get a new one.'

With a new price, thought Crispin, mentally counting the coins he had brought with him. But he was prepared to pay a decent fee for it, more than he would have for an ordinary servant.

The man lectured Jack about this blade or that one. Crispin wandered away, their voices becoming noise in the background as he admired the swords and their elaborately designed hilts. He picked one up, hefted the weapon, and examined the delicate wirework of the hilt and the engraving in the crossguard . . . when he noticed a man in the shop looking at him. He offered the man a nod, and turned away, laying the sword aside. But when he picked up another sword, the man had moved closer and was pointedly staring at him.

'Do I know you, sir?' asked Crispin.

'No. But I think I know who you are. You're Crispin Guest, if I am not mistaken.'

Crispin turned back to examining the blade. 'You are correct.' He offered nothing more.

The man was persistent and drew even closer, almost too close. 'You were once a knight but you plotted against King Richard and were charged with treason.'

Crispin's shoulders stiffened. Why did people insist on spooning him his own history? Did they think he had forgotten it? He evened his shoulders and kept his back to the man. 'You know me, then.'

'But now you find things, don't you? They call you the Tracker.'

'For a price, good sir.'

'Oh yes. Of course.' His voice took on an eager quality.

Crispin set the blade down and turned. 'And . . . do you wish to hire me to find something for you?'

'Why yes! It's perfect. It's divine intervention! For I hadn't thought of you before. But it is indeed the Lord blessing my enterprise. For here you are!'

Crispin refrained from rolling his eyes. 'Yes, here I am. Just what is it you would have me find?'

The man suddenly glanced around. 'Not here. Meet me on Trinity, at the Harper. Within the hour!' And then he was gone from the shop, striding quickly down the street.

Crispin watched him go and wondered. Well, coin is coin.

Jack chose a serviceable dagger, and Crispin paid for it. Jack seemed particularly humbled, which was a feat indeed for so tall a man. 'Master, you should have had that swordsmith grind me old one down. That would have done me well.'

'But not me. I have a reputation to uphold. I can't have my apprentice walking about London with half a blade, sharpened or no.'

They had been walking for a bit and passed their lodgings on the Shambles. 'Er . . . Master Crispin, where are we going?'

'I have a possible client. We're to meet him at an alehouse.'

'Who, sir?'

'I haven't the faintest idea. But it seems to have been divine providence that has put me in his path.'

'Oh. Another of those.'

'Yes. It's best to see what he has to say and get it over with. It might mean a bit of coin. And we'll need it to recover what we spent today.'

'You should take it from me own pay, sir. It was my fault I broke the blade.'

'Nonsense.'

'But sir—'

Crispin halted and faced the man. 'Jack, when will you learn to keep your own counsel. It is done and finished. I am satisfied. Should that fact not satisfy *you*?'

Morose again, Jack lowered his face. 'Aye, sir.'

He spoke no more as they wended their way through the busy streets of London. Late summer was giving way to autumn with a chill wind whipping through the narrow passages of tall shops and houses. The streets were muddy again and foul with the stench of droppings mingled with the mud. He was grateful to move along to the streets with cobbled-stone paving, stamping the mud from his boots, and make his way to the ale stake he saw jutting from the truss ahead. Hanging from it was a sign carved in the shape of a harp.

He led Jack inside and cast about the smoky interior, looking for the man from the swordsmith's shop. When he glanced to his left, the man was waving long-armed at him from the end of a rectangular table.

Crispin reached him and the man swept his hand forward, offering Crispin a seat across from him. They both sat and the man pushed another cup toward him, pouring ale within it.

'And this must be your man, Jack Tucker. I've heard of him, too. Greetings, Master Tucker.'

Jack nodded his greeting, appearing somewhat pleased that someone had acknowledged his fame as well.

Crispin took the cup, drank, and then set it down, resting his arms on the table. 'And you are . . .?'

'Forgive me! I am Carantok Teague.'

'I thought I detected a bit of an accent. Cornish, are you?'

'Yes, indeed. Tell me, Master Guest, are you as skilled as they say? I mean, I have heard some courageous tales of you.'

'You can be certain,' said Jack before Crispin could speak, 'that my master is all you have heard and more. Never has there been a more valiant and trusted man as Crispin Guest. He's like them Knights of the Round Table.'

Crispin cleared his throat. 'No need to spin yarns, Jack. I am an honest man, sir, and do my set task with diligence. I earn my coin well. Anyone in London can vouchsafe for me.'

Teague beamed at Jack. 'I am heartily glad to hear it, Master Tucker. It's strange you should say . . .' He looked around and crouched over the table, leaning in. Jack and Crispin leaned in to match him. 'Master Tucker speaks of Round Table Knights, and indeed, my quest is very likened to those knights of old.' He chuckled. 'Very likened. Tell me, Master Guest, what do you know of King Arthur, his knights . . . and Merlin?'

'As much as any man. Arthur was a king who slew Saxons. Merlin was a sorcerer. His knights did valorous deeds, including search for the Holy Grail.' He glanced surreptitiously at Jack who returned his knowing look. After all, Crispin himself had found the Grail long ago. *Might* have.

'Ah, but you left out something most important,' said Teague with a gleam in his eyes. 'What of the sword?'

'Excalibur? It was said to be a most remarkable weapon.'

'None could pull it from the stone and anvil that Merlin had enchanted. But Arthur did it on Christmas Eve and was hailed as king.'

'Yes, we all know the story.'

'It isn't just a story, Master Guest.'

'No. It is the ancient history of Britain.'

'And a marvelous history it is! Can you imagine, Master Guest, what such a sword would be worth?'

'A great deal. If it could be proved to be Arthur's sword. But was it not also told that the sword – perhaps even a different one – was given to Arthur by the Lady of the Lake?'

'Naturally such tales become embellished with the telling, and by whom. You speak of other poets, do you not?'

'I recall Geoffrey of Monmouth whose history I was taught. Robert de Boron, Chrétien de Troyes—'

'All valuable insights, to be sure. And I have studied them too. Very carefully. But what would you say if I were to tell you that I might know where Excalibur is?'

Crispin raised a brow and sat back. 'I should . . . question the notion.'

'Oh? But are you not a man into whose hands falls many a . . .' He looked around and leaned even closer. 'Into whose hands fall objects of much veneration?' he said in a whisper.

That prickle at the back of his neck was familiar and unwelcome. It meant he was about to embark on yet another dangerous venture that involved something akin to a relic, and he never liked the idea.

Snatching a glance at Jack's face, he saw that he had worked out the same notion, and his eyes had enlarged with worry.

Crispin sat forward and settled his arms on the table again. 'Are you saying you want me to help you find Excalibur?'

'Yes! And an amazing adventure it shall be!'

Crispin stood. Jack belatedly joined him. 'Master Teague, I have no doubt that you feel your quest is sound and blessed by God, but as you say, I have been tasked with searching for relics and venerated objects many times. It does not settle well with me. Good day.'

He turned to go when he heard the sound of a money pouch and its coins clank on the table. He couldn't resist looking back.

Gold coins. Far more than he had seen in many a day.

Teague looked up with a sly smile. 'Yes, Master Guest. This is your part of the payment. There is the sum of sixty pounds here. Enough to buy a . . . a . . . warhorse if you should desire one.'

Jack grabbed his arm and squeezed, for he did not look to be able to speak.

Indeed, it took Crispin's breath away as well. With that sum they could . . . they could do very well for a long time.

Crispin licked his lips and found his way back to his stool. He slowly sat. 'I will do nothing illegal or immoral, sir. If you pay me this sum, I will do as asked, but only within the realm of God's – and the king's – laws.'

'On my oath, Master Guest, I would never ask it of you. For you may have rightly surmised, no man with any ill intent could get hold of Excalibur. The sword would never allow it.'

'Then . . . what would you want of me?'

'I will pay you this prize *after* we have retrieved the sword. And it will take a long journey to get to it. I require your expertise with puzzles and for your protection, for I have heard that you have a facility with weapons.'

It was as if the veil had fallen from his eyes. Crispin raised his head and looked away from the golden coins. 'I see. *After* my task is done. You only trust me so much.'

'It is a great deal of money, after all, Master Guest.'

Crispin nodded. 'That it is. But I cannot undertake such a task without payment of a surety ahead of time.'

The man reached in the pouch before them and grabbed a handful of gold and silver coins, offering them to Crispin. Staring at it, Crispin finally nodded toward Jack, who scooped them up and spilled them into his money pouch.

'Thank you,' said Crispin mildly, though inside he was as thrilled as Jack. 'Where will we have to travel?'

'Cornwall. And we must go immediately.'

'But sir, the weather. Autumn is nearly upon us. Would it not be better to wait for the spring?'

'We cannot wait. It is now, with you and your man, or I must find another.'

Crispin took a deep breath. He didn't need to glance at Jack. He could feel the lad vibrating with tension beside him. 'I should never forgive myself for giving up such a sum. I have a responsibility to my household, after all. And so, Master Teague, you have got yourself the services of the Tracker.'

TWO

I t seemed so rushed, so immediate. They went home to pack and for Jack to make up with his wife. It took only mere moments when he told her he'd be gone perhaps a month. They kissed for a long time with tearful goodbyes. Jack gathered his children and embraced them, kissing first Little Crispin, the oldest at four, and then Helen, nearly two, and then the baby in Isabel's arms, Gilbert. He kissed Isabel again and she clung to him like a vine.

After giving Isabel some of the coins, Crispin made for the door and stood just outside it, having given his farewells to the children who doted on him. He felt uncomfortably like the squire, waiting with the baggage as the knight bade farewell to his ladylove.

Teague bought horses and a cart at the stable down the lane, and with their baggage secured in the cart, and with Crispin and Jack astride their own mounts, they set out along Fleet Street out of London and the long trek to Cornwall.

Crispin rode an elegant chestnut palfrey named Tobias. He seemed to be a good-natured mount, and Crispin couldn't help but pat his sleek neck to encourage him on his way.

Jack's was a black hackney named Sebastian, that Tucker insisted on calling Seb, as if they were old friends.

'How long d'you reckon it will take us, master?' asked Jack.

Crispin angled his head to glance at the sky. 'Ten, perhaps twelve days, depending on the weather.'

Jack whistled.

'Yes,' said Teague. 'It is some eighty-five leagues away. But fear not. We will pass through many a town and village. We will have dry quarters to sleep in, and rest for the horses.'

'You have said very little, sir,' Crispin began, wrapping the reins around his left hand, 'why you are so certain that the . . . the object you seek is there in Cornwall.'

'Oh, but it is! The stories, Master Guest, are plentiful. And I have already discovered . . . well. Once we reach our first inn, I will tell you more.'

Crispin scanned the man's face – placid, pleased even – and reasoned he would extract no more from him. Either it *was* madness or he truly *did* know something. At any rate, Crispin was glad he had demanded a portion of his payment. If it turned out the man *were* mad, he and Jack could make a hasty exit with coin for their trouble. Though – he looked back at the walls of London receding behind him – once he had offered his services, he hated to refuse to do the job.

Teague did not offer more about the sword, but he did speak freely of this and that, stories of journeys he had taken before, ribald tales that he peppered with prayers of forgiveness to the Almighty, and other trifles. He seemed to be a merry man and often given to laughing furiously at his own jokes, even in the midst of telling them. Crispin could tell Jack was charmed, and he had to admit, he was, too.

After some miles far outside of London, they stopped to rest and eat the bread and pasties Teague had brought. The man allowed the cart horse to graze along the verges, and Jack tended to the two saddle horses.

Crispin swallowed the cold meat pie and wiped his lips. 'Will you not explain yourself further now, Master Teague? Is it not better to speak when we are alone, rather than in a full inn?'

'Perhaps you are right.' Teague rose and went to the cart, pulling something from one of his bags. He sat down next to Crispin on a rock and showed him. It looked to be a folded parchment. 'This, Master Guest. This is as precious and as dear to me as my own life, and I guard it as such. It is a map of the wonders of Arthur.' He slowly opened it. A shadow fell over it, but it was only Jack, peering over their shoulders. Teague eagerly laid it flat on his thighs, stroking the old, dirtied parchment with his hands. 'Do you see, Master Guest? Look here.'

He pointed to a spot. The map – if map it was – seemed crudely drawn, but Crispin surmised that it must be of Tintagel. There were certain features marked, with Latin words near each landmark, some as simple as 'Armor' and 'the Staff'. But Crispin couldn't make much sense of it.

'This is what you are going by? For this very long journey?'

Teague winked and placed a finger alongside his nose. 'Only one portion, Master Guest. But with my other parchments I have put together a bit of a puzzle. And I shall surely – with your help, of course – decipher the whole of it. For I have already unearthed finds from King Arthur's knights. I have them in my cart and I shall show you anon. But I am slowly learning more.'

'But . . . what makes you think the sword is at Tintagel? Arthur was born in the castle, but there are no tales of Excalibur being left there.'

The Cornishman smiled. 'I shall show you anon.'

Jack handed Crispin a wineskin and he tipped it up and drank. Glancing into the distance he thought the sky was darker ahead, the direction they planned to travel. 'I do not like the look of that sky, Master Teague. I think the horses have rested enough. It would do them better to find an inn for the night.'

'Indeed, Master Guest. Let us ride.'

Onward they went, and as they rounded a bend in the road, the sky opened up. Crispin pulled his mantle tight about his throat, pulled his hood down over his brow, and rocked with the horse as the cold rain fell.

Late in the afternoon they reached a town and Teague led them to an inn. Wet and tired, the three men tromped into the inn hall to the fire and pulled off their wet things. Teague secured them a room that they would share with others, and they settled at a table near the fire to eat the bean and rabbit stew the innkeeper offered them.

It was there that Teague pulled another folded parchment from his chemise and unfolded it on the table. It looked to be a Latin text, along with illustrations of knights and a king Crispin took to be Arthur. Teague placed his hand on it. 'Here, Master Guest, is the writing that told me to find *what* I have *where* I have. And in it, it talks of Excalibur.'

'And where did you find such a marvel?'

He folded it quickly and secured it inside his shirt again, folding his cote-hardie over it. 'I have traveled much, Master Guest. Encountered many an interesting man with a tale to tell. Not all of them yield me treasure, but this one . . . well.' He patted his chest where it lay. 'This one has.'

'Treasure?' He frowned. 'Master Teague, you aren't a treasure hunter, are you? You know such practices are illegal.'

The naturally ebullient man seemed to shrink. With lowered head he spoke softly. 'Master Guest, I will not lie to you—'

'It's best that you don't.'

Teague raised his face. 'Yes, I see you are not a man to trifle with. And so I will confess that . . . yes, I am a treasure hunter.'

Crispin threw down the bread in his hand and jolted to his feet. 'God's blood, man! I told you I will not be party to illegal activity! And now you have cajoled me out in the wilderness to do that very thing.'

'Hold, Master Guest. You must listen to me. For I have made arrangements with the crown and do my searching on its behalf.' He held his palm out toward Crispin and gingerly withdrew a folded parchment from his pouch. 'See here. Look for yourself.' He held out the parchment bundle. It was festooned with dangling ribbons of leather and wax seals.

Crispin snatched it unapologetically, unfolded it, and read. In a carefully penned hand from an accomplished scribe, Crispin read the decree: that Carantok Teague, gentleman of Cornwall, whose lands encompassed at least one hundred acres, was given permission from the crown to find such diverse treasures across the kingdom as could be found but not by digging in graves or in churches or in barrows of ancient origin with their superstitious intent. All gold was forfeit to the crown. Silver and other such objects could be retained by the said Carantok Teague, gentleman, unless otherwise specified by the crown. The signature was that of King Edward III, King Richard's grandfather. It was dated in 1377, the last year of Edward's reign.

Crispin lowered the parchment. 'How is this possible?'

Jack tugged it from Crispin's loosened fingers and slowly read for himself.

'It is a long story, Master Guest.'

Crispin swept his arm across the inn, but meant to encompass beyond the modest inn and across the barren countryside, whose only features were stacked stone walls, a few gathering clutches of trees, a curving road, and sheep. 'We have the time.'

Teague nodded. 'Yes.' He rose, walking slowly toward the hearth. 'I have no trade, no talent, it seems. Oh, the land keeps my manor well, my servants fed, the taxes paid. At one time I trained for the law, but . . . Four walls, a darkened room, and the study of the law did not suit me. Instead, I traveled. To the Holy Land, to France, to various pilgrimages in England, and what a vast and varied land this is, our island. I found, quite by accident, a trove in the Holy Land. I sold those goods to fund my further travels. I found, since I was a child, that I did have a talent after all, for finding these places where treasure – well, some might say refuse – was discarded. Rusty old weapons and shields. Broken pots. They had no value, but *I* found them interesting. They seemed to tell a story, like those tales of old, of Roman legions and Greek warriors. I wish I knew the tales they told. I shall never know. But I found I got the itch, Master Guest. I have heard the same of you. You are fond of the philosopher Aristotle, are you not?'

Despite the intriguing explanation, Crispin bristled. 'We are not talking of me.'

'Of course,' he said, trying to appease, 'but what if *you* were to uncover something ancient that belonged to your philosopher? Perhaps something as simple as a spoon. Such a thing may not be of great value, but it might mean a great deal to you. Do you see the sort of excitement such finds engendered in me?'

The spark of a thought ignited within him, and Crispin *did* dare to imagine finding such a thing. It was akin to seeing the relic of a saint, for such an object would bring him all the closer to the man that he, in many ways, venerated.

He might have spent a long moment dreaming of such a thing . . . before he abruptly brought himself to the present. 'Never mind about me,' he sputtered, embarrassed. 'How did you come to your agreement with the king?'

'Well, after some years of my travels, when I returned to England, I found some very interesting objects that seemed to tell tales of ancient Saxon kings. I took myself immediately to court and was received by King Edward himself.' He reached into a sack lying at his feet and withdrew a bundle wrapped in canvas. Carefully, he unwrapped it. It was a helm, but of a different design than Crispin knew. It was made of a conical piece that only covered the head with a nasal that protected the nose. It was dented and rusted, nothing a king would want. 'I presented him with a helm such as this . . . as well as the gold coins I found. He took the gold readily, and when I proposed to him that I could find more, he gave me this charter. I was an eager young man then. I daresay, Master Guest, we are something of the same age.'

Crispin flicked a glance at the man, a little pudgy of face and form, but still fit enough to clamber over his cart and around ancient sites.

'At any rate,' Teague went on, 'with this charter . . . and the promise that I could keep a portion that I found to sustain my travels, I have made a good living. I keep my doings . . . restrained.'

Frowning, Crispin paced before the hearth, thinking.

'And what do you do with the treasure you retain?'

'Why . . . I sell them. And gain treasure for myself. But there are some pieces that I keep simply for their miraculous qualities of design. I will show you once we are on the road again in the morning. As I said, Master Guest, I have no trade or talent. Only in the finding of lost things.' He chuckled. 'Much like you.'

'I do not trek across the whole of England, sir. I have plenty of clients in London. And I do not break the law.'

'So you do. London is a crossroads for the Continent. All manner of folk traverse there. I should think it would be rife with treasure, but alas. It is hard to come by when it might sit under the house of a weaver or under a convent. I shouldn't like to try to tread softly around all the eyes in London. And . . .' He raised the charter that Jack returned to him. 'As you see, I am *not* breaking the law.'

'That charter is under King Edward. Why not renew it under King Richard all this time?'

'Well, er . . . King Richard is . . . dear me. He is not King Edward, I fear. I should prefer to ask forgiveness than permission.'

'Richard is not likely to offer forgiveness when his coffers are at stake.'

But the idea that this man might be lawfully or unlawfully cheating Richard out of funds tickled Crispin's sensibility.

'Very well, Master Teague. Gold goes to the king. The rest is yours.'

Teague sighed. 'I'm glad you agree, Master Guest. It is a most
fascinating vocation. I'm certain you will find it so as well.'

I'm sure I will, he thought, sitting again and drinking from his
cup.

'One must have help sometimes,' said Teague. 'This time, it's
you.' He drank, eyes dancing with light over his cup.

'I must admit, I am intrigued,' said Crispin, thinking it over. 'I
do find history interesting and who wouldn't like to discover
treasure?'

'You said you were good at finding treasure as a child,' said Jack,
taking a quick gulp of ale as he turned the rusted helm on the table
before them. 'How did you get started in this hunting?'

'It started as you say when I was a child, Master Tucker, at my
father's own estate – mine now, of course. We have standing stones
down in the meadow but within sight of the manor house. As a
child, I was always intrigued by them, but my mother warned me
to keep away. She said they were put there by the Devil. The local
folk said the faeries put them there. But I have since learned that
it was likely the ancient *druw*, as my people call them. You, Master
Guest, might know them as the *druidae* as Julius Caesar himself
called them. And there I found my first bits of treasure; bracelets
and rings of gold made in a strange style.'

'Eh?' said Jack. He looked to Crispin. 'What is that, master?
The . . . droo?'

'The *druidae*,' said Crispin, fingering his cup, 'were an ancient
people of Gaul and Britain. They were pagan priests and teachers.
But it was also said that they were sorcerers and soothsayers. Merlin
was said to be one of the *druidae*.'

'God blind me,' muttered Jack. 'Pagans?'

'Yes,' said Teague eagerly, taking a quaff from his cup. 'They
were said to perform human sacrifices. They built huge mannikins
of wicker and put poor souls inside and lit them up. So it is said
in Caesar's writings.'

Jack put his hand to his mouth. 'God's blood!'

'When Christianity came to Britain,' said Crispin, 'they were
suppressed and finally either converted or eradicated.'

'Oh, but Master Guest,' said Teague with a merry tone, 'it is said
that they still thrive in the wilder places. Some of my own people
claim to have seen bonfires deep in the woods. They believe that
the *druidae* still do their rituals there, perhaps with the faery folk,

for it is said that the *druw* are close to magic as no modern man could be.'

Jack flicked a worried glance toward Crispin. Crispin chuckled. 'Don't take Master Teague's tales too much to heart, Jack. People see all manner of odd things in the woods and they are nothing.'

'But master, remember when we were near them faery hills nigh Hailles? It made us feel all queer when we saw them. And we heard music from the faery folk.'

Crispin shook his head. 'I think you are misremembering that, Jack.' Jack looked to be about to naysay him when Crispin stood. 'I think it time we get to our beds. We should arise early.'

'I agree, Master Guest.' Teague rose and Jack reluctantly followed.

They shared a room with two other men, one of whom was already snoring on his cot. Jack banked the fire and crawled into his narrow bed while Crispin and Teague shared the larger one.

When morning broke with dull sunshine through the clouds, they took a meal, bought provisions, readied the horses, and began on the road again.

It was slow going for days and days. Each night they stopped in a new village or town, rested the horses and themselves, and trudged on again at daybreak. On the twelfth day, it was raining when they finally reached the village of Treknow, a small outpost a few miles from the churning sea. The cart moved sluggishly through the mud and Jack and Crispin were soaked to their skin under their mantles and hoods.

The village was a scrappy collection of scattered houses and shops down two rows that wove along several crooked lanes, fields, a stone church, and the vestiges of a manor in the distance. Teague pointed out the hill where slate was quarried. 'Has done for centuries,' he said. And as Crispin watched, there came a wain full of slate pulled by several oxen. The large beasts in their yoke didn't seem to mind the downpour as they clopped along the stony road and crushed the mud beneath large hoofs.

There was another wagon coming down the road from the other direction. From the colorfully painted sides it looked to be a pageant wagon with traveling players. Even as soggy as he was, Jack perked up on his saddle.

'Master, do you suppose they are coming to this village to stay?'

Crispin blinked raindrops from his lashes. 'If they are, I pray that the weather is more amenable to them.'

'I should like to see them. I always like the plays the guilds put up in London.'

'Let us hope so. It should be interesting to see what these travelers perform.'

At the mid of the village, they finally came to an inn, a robust structure of stone, with a sturdy story above the ground floor. Teague pulled his wagon into the large innyard and Crispin and Jack got their horses quickly into the stable, giving a coin to the stableman who took charge of the beasts. 'Give them extra feed,' said Crispin. 'They've traveled hard.'

The three men hurried in out of the rain, just as the pageant wagon pulled into the innyard. Crispin had to admit to himself that he was just as excited as Jack at the prospect of the players performing. It would be a welcome diversion from the drudgery of the everyday.

Teague secured them a room and, because the inn was mostly vacant, they had it to themselves. They stripped off their cloaks and unbuttoned their damp cote-hardies – draping them before the smoky fire in their room – and moved downstairs to sit before the fire in the main hall, just as the players entered.

They, too, were soaked to the bone, and one by one, they unbuttoned cloaks and mantles. There were a few women traveling with them who looked to be musicians. Crispin eyed one shapely female as she took off her sodden mantle and cast it to a bench. It wasn't until she turned around that he let out a gasp.

'What is it, master?' said Jack, face full of concern. When Crispin didn't answer, he glanced toward the players with his own, 'God blind me!' on his lips.

Auburn hair, blue eyes . . . Crispin immediately recognized the clever burglar and swindler Kat Pyke.

THREE

C rispin rose, kicking back his stool.

'Master!' hissed Jack, tugging on his sleeve.

Crispin took the warning and slowly lowered himself to the seat. Jack pushed a horn cup of ale toward him and Crispin unconsciously picked it up and drank.

He had not seen her in over four years. She had been involved in murder and theft and had unscrupulously used her obvious beguilements to influence men to break the law for her, even murder, though she had claimed that had not been her intention. Yet Crispin, knowing all this, had succumbed to her charms anyway. He remembered her soft caresses, her intense kisses, and the wildness of her lovemaking. And yet, the moment she left him for good, he knew her unrepentance would lead her into still more trouble.

'Don't think about it, sir,' muttered Jack under his breath.

The man was right. But he couldn't help staring. And in his heart, he hoped she'd look his way . . .

And then she did.

Her eyes held no recognition in them, scanning briefly over him to skim the rest of the room.

He sat back and gulped his ale and grumbled to himself. So much for that. She didn't even remember him. And he had thought . . . Bah! What did it matter what he thought? Until Jack spoke up. 'She don't seem to remember you, Master Crispin.'

'I can see that, Tucker.'

'Oh.' Jack hunkered over his beaker and glanced at her over his shoulder. 'It don't matter, master. You don't want to get mixed up with her again.'

When would the lad know when to shut it? 'We have our own task to contend with,' he said brusquely, hoping that would be the end of it.

Jack drank quietly with him, until Crispin rose and took himself outside to the privy. He shivered, having left his cote-hardie back in their room, but he hiked up his chemise to do his business when a shadow came through behind him. Suddenly, arms encircled him and a distinctly feminine form clung to his back. He turned and was about to object when lips covered his. He pushed and dislodged the interloper.

'Crispin,' said the familiar voice. 'Is that any way to greet an old friend?'

'Kat,' he breathed, exasperated. 'When you saw me in the inn's hall, I thought you did not recognize me.'

'What was I to do? Wave my arm about and shout your name? Don't be absurd.' She hitched up her skirts and sat on the hole next to his. 'Truly, Crispin. Sometimes you can be as puzzling as the fools I swindle.'

He glared at her.

'Mind your aim,' she said calmly, and he did, finishing quickly and securing his braes again.

She finished and shook her skirts back into place. 'Come. Let us leave this place. It stinks.'

She took his hand, trotted around the corner of the privy, and pushed him up against the wall. 'That's better.' She hauled him in by his shirt and kissed him again.

He tore away, fastening a harsh glare on her. 'Kat!'

'Crispin! Why do you resist? You didn't before.'

'That was years ago.'

'Oh.' She drew back, putting a hand to her hip. 'And you think of me no more?'

He shuffled, but paused too long.

'You *have* thought of me!'

His cheeks burned and he turned away. 'It's not that. But it has been some years.'

'And now here I am. And here *you* are. What *are* you doing here, Master Guest?'

'Business. My own.'

'Come now. What sort of business? Has it to do with that man I saw you with?'

'Yes. And I see you have found your calling. A troupe of players, masking who you truly are.'

She chuckled. 'Alas. I only play music.'

'Music? I didn't know you played.'

'I didn't. But I learned.'

'You always seem to learn quickly.'

'A woman in my position must. And so I play. I hope you come to watch us. We'll be doing the story of King Arthur.'

'How apt. I would be pleased for the diversion.'

'The play . . . or me?' She sidled closer. 'I hope we can find some place to be alone,' she said, edging still closer, laying a hand to his chest.

He glanced down at it, at the pale hand on his linen shirt. Which was creamier? 'We'll see,' he said mildly. He hoped she hadn't detected his heart skip a beat.

'Oi, Master Crispin! Where did you . . . oh.'

She smiled at his apprentice. 'Jack Tucker? Look at you. What a handsome young man you've become.'

He pulled uncomfortably at his collar. 'Demoiselle.'

She looked from Jack to Crispin. 'Well. We all have places to be. I shall see you anon, Crispin.' She gave him a beguiling smile and flounced back into the inn.

'So she did remember you.'

Crispin pulled at his shirt, straightening it. 'Yes. She simply did not want to appear obvious.'

'I need not remind you that—'

'No,' he said curtly, cutting him off. 'You need not.' He pushed past Tucker to find Teague back at the inn. The sooner this business was over with, the better.

It wasn't long till they all retreated to their room to settle down for the night. And though Crispin was tired, he could not find rest.

In the dark of the night, he rose, slipped on his smoky coat, leaving it unbuttoned, and crept down the stairs to sit in the main hall.

There were servants and others lying near the fire on the floor or on stiff cots, the only light in the room from the glowing coals in the hearth.

He made his way quietly away from the others, and brooded in the corner, just close enough to reap the warmth from the stony fireplace. He hugged his coat about him and couldn't help but let the varied parade of thoughts tramp through his mind: this venture to Cornwall in which he had no hopes of succeeding; the unexpected and not altogether unwanted appearance of Kat Pyke . . . which led him to thoughts of his lost love, Philippa Walcote, who had been married to another for so long that their bastard son was now twelve years old and called another man 'father'.

What a strange life he seemed to lead. And how would it end? Likely in the care of his generous apprentice, of all people. A one-time cutpurse and orphan who had lived at the mercy of the streets of London. He chuckled, couldn't help it. Maybe his old friend Geoffrey Chaucer *should* write a poem about it.

But then his thoughts took him to the old days when he and Geoffrey were friends in the Duke of Lancaster's household.

That was certainly a long time ago, he mused.

'The mid of night is a time for long-ago musings,' said a voice at his ear, startling him. He jerked nearly to his feet until the man put a gentle hand to his shoulder. 'No need to take up arms just yet, young man.'

'I did not know you were there . . . or that I had spoken aloud,' said Crispin, studying the stranger in the dim light. He was an old man with a careworn face and a gray beard flowing nearly to his chest. His gown was dun-colored and patched. A staff lay on a bench beside him.

'You need not worry over an old man. Besides, I like to sit in the quiet of the dark . . . and think of old times.'

Crispin snorted. 'It must be dark indeed to call me a "young man".'

The old man waved his hand. 'At my age, everyone else is indeed "young".'

Crispin had nothing to say to that.

'You're a stranger here. What business brings you nigh Tintagel?'

'I . . . work for another whose business brings him here. I am from London.'

'Ah! I haven't been in London town for many a year. Tell me,' he said, leaning closer. 'Is it as fair and as bold as ever?'

Crispin could not keep the pride from his voice. 'She is as bold and as buxom as always. The Thames churns, the ships sail, the streets hum, and the gates are tall and strong.'

'Spoken like a kinsman of the old town. And you speak well and in a fine tone. If I did not know better, I would take you for a lord.'

Crispin's cheer died. He frowned. 'No, not a lord.'

'Your tone has suddenly gone bitter. I did not mean to offend.'

Crispin rubbed at his cheek, felt the scruff of beard growing there. 'I . . . apologize for my tone, sir. It seems the march of time will never erase my bitterness at my fate. My name is Crispin Guest, if it is at all familiar to you.'

'Crispin Guest? Ah. Your name seems to spark a memory, though, as I said, I have not ventured to London in many a day. My place is here. But I seem to recall tidings of a knight . . . who is no longer a knight from treason . . . and yet lives.'

He grunted his reply. His gaze never wavered from the fire several feet away.

'Surely it is not that long-ago event that keeps you from slumber. Only two things keep men from sleep: an impending battle . . . or a woman.'

Crispin chuckled. 'The latter, I should think.'

'Yes, the sweetest of embraces. I have not considered a love for many a year. That is a dance for younger men.'

'I don't feel so young these days.'

'Nonsense. You are hale and virile. No wife?'

'No.' He tried to keep the bitterness from his tone this time. 'I don't think it is for me. I might have been a knight and lord, friend, but I am not wealthy as I used to be. Which is why I am not snug in London and must traipse over the countryside to godforsaken outposts . . . Oh, forgive me. I did not mean to insult your country, sir, if you are from Cornwall.'

'I am, but I understand where it lies. Cornwall, in its isolation, its jarring coastline and angry seas, its desolate plains and deep forests are not fit for all men.'

Crispin angled to gaze at the old man in the dark. 'But you love it, just the same. Your words tell me so.'

'As any man loves his own country, the place of his birth. And mine was long ago.' He fixed his pale blue eyes on Crispin. 'And I have not introduced myself. I am Marzhin Gwyls, one of the caretakers of the castle.'

'Indeed. My employer will surely insist we go there on the morrow. That is where our work lies.'

'Well, you are welcomed, then. I will look for you.'

'Tell me about the place. It isn't like any castles I am used to.'

'No, I imagine it isn't.' He moved, settled in, and Crispin saw him cradling a beaker in his gnarled hand. 'The castles you've visited are inhabited by servants, knights, workers – the many who must upkeep such a place for their lord or king. Foodstuffs must be stored, animals tended. But there is no grand hall any longer at Tintagel, no great bailey full of activity and men. Tintagel is merely a ghost.'

'How so? I thought – it seems I had heard long ago that Prince Edward of Woodstock took it under his wing as the Duke of Cornwall, as so many earls of Cornwall had done in the past.'

'So it seemed. But the challenges of Tintagel proved too much for him as they had for others. It remains derelict, with the minimum of attendants. Caretakers like me – crumbled old men that we are – as well as a few men-at-arms, who are being punished by being sent to such an outpost, and a constable who watches over all; these are the only inhabitants. The rest are ghosts. There are few buildings with roofs, and those are taken up by the men I have mentioned. What could your employer possibly want to come here for?'

Crispin made a sound in his throat. 'Perhaps he is chasing ghosts as well. Who am I to question it, when I was promised my pay?'

'You are a practical man, then.'

'I must be to survive.'

'Then take heed, Master Guest. The men of the castle are not alone. For there are those outside the walls, too, who haunt the demesne. They are . . . undomesticated, unvillaged. What one might call wild. In another century, my people would have called them the *druw*, or as the Romans called them, the *druidae*.'

He shivered at the word so lately spoken by Carantok Teague. Could there be any truth to such tales? This man seemed to think so.

'Surely this must be rumor. Could there be pagans living out in the woodlands of Cornwall in these times? Is Cornwall so foreign to the rest of England that it harbors pagans?'

'I wouldn't rule it out, Master Guest. In my experience, nothing is impossible.'

Crispin fell silent. He had felt a little sad and anxious when he had slipped downstairs, though Kat's appearance and her accosting him in the privy had made him feel a little better. He watched the glow of the fire, cast his gaze over the men sleeping before it, heard them grumble and snore and break wind. When he turned to Marzhin again, the man was gone.

Well, it *was* late. He decided he could return to his bed and sleep now. As he trudged up the stairs and looked down upon the men below again, he no longer viewed them with a twinge of loneliness, but with a sense of the snugness of the fire, the close companionship, and other fool notions his weary mind put upon it.

In the morning, Jack was up first, as usual, poking the fire in their room, heating water, and fetching Crispin and Teague ale. Though Crispin looked for Kat, he did not see her, even as they saddled their horses. Teague hitched his horse to the cart and they all headed toward the castle.

It was no shining fortress on a hill, white and gleaming from fresh limewash, with towers and pennons flapping in the breeze. If they hadn't been looking for it, they wouldn't have noticed it.

A long, muddy, hollow way cut through the green hills, first dipping down and then rising up until a small scattering of stone houses came into view. Most looked deserted and derelict. Leaving the empty hamlet, they came to a plateau with a high crag to the left and built up with stone. It narrowed from a natural valley of hill on one side and stacked rock on the other. Before them was the first natural defense leading to a large square gatehouse.

'The narrow gate of the Lower Ward,' said Teague cheerfully. 'Know you that this is the meaning of the name "Tintagel". *Din Tagell*. It means "Fortress of the Narrow Entry".'

'Seems like a foolish name,' said Jack. 'Why not for its solitude or dangerous sea? Or for the stones around us?'

Teague shrugged. 'Such names are put upon these places by warriors and kings. Perhaps they have less imagination than your young squire, Master Guest.'

'I think you have the right of it, Master Teague,' said Crispin with a neutral expression. 'But it would be, strategically speaking, the best entry. Only three men abreast would be able to enter, and so it could be easily fortified with the minimal number of men.'

They passed through the first fortification without a man in sight. Where was the porter? And the heavy wooden portcullis lay wide open like the maw of some great beast. They came to a stone court-yard flanked by wooden structures, a stable where shaggy horses nibbled on the stall sills and poked their heads out to watch the men. A battlemented wall facing toward the sea rose up above them. Crispin heard the roar of the waves echoing up the stone face of the battlement and smelled the salt spray on the wind. No one greeted them to challenge their presence or to see to their horses. But even so, Teague plodded on, moving the cart horse through another stone gatehouse toward a road.

Where are we going? Crispin wondered. Hadn't they just left the castle? But no. He saw ahead another green and rocky place with more battlements and stone towers.

A low, narrow saddle of land spanned a sudden chasm before them. The cart and horses moved over its crumbling rock, dislodging rubble as they passed, and Crispin worried it wouldn't stay intact, looking down with some consternation over the side and below to a sheltered harbor of pebbled sand with waves licking at the rocky shore. The narrow passage seemed to be the only way to reach the rocky spit of land jutting into the sea.

Ahead, rising into the bleak sky, was the Outer Ward of the castle itself, the island. The gate tower, whose stones were crumbling into their path, seemed to have chambers above. From the few who occupied the fortress, Crispin reasoned that this might be some of the only places to sleep, possibly for the men-at-arms. Smoke drifted from its tiled roof, seeming to justify his assumptions.

'There is the constable's lodgings,' said Teague, gesturing to a structure built in what had obviously once been the great hall. Smoke rose from a kitchen chimney. The walls rose solidly and Crispin could see the remaining holes where the roof beams had been removed.

He peered around, surprised that there was no guard, that they were still unchallenged. There *were* two men-at-arms nearby, huddled around glowing braziers and passing around a skin to drink from, but they never glanced toward them.

'Here now,' said Jack, with a quiver in his voice. 'What's all this, Master Teague? What manner of castle is this?'

'An old one, Master Tucker. Forgotten. Disowned. That is why I may come and go so freely.'

'Blind me,' Jack muttered. He twisted around on his saddle, eyes scanning the broken walls, the shuttered buildings barely paved with roof tiles. Indeed, many of them bore naked rafters where birds and the weather imposed upon their ruined rooms.

Crispin wondered just what Edward of Woodstock had done to rebuild the castle when there was so little evidence of fresh structures or occupation.

Teague pulled the reins, halted his cart, and pointed across the courtyard. 'There, Master Guest, is our destination. You see that broken gate at the other side? We will go through it to the hills beyond the castle, where we shall begin to look for our quarry.'

'Will we be detained? Questioned?'

'Not a bit of it. The men that are posted here . . . well. The less they do, the happier they are. They gamble, they drink, and gain the company of the occasional woman in the village. They will not trouble us.'

'It has been my experience, Master Teague, that many a bored knight will harry a stranger to quell their restlessness.'

'That is why you are here, Master Guest.' He eyed Crispin's sword as he snapped the reins again, urging the beast onward. 'I have not found it that way at Tintagel, Master Guest. In any other place, I would say that a certain level of vigilance is usually proper. But be at ease. They will not trouble us.'

But Crispin wasn't at ease. He couldn't help but glare back at the men-at-arms in their drunken laughter.

They passed through a broken stone passageway and out into the verdant hills of the rest of what seemed for all the world to be an island.

There were tracks winding up the hill and around, ancient tracks, by the look of them. Possibly trod on by Arthur himself. It gave Crispin pause, and he turned this way and that in the saddle, gazing at the land that this ancient king had also gazed upon. He turned lastly toward Teague on his rocking cart. With a little excitement in his voice that even surprised himself, Crispin asked, 'Where do we go?'

Teague pointed onward. 'There, Master Guest. To a mound of old foundations below the chapel on the top of yon hill. According to my maps and the old tales, these were the places King Arthur and his men sheltered.'

Sheep grazed there now where Arthur's knights might have walked. It seemed strange, but who was Crispin to question? In Arthur's day, this whole island was likely protected by that narrow passage – *Tintagel*, indeed – to prevent armies from marching through. It was very likely that the castle itself was not all there was to this place. It had been Arthur's home, the castle of Gorlois, the Duke of Cornwall, before Uther Pendragon had urged Merlin to weave his magic and disguise *him* as the duke, so that he could lie with Gorlois's wife and beget Arthur. Deceit after deceit had doomed the place. For the duke had died miserably in battle the very night Uther lay with his wife Igraine, and Uther was later poisoned, for he had broken his promises and dishonored himself. The castle had fallen to ruin and, though Earl Richard of Cornwall had tried one hundred years before Crispin's time, no one had restored it since, even as the doomed Edward of Woodstock had promised . . . and failed to do.

A shudder slithered down his spine. Were the very stones cursed? What in God's name was *Crispin* doing here?

Carantok Teague seemed to care little for this history spinning in Crispin's head, even as the man hummed merrily to himself and drove his cart down to a freestone half-structure.

He threw the reins aside and jumped off. 'And now, Master Guest, Master Tucker, I shall show you the wonders of what I have found. I have taken the jewelry – the bracelets and arm rings – for safekeeping. For, er, the king, of course. Some of the rest remains here. Old rusted swords and axes. I was certain they would not be disturbed. Let us have a look. I'll need your help to move the stone covering the hole.'

He marched toward the low wall or foundation and stepped over it.

Crispin glanced at Jack and signaled for him to dismount. They followed the man over the stone foundation and found a flat, squared stone covering what could have been a well. Crispin's cloak flared with the cold and salty breeze, sweeping over the desolate green and rocky land.

Each positioned themselves at a side, bent over, and lifted. Walking backwards with the heavy stone, Crispin and Jack lowered it as Teague instructed.

Teague had covered the hole with a sheet of canvas. He stepped toward it, grabbed a corner, and whisked it off. A gasp halted his breath.

Crispin turned at Jack's squeal of surprise. But he quickly trotted to the edge of the hole and looked down with the others.

A man-at-arms lay folded tightly, as if trying to make himself as small as possible, arms wrapped around knees held up to his chest, with his whole body lying on his side, sword still in its sheath, and dagger there as well.

And quite clearly dead.

FOUR

C rispin heaved a sigh before stepping down, and with one foot in the hole, he leaned in and looked the man over. Coshed in the back of the head, which was still covered in dried blood and brains, with the skull neatly dented. But, by the bloated look of him and the smell, he'd been there a few days at least. He was wearing mail and a surcoat. Something was in one of the hands clasping his legs. And because the rigor had come and gone, Crispin could easily loosen the fingers. He reached down and took the object from the dead man. A gold brooch with a horse's head and wrapped gold wire. He turned it in his hands, looking it over. He showed it to Jack, who peered at it before he shrugged and looked up to his master. 'Master Teague, some of your treasure?'

Teague looked at it with a stark, white face and shook his head.

Crispin slipped it into his money pouch and stood up. 'Jack, why don't you fetch the constable. I fear they have lost a member of their company.'

Jack nodded and, mounting quickly, spurred the horse back up the trail in a trot that became a gallop.

'How could this have happened?' said Teague in a whisper. It was the first thing he had spoken after a long interval.

'I don't know. You say no one knew of this place.'

'I had no help and those in the castle were not interested in my diggings here. They had no idea what I was doing. For as I said, any gold or gems I had already liberated. Only rusty swords and axes remained. Hardly of any interest to those fellows.'

'The question is was he murdered here, or murdered and dumped here?' Crispin crouched down again and examined the place where the man lay. The soil around him was covered in a rusty color. He scooped some into his fingers and rubbed it between them. Blood. So he had bled out here and was likely killed here. With a cursory glance, there was no evidence remaining of footprints. The weather and time had taken care of that.

He wiped his fingers on his cloak. 'He died here, and was deliberately stuffed within and hidden. Perhaps the murderer did not know that you would return.'

'This is awful. Disgraceful. What's to be done?'

'Little, until the authorities come to examine the body.'

'We have no coroner. And my work!'

'A man has been killed by foul means, sir. Surely that is paramount.'

'Yes, yes, of course.' Teague remained quiet, only ruminating under his breath with a hand to his mouth, until Jack returned with two men-at-arms behind him. Jack dismounted quickly, clutching the horse's lead with a cold-chapped hand.

A man Crispin took to be the constable looked down at the scene from his saddle. 'What goes on here? Who are you?' He was looking directly at Crispin and at the sword hanging from his hip.

Crispin bowed and stepped up to his stirrup. 'I am Crispin Guest, known as the Tracker of London.'

'And what the devil is a "tracker"?'

'I can speak to that, Sir Regis,' said Teague, dragging his cloak tighter over his chest as a gust blew up from the sea, full of cold, salt and isolation. 'I have hired Master Guest. He has a fine reputation in London for solving crimes. His patron was the Duke of Lancaster himself.'

Sir Regis's dark eyes roamed over Crispin again with suspicion. 'Is that so?' He threw his reins to Jack, who grabbed them with one hand, and dismounted. He strode to the edge of the makeshift grave and peered down. 'Why, that's Roger,' he said softly. 'Roger Bennet.'

The other man-at-arms made a sound of surprise.

'So you know him,' said Crispin. 'Then you were aware he had been missing for some days.'

'He wasn't missing,' said the knight. 'He was making a trip to see his sweetheart in Treknow.'

Crispin watched the man rub his bearded chin, eyes staring at the dead man, unable to tear his gaze away.

'And when was that?'

'It was . . . two days ago, wasn't it, Thomas?'

The other man, Thomas, nodded from his perch on the saddle. 'Yes. Monday. God have mercy.' He crossed himself.

Sir Regis belatedly crossed himself.

Crispin dug into his pouch and pulled out the brooch, holding it up. 'Do either of you recognize this?'

Regis passed his gaze over it but soon returned his stare to the dead man. 'No.'

Thomas shook his head.

Crispin punched it down into his pouch again. 'Did anyone see him leave? His horse?'

That made Sir Regis lift his head. He and Thomas exchanged glances. 'I saw him leave,' said Thomas. 'On his horse, as he always did.'

They all seemed to scan the hills, the rocky cliffs at the same time. 'Then . . . where is the horse?' said Crispin.

'Look here.' Sir Regis stared again at the dead man. 'If you are this "tracker" then you can find the killer.'

Crispin glanced at Teague, who nodded vigorously. He supposed Teague's fee would cover his time. 'Yes. But what of the coroner?'

'We don't have the luxury of London to have a coroner at our beck and call. You'll have to get along without one.'

'Then you are the law in this region?'

'As good as, I suppose. You there. Teague, is it? When did you arrive?'

He stood upright, putting a hand to his breast. 'You must have seen us arrive today. Only just now.'

Regis nodded distractedly. 'Yes, yes. I suppose so. Well, then. We'll need your cart.'

Carantok looked shocked at first, but then acceded to it. Crispin reckoned the man was worried about his secrets and whatever bounty he had stowed away in there, but a dead man would have little to say about it, and these two men-at-arms were too befuddled to make a search of the man's possessions.

They all helped to gather up the stinking corpse and hustle it to the cart, wrapping him in his own cloak. The constable ordered them to take him to the parish church. The stone church with its tower was just visible at the horizon of a distant crag on the mainland.

'It would help, Sir Regis,' said Crispin, standing at his stirruped foot, 'if you and your men scoured for the horse. Perhaps in Treknow, the countryside, the beach.'

Regis nodded, bearded jaw tightening. He nodded to their company, and Carantok snapped the reins, moving the cart slowly up the road.

Jack was about to go with him, when Crispin held him back. 'There's no need to follow their solemn trek, Jack. We need to do some thinking here. He's only a corpse now. He's told me all he could.'

Crispin tied both mounts to a stump and began walking slowly around the site.

'What could have happened, Master Crispin?'

'Could he have returned on foot?' he muttered. 'No, it's too long a trek, and in any case, why leave the horse behind? If Thomas saw him leave, then something brought him back here.'

'Thomas could be lying.'

He looked at Jack, studied the man, that flaming red beard of his, and nodded. 'He could be. I shall have to see if he were. But if he hadn't, what could bring Bennet back?'

'The woman? They talked of him seeing a woman in the village.'

'But why would she take the trouble to lure him back here to murder him?' Crispin bit his lip in thought. 'Wouldn't it be just as expeditious to murder him secretly in the village?'

'You never know with women.'

Crispin turned to stare at his apprentice again . . . and laughed.

Jack shuffled uncomfortably.

'Tucker, if you plan on being a Tracker after me, it's best you leave the more radical musings behind. Could a woman move that stone back over the body?'

'No, sir. Only if she had help. But something brought him here, that's a fact.'

'Indeed.' Crispin looked out over the whole area, back toward the road from which they themselves had traveled, to the higher road where the stone chapel sat, just peeking over the hill, to the lonely jagged hills that dropped off to the sea. 'He could have been lured, so you say, but by something else. Master Teague seems to think that his own doings are secret . . . but are they?'

Jack's eyes widened. 'Oh! Him looking for treasure?'

'Possibly.'

'And that don't bode well for the presence of Kat Pyke, now does it.'

Crispin hadn't wanted to consider it. After all, she *had* killed a man. In self-defense, so she claimed. He had believed her . . . up to a point. But she was a mistress of lies and he couldn't quite dismiss the notion.

'I suppose I shall have to talk to her.'

'Er . . . perhaps, sir, *I* should be the one to talk to her.'

He turned a scowl on Jack. 'And just what are you insinuating?'

'I'm not insinuating naught, sir, it's just that . . . you have a weakness for women.'

Crispin doubled his scowl and crossed his arms over his chest. 'A weakness. Are you saying I'd be compromised?'

'We-ell, sir . . . it's . . . it's . . .'

Blowing out a breath, Crispin stalked up the trail away from the bloody pit. The man was right, of course. He was always compromising himself because of a pretty face. And how her face made him think of . . . of their past liaisons. Even now his cod stiffened at the thought of her.

He ground his teeth and nodded reluctantly. 'Much as I hate to admit it, you may be right. Yes. I will send you to speak with her and investigate this other woman in Treknow. I'll talk to others here.'

'I'm sorry, sir. I'm . . . I'm just trying to be a good Tracker, like you said.'

'No need to dwell on it, Tucker,' he rasped.

Jack needed little prompting. He mounted his horse and urged it up the road and back through the castle toward Treknow.

Crispin turned to watch him go and smiled grimly. That man knew him too well. But he conceded that he had the right of it. It was a good thing, after all, that Jack understood his master, for they would get much farther with a clear head.

Crispin sighed, adjusted himself, and turned to look down into the makeshift grave once more. He hopped down into it, now that it was devoid of the bloated corpse, and crouched down. The blood had spread all around under where the body had been, but he could detect the spade marks that Teague had no doubt left behind. But if it had been treasure someone had been seeking, there were no additional holes made, no dug-out corners and upturned soil. Had they killed Roger before they could look for the treasure that Teague claimed was here? If those plans had been waylaid, why not move the body? And why, if there was such desolation here on these plains and rugged hills, would they need to be bothered with a dead man? They could easily dig for their treasure and drop him back in the hole when they were done. Yet, clearly, this had not been the case.

'What intrigue is here?' came a voice from above him.

He scrambled for his dagger and spun clumsily in the hole. When he looked up, it was only the old man, Marzhin Gwyls. 'God's blood, man! You startled me. Where, by all the saints, did you come from?' He swept his gaze over the empty plains and hillsides.

'I was beyond yon hillock,' Gwyls said, and gestured behind him. The land undulated with hills and rocks, like an ocean wave. 'I came to see what the commotion was.'

'A man has died. Murdered.'

'Oh, blessed soul! Who, then?'

'One of the men-at-arms. Roger Bennet, so he was called.'

'What a shame. Murdered, you say? It is a very great sin to murder a man.'

'Indeed it is. Did you see anything of it? It happened two days ago.'

'No. But just a few hours ago, I did note a dead horse upon the beach. Just there.' He pointed behind him toward the eastern cliffs.

'Well, there is the mystery of the missing horse solved.'

'Dear me. Dear, dear me. Such a thing should not be.'

Crispin levered himself from the hole and dusted off his hose and cloak. 'So *did* you see anything two days ago? A man on a horse hereabouts, with others?'

'Is this where he was found?' Gwyls stepped gently into the hole like a much younger man and scoured about, kicking at the chalky earth and at the blood-soaked soil. 'Such a terrible thing in such a terribly lonely place.' He raised his chin and looked skyward, as if beseeching God, before he surveyed the squared hole again. 'What goes on here, Master Guest?'

Should he say? It wasn't his story to tell. But surely Teague had discussed his comings and goings with the caretakers. 'My employer likes to . . . dig. To . . . find things.'

'Rather like you. Only you find people and sin.'

'Perhaps it would be a better life searching as Carantok Teague does, for the past.'

'Does he? Look for the past? How extraordinary.'

'He . . . finds things of worth. Objects.'

Gwyls's pale blue eyes seemed to glitter from the sun's passing in and out of the rush of clouds. 'Objects from the past? Ah, now I see.'

Crispin said nothing more, feeling perhaps he had spoken too much already.

Gwyls crouched down, looking at the soil beneath his feet in the hole. 'Look here!' He scratched away at the soft earth. Fingernails now lined with dark dirt, he uncovered what looked like a rusty sword pommel.

Crispin quickly joined him and dug away with his hands, revealing more of the crusted hilt. It couldn't be, could it? Could this be the fabled Excalibur that Teague had been hunting for?

They both dug it out . . . and found a decayed blade with not a bit of shine remaining. The wet earth had done its damage, turning it to rusty, pitted iron. When Crispin pulled it free and held it aloft, it was a pitiful remnant of a weapon.

'Isn't that a shame?' said Gwyls. 'Why would someone leave a weapon in the ground?'

'There could have been a battle and it got buried accidentally. Or . . . this could have been a grave, I suppose. After all, there was much found with it . . .' He stopped. Now he'd truly spilled it. He winced as he looked toward the old man.

He was smiling, damn him. 'A hoard, was it? Jewelry and the like? Do you know, I once found a coin with the head of a Roman emperor on its face?'

'I've said too much. I beg you not to tell anyone.'

'Fear not, Master Guest. I would not impede your employer nor get you into any trouble. If your man wishes to search for lost legacies, he may dig all the holes he likes. He'd just better make sure no more men are left for dead in them.'

Crispin shook the mud from his hands. How could he have forgotten? One glint of some secret trove and all thoughts of the dead man and his murderer had flown out of his head. What was wrong with him? A lust for the secrets of the treasure, perhaps? Or was it just to solve another mystery? He'd rather it were the latter.

'Tell me, Master Gwyls. Have you ever . . . has it ever crossed your mind that King Arthur might have left behind, well . . . relics, for want of a better term?'

'Arthur?' He stroked a hand down his beard. 'There have been many men since, remaking Tintagel over and over, turning the earth as well as moving stones. How could anything remain?'

'Still, it is rumored.'

'That's what your man seeks, eh? Well, it should prove interesting. Though I should caution him . . . and you. There are relics of the past that are best left in the earth. The others, the watchers, guard them. They do not desire that the eyes of man should look upon them again.'

Crispin frowned. 'What . . . what manner of thing are you saying, Gwyls? Who watches? Who guards? Not those men in the castle?'

'Oh no. Not them. They are . . . well. I shouldn't like to speak ill of the dead – bless the dead man's soul – but the others. The *druw*.'

'So you said before. Pagans? Truly?'

'I am saying, Master Guest, that there are some mysteries that cannot be solved.'

He eyed Gwyls critically. Anyone could have slain Roger for all sorts of reasons. Could Gwyls be capable? He scoured the man's staff with its heavy wooden head. Where was the instrument that caused Roger's death? No club was found. It could have been a rock, he supposed, but that staff might have done the job if swung with power and taken the man unaware.

Marzhin laughed suddenly. 'You think mighty loud, Master Guest. No, I didn't kill your corpse.'

Crispin narrowed his eyes. 'One must entertain all possibilities—'

'*Plausible impossibilities should be preferred to unconvincing possibilities*.'

Crispin's tense shoulders relaxed. 'Aristotle,' he murmured.

'Indeed. I subscribe to all philosophies. I find truth in the strangest of places.'

Crispin nodded. 'So do I.'

Gwyls chuckled. 'I suspected you did. You cannot hope to be as successful as I have heard you are without having an open mind.' He tapped at his own temple.

Pagans, eh? He dug in his pouch and brought out the brooch. 'Have you ever seen the like before?'

Gwyls took the brooch in his lined palm. 'Yes. Yes, I have seen similar pieces. It is an unusual design these days,' and he pointed with his other hand to the horse head. 'A symbol from the Saxon days of Britain.'

'Are you saying it is old?'

'Could be. Did you find this in the ground?'

'No.' He took it back and studied it once more, turning it in his fingers. Finely wrought, he did not think anyone nigh the castle could afford such a piece. He stuffed it away again.

'It seems old. Of the *druw* style.'

'I keep hearing mention of these pagan people. Do you still insist that they are living today?'

'I entertain the notion, Master Guest.' Gwyls wore a half smile curving the edge of his mouth, but said nothing more as he leaned on his staff.

'Enough of this,' said Crispin, scowling. 'What of this dead man? If he left the castle so openly, how is it he returned so secretly?'

'Who has said he left openly?'

Gesturing up the hill toward the parish church, Crispin saw the cart's slow progress. 'Your constable and his man say so.'

'Did they? What was it they said?'

Pondering now, Crispin walked through their response. 'You're right. They only said he left two days ago. Thomas said he saw him. I suppose I shall have to enquire if there are more witnesses to that, or merely that it was known he was to leave.' He gave a lopsided grin. 'Thanks for that. I seem to have grown impatient in my enquiries these days. Not as careful as I used to be.'

'I find that difficult to believe. You are hard on yourself, sir.' He nodded and turned away.

Crispin watched him go in his slow amble, thinking that the old man was much too charitable to him. But if he were to truly redeem himself, he'd best get back to the castle and make enquiries.

FIVE

J ack Tucker rode unchallenged back through the gate and out of Tintagel to the main road, before turning on his saddle to look back. Such a strange place, where no one seemed to care who came and who went. He'd have to mention that to Master Crispin, for perhaps no one had truly noted when or *if* Roger had left at all to find his sweetheart.

His horse plodded along the road, and he rode lazily with it, a little proud of himself of how he sat on a horse these days.

The wagon with the players was still there at the inn. He tossed his horse's reins to the stableman and walked through the mud to get inside. The cold fell away, and the smells of food and smoke filled his senses. He loosened his mantle and relaxed in the warmth, and when his eyes adjusted to the darker interior, he scanned the room and found Kat Pyke sitting in a circle of men. 'Naturally,' he muttered, and strode toward her.

It took her a long while to finally look up, and when she did, her eyes traveled over him in a way that made him most uncomfortable.

'Master Tucker. My, my. How you've changed.'

He self-consciously ran his hand through his ginger beard and shuffled his muddied boots. 'No more than I should have. I beg, demoiselle, to speak with you. In private.'

The men made remarks and laughed when she gave them all a wink and rose, walking between them to reach Jack. She stood toe to toe with him and looked up at his tall frame. 'Wherever shall we go for this private . . . talk?'

The men made more salacious noises as Jack rolled his eyes. 'Outside, then,' he grumbled, clutching her arm. He dragged her out and it wasn't until they made it to the courtyard that she wrestled her arm away from him, kneading it above the elbow. 'Your grasp is tight, Master Tucker,' she said stiffly.

'I beg your mercy, demoiselle. But I am here on serious business. When exactly did you arrive to town?'

She clenched her cloak around her and leaned against the stable wall out of the wind. 'You and your master saw me yourselves. We arrived at the same time. Oh yes, I saw you two on your horses with that man and his cart.'

'Very well. And what brings you to Treknow?'

She made a face and shook her head. 'Master Tucker, this sounds very much like an inquisition, rather than a talk among old acquaintances.'

'It is that, Mistress Pyke.'

'Whatever for? Has someone died?' She said it in jest. He was almost sure of it.

'In fact, yes, they have.'

Her flirtations halted. She pushed away from the wall and rushed up to him, anxiety framing her eyes. 'Who? Where is Crispin?'

'My master is well and investigating elsewhere.' She seemed to relax at those tidings. 'He asked me to come here to talk to you, because it involved a man and perhaps items of worth . . . the kind you are fond of stealing.'

'Shush!' She glanced about, but no one, not even the stableman, was near. 'Master Tucker, I'd rather my past did not come to light in this company. They hired a musician and that is what I am. Why would I be suspected of such foul play?'

'*Because* of that very past, demoiselle.'

'Why didn't Crispin come himself?'

Jack hesitated. But like any soldier looking for the merest chink in the armor to thrust her dagger, she pounced. 'Oh ho! He didn't *wish* to come himself. Afraid of such a little slip of a thing as me?' She threw back her head and laughed, full-throated.

Jack felt his face heat and he longed to shut her up, but he couldn't get up the nerve to strike her. 'Keep quiet, or I'll be forced to quiet you.'

The look in her eye told him he had used the wrong words. And when she laid a hand to his chest and gazed at him with sultry eyes, he was certain of it. He grabbed her hand, squeezed it hard and tossed it away. 'I am a married man, wench, and proud to be a sinless husband. Keep your wiles to yourself. Oh, there is a devil in you, and I'm glad I spared my master from the likes of this.'

She laughed. 'Oh Jack, you silly man. You must know that my heart is set on Crispin. Any other man is a very poor substitute.'

That made him scowl all the more. 'Enough of this. Now answer me quick before I forget I am a calm and gentle man. Did you have aught to do with the death of Roger Bennet? Did you do it for the treasure?'

She seemed shocked at first, with moist lips open and eyes like bezants. But then the word 'treasure' appeared to have broken through, and her eyes narrowed with calculation.

Christ, Jack, he admonished himself. *What have you done?*

'Treasure? What treasure could that be?'

'Erm . . . keep your mind on what's important. Did you kill – or cause to be killed – that man?'

Her jaw tightened. 'When I killed in the past, Master Tucker,' and she poked him in the chest, 'it was to protect myself. Have you got that understood?' She stopped poking and raised her hand. 'I swear by God Almighty, I never would have killed a man for anything. Even his treasure. Only to protect myself and my honor.' She straightened her cloak and rolled her shoulders. 'I don't know nor have I ever heard of Roger Bennet until this moment. Now then. Have I answered your questions, Master Tucker?'

'So . . . so you know of no, er, treasure? That's not why you're here, then?'

She carefully folded her arms over her bosom. 'If I were – which I'm not – why should I tell you?'

'Demoiselle, you make it most difficult to believe you.'

'Believe what you like. I murdered no one. You haven't the right to throw accusations at innocent women. I think we're done talking.' She turned to leave, but then came at him so suddenly he wasn't prepared for her to grab the front of his cloak and drag him forward. He stumbled, ending up looking her in the eye as he bent forward, helpless under her assault. 'And if your master has any more questions for me, he can grow the bollocks to ask them himself. And not send an errand boy.'

'Oi!'

'You can tell him that. Or I just might do so myself.' She let him go, dusted her hands, and stalked across the courtyard back to the inn.

He straightened his cote-hardie and rubbed his beard again. 'God's blood,' he muttered, feeling strange and discomfited. She did have a way about her.

It had begun to drizzle. He looked up accusingly into the gray sky and pulled his hood up. 'What, by all the saints, will I tell Master Crispin now?'

He mulled it for a while before girding himself and venturing into the inn once more to seek out the innkeeper. He ignored the whistles and catcalls from Kat Pyke's male friends, and found the man near the back door. 'Good sir, would you know of the woman in the village who spends time with a soldier up at the castle, a man called Roger Bennet?'

'Well, lad, that isn't my area of interest. But I'll wager the wife knows. She likes that sort of gossip. Here! Gertrude! Where are you keeping yourself?'

'I'm keeping m'self where I always keep m'self,' said a slim woman with a white kerchief pilled on her head, arms full of crumpled linens. 'Doing the work.'

'Here, Gert. This man wishes to know who the girl is that keeps a man from the castle busy on Mondays.'

'What man?' She looked Jack over. 'Why'd you want to know?'

'It's very important that I speak with her. The man in the castle is called Roger Bennet.'

'Oh, him! Well then.' She shoved the laundry into the innkeeper's hands, and wiped her own chapped fingers down her apron. 'I seen him – and a right handsome lad he is, too, like you, young sir.' She winked. 'And that milkmaid, Janet Penhall. She's a fair lass. Red hair . . . like you.'

'And where can I find her?'

'What you want to be finding her for? She's already got a sweetheart.'

'I . . . I merely mean to impart important information to her.'

'I tell you what. You tell *me*, and *I'll* tell her.'

Jack straightened, glancing toward the man for help . . . but there was none to come from that quarter. He was plainly besotted with his wife, and looked on at her with a smile of contentment. 'Madam, I cannot do that. If you please, tell me where I can find her.'

She sagged. 'Oh well. Then you can find the lass up the lane. The dairyman's manor lies just over that hill, where the road curves. You'll see the cows grazing.'

Jack bowed. 'I thank you.' He offered a sympathetic expression to the man and turned on his heel. Before he could leave the inn, Kat called out to him, 'Jack! Make certain you tell Crispin what I said.'

He winced, but did not turn to her before leaving the inn to the laughter of the men around her.

Taking his horse from the stableman, he headed out of the courtyard and followed the muddy road. The rain came down heavier now with an icy hand, stripping the warmth from his sodden hands on the reins. He looked to his right, toward where the road curved behind a hillock, and took that fork. He rode a little way until he saw cows grazing behind a wattle fence. Behind the house, through a veil of rain, stood a wide barn. He urged the horse forward through the gatehouse that was little more than a wooden structure and took that gravel lane up to the manor.

When he reached the courtyard, a man emerged with a pitchfork leaning on his shoulder. He wore a hood with a hat over it, its brim dripping from the downpour.

Jack nodded to the man. He spared a hand to wipe the rain from his beard. 'Good day, sir. I'm looking for the maid Janet.'

'And why would you be wanting to talk to my daughter? I don't recognize you.'

'That is true, sir. I've come up from London with my master, Crispin Guest. Perhaps you've heard of him. They call him the Tracker of London.'

'Tracker? What the devil does he track there?'

Jack was unused to people not knowing who his master was. He settled his face as he'd seen Master Crispin do many a time when interrogating a witness. 'He tracks down crime, sir. He recovers lost objects, stolen goods . . . and finds murderers.'

'Eh? What would you want with my daughter?'

'Is she here, sir? It is a matter concerning Roger Bennet.'

The man frowned. 'He's betrothed to her. Or nearly so. Why doesn't he send the message himself?'

'Did he come round this way about two days ago, sir?'

'No. We've not seen him since a fortnight.'

Jack huffed a breath and dismounted. He clutched the horse's reins with icy fingers and looked the man straight in the eye. 'Then it is my misfortune to tell you that Roger Bennet has been murdered up at Tintagel, about two days ago.'

'No. Oh no. God have mercy.' He crossed himself and lowered the pitchfork.

'I am sorry to be the bearer of these tidings. But as you see, I must speak with your daughter.'

'You mustn't tell her. She . . . she'll be devastated.'

Jack reckoned the man was in a similar state. He looked as if he'd lost a bag of gold, and he very well had. 'I won't, sir. I am my master's apprentice and I was taught discretion.'

'I'll tell her. Gently.' The man seemed to gird himself and motioned for Jack to follow toward the barn. Its doors were open wide, and cows, a donkey, a dog, and several chickens trotted here and there, in and out of the barn's dark interior, smelling of wet barnyard.

Janet was on her stool, milking a cow that was chewing on long stalks of straw. She hadn't yet noticed them as she picked up the bucket, carried it to a barrel, and poured the milk in. It steamed as it poured in a pillar of white.

She raised a hand to her brow and noticed them approach, lowering the wooden bucket.

'Daughter, this man wishes to speak to you.'

Jack bowed. 'My name is Jack Tucker, demoiselle, and I am apprentice to Crispin Guest, Tracker of London.'

Her ruddy cheeks seemed to pale as she stared at him. Jack knew that an official coming to call was never good news, so he tried to maintain a professional air, giving no emotion one way or the other.

Since she said nothing in reply to him, he cleared his throat and went on. 'Is it true that you have seen nothing of Roger Bennet since a fortnight ago?'

Finally, she looked to her father.

'Answer the man, girl,' he said gently.

'Well . . . aye. A fortnight at least.'

'No message? No note?' Though now he wondered if either could read.

'No. My lord, what is this about?'

He gave a small smile. 'I am no lord, demoiselle. Just . . . making enquiries.'

'Has something happened to Roger?'

Before Jack could say, the man began to wail. 'Oh child! All is lost! He's been murdered!'

That's what he calls telling her gently? Jack sighed.

She wailed, too, and fell into her father's arms. The both of them wept and cried out, and soon the donkey joined them in its own braying, and Jack, standing like a useless post, decided enough was enough, and pulled his horse's lead away and back toward the road.

He mounted and looked back at the dairyman and his daughter. Other workers began to gather and watch them curiously. He wasn't certain what Master Crispin would do under such circumstances, but he wasn't prepared to wait them out.

'Come on, Seb,' he said, kicking the horse's sides and traveling back along the road. He swore he could still hear them wailing on the wind.

SIX

Crispin rode through the eastern gatehouse just as the heavens opened. He tugged his leather hood low over his face but it seemed his heavy cloak did little to discourage the wet permeating to his bones. He hunkered down over Tobias, grateful to have the horse. At least he wasn't walking all that way in the mud.

He reached the mainland of the castle and its nearly empty courtyard. Smoke lingered near the rooftops . . . when there *was* a roof. He glanced again at the stable with the shaggy horses, toward the lodgings of the men-at-arms and urged the horse there. He dismounted, threw the reins over a post ring, and trudged up to the door. He knocked.

The door opened heavily, scraping the floor, and the burly guard filled the doorway. 'Eh? Who are you?'

Crispin gave a cursory bow that was little more than a nod of the head. 'Good sir, I am Crispin Guest, Tracker of London. Sir Regis—'

'Yes, we were told of Roger.' Another face behind the man emerged from the gloom.

'May I come in and talk with you and your fellow?'

The man shrugged and stepped aside.

Crispin entered and shook off the rain from his cloak. He was invited to the fire. The room was close and dark except for the flames in the hearth. The two men's appearance was rough and slightly unkempt. It was not entirely unexpected for men living at such an outpost. Teague had told him there were four men-at-arms, one porter, and one constable. A chaplain lived in lodgings near them in the mainland ward. Crispin had seen for himself the two caretakers, and this was the entire complement of the wretched castle.

The two men faced him, looking on anxiously. With his back warming at the fire, Crispin eyed them. 'Roger Bennet ventured out two days ago. Did either of you see him leave the castle grounds?'

'I saw him get his horse,' offered one man with dusty blond hair.

'Did you see him leave through the gate?' asked Crispin.

He scrubbed his hair and stared down at his boots. 'Come to think of it . . . no.'

'He was going to see his girl,' said the other man, wearing a leather tunic dotted with iron studs.

The blond man elbowed Leather Tunic. 'But which one, eh, Stephen?'

They chuckled but soon returned to solemnity, remembering that Roger was dead.

'Oh?' said Crispin. 'Was Roger known to keep the company of *two* women?'

The men exchanged glances. Who was Crispin but a foreigner, a man from another place; distant London?

Crispin raised his chin. 'Well then?'

The blond man, somewhat chastened at letting loose such information, cleared his throat. 'Well, there is the one in the village, and the one from . . . outside the village. The wilderness. No one trifles with that folk, but Roger did.'

'Why does no one "trifle" with the wilderness folk?'

It was Stephen's turn to speak. 'Some say they're pagans. I don't believe it. But Arno does.'

The other man nodded. 'Arno Leverton. And he's Stephen Kettle. Yes, I've seen them in the woods with their bonfires. I saw the men wearing antlers. There's something devilish going on there.'

Crispin crossed his arms over his chest. 'I have heard of villagers in all parts of England with rituals of antlers and bonfires. It is as old as the land itself. It means nothing.'

'Is that so?' said Stephen with a sneer. 'And I suppose you heard them chant in a foreign tongue and make the fire dance with them? That's what *I've* seen.'

'Be that as it may, do you know the woman's name? And where their settlement is?'

They exchanged looks again. Neither one seemed inclined to say until Stephen Kettle stuck his thumbs in his belt. 'I think her name is Eseld. And where their village is . . . well. That's anyone's guess.'

'No, I think it's to the west of here, in the forest,' said Arno Leverton. 'No one goes that way. And if you've got any brains, Guest, you won't either.'

'Justice for the dead is my consideration, gentlemen.'

They stared at Crispin as if he'd spoken like a pagan. He shrugged and made again for the door. 'West, you said? Into the forest?'

Kettle stomped toward him. Crispin braced himself for a blow, for the man's hands had curled into fists and his face was red and twisted. 'I beg of you, sir. Don't go there. At least . . . don't go alone.'

'Then come with me.'

Kettle stepped back to the fire with his friend. 'Find a man in the village to show you the way. If they dare.'

He felt a chill shiver down his spine. Men were often afraid of their own superstitions, and there was usually nothing to fear. But . . . in the last few years, Crispin had come to question his staunch beliefs that there was little but God's wrath – or the king's – to fear. There might *be* something to this settlement in the wilderness. Or it might just be tales told to keep the curious away. Whatever it was, he had to speak to this Eseld.

'Thank you,' he said with a cursory bow, and left them.

He stood in the rain in the courtyard, looking back at the smoky warmth just beyond the door and sighed. Best to head to the village and find Jack. It was probably wiser not to go to the woods without an escort, as they said.

He mounted the soggy horse, apologizing under his breath to the beast, and urged it on through the courtyard and to the gate beyond. Out onto the road he went, lifting his eyes only enough to look for the sodden rooftops, the lazy smoke rolling along the slate and thatch in the gray distance.

Jack was, no doubt, out doing his task. And Crispin decided that a little warmed wine at the inn might be advisable before heading out to look for the man. His horse plodded along until they reached the innyard. The mummer's wagon was not there, and he felt just the merest disappointment. Because he thought of Kat and of her recent kisses . . . and that stupid feeling again.

'I'm getting too old for this,' he grumbled, and left Tobias for the stableman.

The inn was warmer and dry, and he shook off his cloak and hung it by the fire. He asked the innkeeper for a bit of warmed wine and the man went in haste to prepare it. Crispin settled back by the fire, putting his feet up on a stool in the empty room, and even closed his eyes. The warmth made him drowsy and he sensed the innkeeper near him, setting down the cup on the table. He jerked with a start when lips dropped to his.

With eyes wide and his body halfway from his seat, it took a moment to realize the sound ringing in his ears was Kat, laughing at him.

'You should see your face.' She giggled. 'You thought it was the innkeeper, I'll wager.'

He straightened his coat, lowering his face. 'Nothing of the sort. You surprised me is all.' He saw the wine and grabbed it, spilling some in his haste. He gulped it. It was too hot, and he choked, coughing. Her little hands slapped his back.

'Steady there, Master Guest.'

He shrugged out from under her and sat hard on the chair to avoid her touch. Except that she drew in close and poked him in the chest. 'You sent your man to interrogate me,' she said, face far too close to his. 'That is unacceptable. *Don't* do it again!'

He sipped the wine before setting the wooden goblet aside. 'We needed to know.'

'Then have the bollocks to ask me yourself next time.' She sat next to him and even scooted the chair closer. The firelight glowed on her cheek, scattering the light in her eyes, touching the edges of her hair. There was no question that she was a beautiful woman. And he well knew how she had used it to her advantage. 'Need there *be* a "next time"?' By the flair in her eyes he knew it was a mistake saying so.

She rushed him again, hands placed on each chair arm so that she was leaning in, with her bosom just under his nose. 'No next time? You have no interest in speaking to me? How have I offended you? When I left London, I thought . . .' She sighed, heaving her chest . . . which his eyes could not help but watch. She moved away from him and slumped back into her chair. 'You haven't thought of me at all, have you?'

'That's not true. I . . . worried about you.'

'You *worried* about me. And that's all?'

'Dammit, woman, you said for me not to follow you!'

'I didn't mean it.'

He knew his mouth had dropped open and he snapped it shut. But then he couldn't help but laugh. He sat back more comfortably against the chair. 'Kat, Kat. What is a body to do with you?'

'If we are speaking of *your* body . . . much.' There was that sultry glint to her eye again and she measured him from under her lashes.

'I find myself . . . busy.'

'Too busy for me? With your . . . *treasure*?'

He let out a long breath. 'Jack,' he growled.

'Oh, don't blame him. He hadn't *meant* to say anything. I just seem to have a way with loosening men's tongues.'

His hands tightened over the chair arms. 'You . . . you didn't . . .'

She waved her hand in a carefree manner. 'Don't vex yourself. I never broke the virtue of your apprentice.' She put a hand to her heart when she said, 'He told me he is a faithful husband with no desire to sin.' She smiled. 'He's a good man.'

Crispin's hands eased and he sat back again. 'Don't use your wiles on him. He means what he says.'

'I know. I told him my heart is set on you and only you.'

He sighed again. 'Kat . . .'

'Crispin.' She leaned forward in her seat. 'Tell me something. Why are we wasting our time here, when you have a perfectly good *empty* room at your disposal?'

He laughed again. 'Because I have no intention of bedding you, demoiselle.'

'But I have every intention of bedding *you* . . . Master Guest.'

He smiled, the humorous edge coming off his laughter. '*Do* you?' He didn't mind these playful games, but he was certain he couldn't trust her with more.

She rose in challenge but instead of rushing at him, she slowly moved across the floor, plucked the goblet from his hand, and drank from it. She seemed to stand in a position for the best advantage, allowing the flickering hearthlight to play over her curves, her cheeks, her hair.

He swallowed, watching her. Yes, he'd thought of her. In the darkest of nights, when his cod ached from lack of a woman. When he satisfied himself and pictured a female form, often it was Philippa, but lately, it had been Kat.

'I am older now, not as easy to seduce,' he said, though his voice sounded uneven to him.

She looked up and set down the wine. 'No? Perhaps . . . it is I who is lonely.'

He mulled it. She was right. The room was unoccupied and here they were. *What the hell?* He rose, took her by the hand and led the way up the stairs.

He unlocked the room, and when they were inside, he laid the bar over the door. The hearth was cold, but it didn't matter. He felt warm, and his breath caught as she touched the buttons of her bodice. He strode forward and pushed her hands away. He took the buttons of her cote-hardie himself and undid them, before leaning forward and taking her mouth in a kiss.

As sweet and as compliant as he remembered. She tasted of the wine from downstairs, of the spices from the brew and the currants of the berry flavor. He felt her arms around his neck and his own hands skimmed through the bodice to her back, holding her through only her chemise.

She shrugged out of the gown and let it fall to the floor. As they continued to kiss, she worked on the buttons of *his* cote-hardie. He moved incrementally back so that she could finish, and she looked up at him with a smile.

He smiled back, remembering how she'd be, and allowed her to pull off the coat and then his chemise. She ran her nails up his torso before relieving him of his braies and hose.

She looked him over approvingly before she grabbed the hem of her chemise and pulled it up and over her head. Now it was his turn to give *his* approval.

He moved in and took her in his arms, reveling in the soft feel of her, her hands and fingers running over him, her kisses and the way she nipped at his earlobe when he bent to kiss and caress lower. Finally, he pulled her toward his bed and yanked her up onto his lap as he sat on the edge.

Her arms twined around his neck, her thighs open around his waist. With her warm breath hitching at his ear and his hands beneath and behind her, she sighed. 'Crispin, Crispin. How I've missed you.'

'You scarce remembered me,' he said, bending his neck to taste her throat.

'I did remember. I had wicked thoughts of you.'

'Shame on you, Mistress Pyke. You should confess it.'

She tossed her hair back from her face and kissed him loudly.

'Oh, I did,' she purred. 'Often. But then the priest tired of me, sent me away.'

He shook his head, nose in her fragrant hair. 'So much sin.'

'And touching myself when I thought of you . . . like this.'

His breath caught and his eyes blazed watching her, until he couldn't stand it any longer and grabbed her to toss her back to the bed. When he bent over her, she smiled in triumph.

'So much sin,' he whispered before they stopped talking altogether.

SEVEN

Kat lay on Crispin's chest, fingers teasing his chest hair. He didn't mind. His eyes drooped and his lazy smile seemed permanently painted on his face. Her hands moved over his torso, fingers stopping at every scar.

'There are so many more of them,' she said with a sigh. 'Crispin.' She shook her head, leaving a trail of her hair swathed over him. 'You do get into trouble, don't you? I don't want you to be hurt. You must let Jack take on more of the responsibilities.'

'And let *him* get hurt? I think not. I need Jack.'

She sat up, hair framing one breast and hiding the other. 'But look at the state of you!'

He looked down along his chest and ribcage. There did seem to be more these days. Bruises, too. He didn't take a punch like he used to when he was younger. There were the old torture scars from the inquisitor's pincers, cuts from daggers, from swords, and from everything in between. He picked up her hand and yanked her until she fell on him, her face close enough to kiss. He did, savoring those pouting lips. 'No more than if I had remained a knight and fought in battles and jousts. I could even be dead by now.'

'Don't talk of death. Not you.' She hugged him, kissing his neck, his cheek. 'I will not entertain such a possibility. You are Crispin Guest, Invincible.'

'I'm very much not. I feel my age. I am far from invincible.'

She sat up again and cocked her head. 'How old *are* you?'

He pulled her down again. 'Never you mind.'

He felt her laugh against his chest, and stroked her hair, gliding his fingers through it, watching the gray light from the window catch on the soft smoothness of her tresses, and fall on his gnarled knuckles and calloused hand. He stopped and rested his fingers on her backside. 'We can't stay here all day. I must do my business.'

She sighed petulantly. 'And I must do mine.' But she whirled up and over him, balancing on her hands on either side of his shoulders while her knees spread over his hips. 'But how I have missed you. I'm glad you're here. Will you come tonight and watch our play? We'll be at the village green at sunset.'

'I wouldn't miss it.'

She smiled and slowly lowered herself. When she was on him, skin to skin, he moaned. 'I can't.' He grabbed her upper arms and gently shoved her aside. 'I must rise.'

She glanced down. 'Looks like it to me.'

'No, you minx.' With great reluctance, he rolled up and threw his legs over the side of the bed. 'I must go back to work. We've tarried too long here.'

'But it was such a good use of time.'

She threw an arm over his shoulder. He could feel her breasts pressing against his back, her lips at his ear. He turned and kissed her leisurely before he pulled slowly away. 'It was. But now I must to my work.'

He rose, adjusted himself, and bent to retrieve his clothes. She lay in the bed, tumbled amid the sheets, and watched him through the curls of her hair. He looked back only once, and cursed under his breath. When had he become such a weak man?

He'd just pulled his hose in place, still tied to his braies, when she asked, 'So . . . what is this treasure, Crispin?'

He paused only a moment before he upended his chemise and shook it down his body, punching his arms one at a time down the sleeves. He said nothing.

He could hear her get up from the bed. He tried to don his cote-hardie, but her naked body was in the way. *Don't look*, he admonished himself, and didn't, except for a glimpse of pale, white skin. 'Crispin,' she said, cloyingly. That was easy to ignore.

But when she spun him and he got tangled in the coat's sleeves, he had no choice but to gaze at her. 'Crispin Guest! Answer me.'

Calmly, he continued to straighten his coat, and buttoned it from the top down. 'I have nothing to say.'

'Your Jack mentioned a treasure. Something that I'd likely be interested in stealing. What is it? Just out of curiosity.'

He found his belt with its scabbard still attached and hefted it to his hips. 'Why is it, Kat, that I suddenly feel that you already know what it is? That perhaps you joined this troupe of players because they were coming to this very village . . . or better still. You *encouraged* them to come to this village?'

Her lips were twisted tightly, and her lids had drooped over her eyes.

He buckled his belt and smirked. 'Oh ho. Did my dart hit true?'

She swiped her chemise from off the floor and flung it over her head, wriggling it down over her body. 'You don't know anything about me.'

'I think I do.'

The gown was next. She slipped into it and began furiously buttoning. 'You don't. You may think you do, but you don't.' She mismatched buttons with buttonholes, and with an exasperated puff of breath, undid them and began buttoning again. 'Just because you are this "tracker", you think you know everything. All men are vain that way.'

'I see.' He sat on the bed to draw on his boots. 'Then it's an incredible coincidence you coming to this godforsaken village at the edge of a civilized kingdom?'

She stopped and looked up, pushing her hair out of her face. 'Well, not when you put it that way!'

'Kat, I tell you now . . . no, I am ordering you, to stay away from my employer. As usual, you don't know what you are getting into and I will not allow you to interfere.'

She finished buttoning with a flourish and looked up, chin raised. 'There are two things you must know about me, Crispin. One, I don't take orders. And two, I do what I like.' She raised up her hand. Not to strike him as he thought she might, but to show him his money pouch . . . in *her* hand.

He reached over and snatched it. Looking inside it, he was satisfied that most of it was there. 'That's not funny.'

She chuckled. 'It truly is, though.'

'No, it isn't. If I catch you anywhere near me, or Jack, or my employer, I *will* take you to the nearest sheriff.'

Her stiff posture softened and her smile curved her lips. 'You'll turn me in? Me? Oh, Crispin. Haven't I told you how many times

I've been delayed by sheriffs, only to be let free again? They can't hold me. They won't.'

'We'll see about that.' He darted in and kissed her on the forehead before her nails could sweep over him.

He laughed when he reached the door. 'Hadn't you better get along to your troupe?' he asked in the doorway.

She tied up her hair with a veil and stomped through the door, making sure one of her steps mashed Crispin's boot.

He grunted with pain and he could just see her smile as she retreated down the steps.

On his way again, he allowed Tobias to saunter through the village. The rain had stopped at least, but the path was muddied and stirred up from wagons and carts. He let his eyes wander over the few shopfronts and people picking their way over the mud with burdens over their shoulders.

When he got to the green, the players' wagon was there, setting up for the evening's play. He tried not to pick her out among the people milling about, and ended up turning away. When he met up with Teague again, he'd have to ask about her.

He glanced toward the small church and began to wonder how on earth he was to find Jack again. Perhaps it was best to return to the dry warmth of the inn. And just as he decided it, he spotted the man coming down from a small northern road.

He nudged the horse's flanks and trotted forward to meet Jack in the middle.

'Master!' Jack called out, waving.

Crispin met him knee to knee. 'Well? Have you discovered anything?'

'His sweetheart here in the village was devastated that he should be dead. It looks like her and her father expected that he would marry her and bring an income to them.'

'Did you ask about their acquaintances? Who else knew of their possible betrothal that didn't approve?'

'Well now . . . there wasn't time. You see, the father let it slip when I told him in confidence and there was no more use talking to her.'

Crispin sighed. 'You'll have to go back at some point.'

'Aye, I know it. What have you discovered?'

'That she wasn't his only sweetheart. There was another from a village in the forest. The woman's name is Eseld.'

'Oh. That is another matter, isn't it?'

'Indeed. We must explore this village. I've been warned that they are pagans. Even the men-at-arms in the castle fear them.'

Jack's eyes widened. 'Well . . . m-maybe . . .'

'We *must* go. Are you frightened?' He elbowed toward Jack and grinned. His apprentice tried to smooth his expression.

'Course not! I'm just . . . wary. As any good apprentice would be. I need to protect you, master.'

'You need to protect me. Of course.' He enjoyed Jack's grumbling, and grinned as he turned the horse back to the inn.

'Why there, sir?' asked Jack.

'Because we must find someone willing to take us to this village. We might be lost for weeks in that forest.'

Crispin called for food and settled down at a table close to the fire.

'Have you seen anything of Mistress Pyke today, sir?' asked Jack nonchalantly, sipping his ale from a wooden cup.

Crispin drank, set down his cup, and settled back in his chair. 'As a matter of fact, I did.'

'And?'

'And . . . I have reason to suspect she is here for Master Teague's treasure.'

'God blind me! I knew it.'

'I have no proof, of course. Only a suspicion.'

'I'll wager all, that you are right, sir.'

'We shall have to see. Ah. And here is Master Teague now.'

The man looked worn out. Little wonder, with finding a dead man in his barrow, and having to haul him up to the parish church above the village. He sat heavily at Crispin's side.

'Lord help me and all who survive the Devil's mischief,' he said with a deep sigh.

'Here.' Crispin shoved his own cup toward Teague and filled it from the jug. 'I've ordered food. Looks like you could use some.'

'Thanks, Master Guest.' He drank and didn't lower his cup till it was empty. 'What a horror. Such evil. Who could have done such a thing? Are you any closer to knowing who, Master Crispin?'

'Not yet. My enquiries have only just begun.'

'That Sir Regis at the castle. He's a hard man indeed. He's left it all to you, hasn't he?'

'It's best left to me. Some men make grievous mistakes when they try to investigate crimes. They destroy evidence and let scoundrels go free if it suits them. Especially when a bribe crosses their palms.'

Teague seemed appalled. 'Oh, you've seen some bitter things, have you not, Master Crispin? And that you can keep your honor doing it! And you, too, Master Jack. It takes a man of integrity to keep his head.'

Crispin borrowed Jack's cup to drink from. 'Deception is the stock-in-trade of the outlaw. No man wants to hang, even if he knows he deserves it.'

'I thank God for His timely intervention on your part, Master Crispin. For though traitor you were, you have redeemed yourself in God's eyes.'

Crispin choked only a little on his ale, but he continued to drink.

'Yes, it was a happy day indeed when He spared your life,' Teague went on. 'Look at the good you've done since.'

'The Duke of Lancaster saved my life,' he said, pushing the cup toward Jack, who filled it again. 'And I am ever grateful to him for it.'

'Ah, but the Holy Ghost must have come upon him to give him the strength for such a dangerous move. Yes, Master Crispin, you are blessed many times over.'

Crispin drank, saying nothing.

Their food arrived, a hot pottage with a cheese board and heavy brown bread. The three dug into their bowls, none speaking as they ate.

With his belly full, Crispin set his bowl aside. 'Master Teague, I wonder if you have ever encountered a woman named Katherine Pyke. She sometimes goes by the name Kat.'

Teague choked and began coughing, doubling over so that Crispin pounded upon his back. 'Come, sir. Are you well?'

He raised a finger before grabbing his cup and downing the ale. Teague sat back, clearing his throat. 'Ha. Well. Sorry about that. I, er . . . what did you say?'

Crispin eased back into his chair, folding his arms over his chest. 'I asked whether you had encountered a woman named—'

'Yes, yes. So you said. Well . . . it's strange you should ask. I . . . did encounter a woman of that name, some months ago.'

Blinking slowly, Crispin sighed. 'And did you by any chance mention to her your journey to discover these treasures?'

'Of course not! Why, I would never do such a thing.'

'Were you drunk? Did you bed her?'

'Master Guest!' He stumbled to his feet, setting his cup down hard. 'You forget yourself. You are under my employ. I beg you to remember that.'

Crispin hadn't changed his posture. 'My apologies,' he said, nodding slightly. 'It's just that I am acquainted with the lady and she has a way about her. And she is a seductress. She can loosen a man's tongue with drink and . . . other things. And . . . she is here.'

'What!' He whipped his head around, but seeing only a few men, and an elderly fellow sitting in the corner, he slowly sat again. He cradled his head in his hand. 'I . . . I regret to say that I did meet this woman . . . that I did drink perhaps a bit too much . . . and that . . . well. Her charms were . . . enticing to a lonely traveler long on the road.'

Crispin resettled himself at that. Teague was a slightly round man with the beginnings of jowls. Not an unattractive man, but not one she would take as a paramour simply for love. And she had done the same to Crispin, just to find out more of the treasure. He needn't flatter himself that she had worked her wiles for any other reason, even though he had wished it were so.

Had she already been to the castle? Had she enticed Roger Bennet to show her where the treasure was and killed him for it? But no. If she had and had gotten the treasure, she would be long gone. She said she had arrived with the troupe and Roger was killed two days ago. Could she have slipped away from them and somehow arrived here sooner? He'd have to talk to the mummers to find out.

Jack elbowed him, and Crispin got the impression from his face that this hadn't been the first time his apprentice had tried to draw his attention.

'Master, *could* Mistress Pyke be part of this crime?'

'I was just considering that, Jack. But the murder happened two days ago, and the troupe arrived the same time we did.'

Jack said nothing but he didn't look as if the story was over. He was surely having the same thoughts that Crispin had.

'In any case, Master Teague, do stay away from her.'

'You don't have to tell me twice, Master Guest. I felt the fool the first time. I shan't make myself the butt of any more of her foolery.'

'That is wise.'

'If you will excuse me, I think I will retire to our room to look over my maps. Come up when you can and we can scour them together.'

They both watched the man rumble up the stairs until he disappeared behind the door to their chamber.

They sat in silence for a time, until Jack, sitting back in the same posture as Crispin, ticked his head. 'You slept with her, didn't you?'

'Insolence, Tucker?'

Jack leaned forward and whispered harshly, 'You *slept* with her! Right under me nose.'

Crispin sighed and refilled his cup. 'And what if I did?'

Jack made an exasperated sound. 'You made a fool of yourself as much as Teague has.'

Crispin scowled. 'You're overstepping yourself.'

'I–I'm sorry, Master Crispin. I mean no disrespect . . . but . . .'

As quickly as his anger bubbled, it died again. 'No, you're right. She's just so . . .' He mused on her passionate embraces. Even now, given the chance, he'd— 'God's blood, Jack,' he hissed. 'But I told her nothing, put her on notice that I'd be watching her.'

'That's something, at least. How can we protect this treasure then?'

'It will have to wait. We need to get to this other village.' He stood. 'Men of Treknow,' he announced. People turned toward him, curious at the stranger. 'I have heard tell there is a village somewhere in the forests. I will need a man to take us there. I'm willing to pay.'

Silence.

Crispin scanned the crowd and they only greeted him with curious expressions. He stalked over to a table he took to be filled with locals. 'You men. Who will take us to this village?'

They turned away.

'Is no one brave enough?'

Even that didn't bring a response.

'Maybe this village doesn't exist. Maybe it's all lies.'

'It does exist,' said a man in the back of the room. All eyes turned to him.

'Then take me there.'

He glanced at his fellows, shook his head, and lowered his face.

'Master,' hissed Jack.

He looked the men over. Seldom had he seen such intense fear as they seemed to exhibit. It made him think twice . . . and that was a new viewpoint for him. *I must be getting old.* He had never feared to tread where danger lay before. But the looks on these men's faces certainly gave him pause.

'Maybe it's best to put this aside for now,' he said to Jack quietly.

It seemed the better part. After all, these tales of this invisible village with pagans inhabiting it did seem, on the face of it, outlandish. Superstition could make a man quake. 'Let us join Master Teague to see where he digs next. It is not so easy to hide on the island. Perhaps we can ask that the men-at-arms refuse entry to any women from the village.'

'That's a start.'

They rose and trudged up the stairs.

EIGHT

Teague had laid out the maps along the bed. 'Look here, Master Guest.' He didn't bother looking up. He merely smoothed the parchment and pointed. 'The next place to dig appears to be here.'

'Why do you think the sword was buried?'

'All the clues lead me to think so. They speak of earth, of caverns, of darkness. And the constellations here . . .' He pointed to a drawing on the map that delineated a star pattern depicting two brothers swathed in Greek tunics. 'According to my star charts, we should see Gemini over the next area to dig. But look here,' he said, pushing the map aside to reveal another parchment, covered in circles and other marks very like alchemy symbols, with more tiny script here and there on the margins and haphazardly in the middle, even overlapping the symbols and sigils. 'Here is the clue that took me long to decipher and I think it is the crux of it:

> *In the sanctum it abides,*
> *the undercurrents of time do guard*
> *the hollow of Caliburnus,*
> *until the King rises again.'*

'Caliburnus?' asked Jack.

'Yes,' commented Teague. 'The Latin name for Excalibur. Indeed, it has many names.'

Crispin couldn't remember the last time he'd been required to use a shovel . . . except when he was first banished from court and got the job as a gong farmer, cleaning out the latrines along the Thames. And he was lucky to get it. At least this was clean, fresh earth and not a privy. As long as there were no more corpses.

'If I were hiding a sword, I would not bury it.' He found that his hand lay on the hilt of his own sword, the one given to him by Henry Bolingbroke, the Duke of Lancaster's son. 'The earth would degrade it, rust it. No, a sword so prized would be encased in a coffer and secreted away. I wonder if you have ever investigated the chapel, Master Teague.'

The man stared at Crispin, jaw open, eyes wide. 'Bless me, sir. I never would have thought. Leave it to a man who has a sword for himself to think of such a thing.' He glanced down at his maps, searching out the clues only he seemed able to decipher. 'The *sanctum*! The chapel, Master Crispin. You are a marvel!'

For the first time, Crispin began to think that this search might prove viable. Would they truly find Excalibur?

'Shall we head back to the castle, Master Crispin, to look in the chapel? It is unoccupied, for the chaplain resides in the mainland ward.'

The spark of a quest warmed his heart with excitement . . . until he remembered his other task. 'My man and I are still in search of a murderer.'

The look on Jack's face reflected his own disappointment. They needed to talk to the men of the players' troupe. Had Kat urged them to come here? Had she left the wagons earlier than she had said? For even as he thought warmly of her, his suspicions of her motivations still haunted him.

And yet . . . this treasure-seeking reminded him of his days in Lancaster's company, when they went on their pilgrimages, and found adventure there. 'And yet,' he said, tentatively, 'I suppose further investigation could wait for a few hours.'

'Excellent!' cried Teague. He slapped Jack on the back. 'Let us go up to the castle, for a few hours at least, and investigate the chapel.'

Crispin regretted it the moment he gave in. Oh well. If there was a murderer, he doubted they'd be leaving anytime soon. If Kat had a hand in it, she would have been long gone. Maybe.

They set out again for Tintagel. This time, Crispin scanned the countryside past the mainland ward with his mind on two tracks:

one for a murderer and what his business had been, and two, for a place to hide a sword for hundreds of years.

Maybe the chapel was an obvious place, or perhaps not, for he could recall no story or history that would place the sword at the birthplace of Arthur. Wasn't it more likely to be at Camelot or Avalon . . . wherever they were?

For a man who had come across the Holy Grail, the Crown of Thorns, the Blood of Christ, and countless other relics, what was a simple mortal sword to that? And yet he felt foolish at the thought, for he had never looked for those other things. They had come to him, fallen into his lap for no earthly reason other than God had wanted them to. Or had He? Had they truly been authentic relics with mystical powers?

But even as he thought it, his hand went to his scrip that still contained a thorn from the Crown of Thorns. He'd never had the courage to use it again since that first accidental time, but he couldn't deny it was a comfort to have on his person, even though he wasn't entirely certain he believed in it.

The road up to the chapel wound around the hills and rocky outcroppings of the diamond-shaped spit of land that served as the island fortress. Crispin smelled the sea, could certainly hear it when the wind was right. Seabirds called from overhead, spinning on air currents, round and round like a whirlpool.

He saw Jack watching them and then casting his eyes across the lonely green hills, broken only by sheep and low stone houses, empty as the plateau itself.

'Such a solitary place,' said Jack, wind whipping his mass of curly, ginger hair. 'It's little wonder no one abides in the castle. It isn't like other castles, is it?'

'No,' answered Crispin before Teague could. 'Most are built of stone. I suppose this is a natural fortress, guarding the way from the sea.'

'Who'd be fool enough to try to land a boat out there? It's rocky, with waves crashing against it. I can hear them.'

Teague nodded. 'It's not a very hospitable place, but castles seldom are. But there is a beach, the Haven, where the ships came in to supply the castle. At least in an earlier day when the inhabitants were more numerous. The "Iron Gate", so it is called, was a defended wharf that protected the landing. But it is seldom used today. Though I daresay that Master Crispin has had his fill of castles, isn't that true, sir?'

He didn't know if he liked the man's familiar use of his name, but he didn't see the sense in making a fuss. 'I have lived at Pontefract with Lancaster. It's his favorite of his many manors and castles.'

'He's a very wealthy man, is he not?'

Crispin couldn't keep the sneer from his voice this time. 'I do not discuss my lord's finances. My . . . former lord's.'

'Of course not, Master Guest. I did not mean to offend. I only meant that you have lived in castles of stone and castles like this one, mere fortresses.'

'I've had my share, yes. But I was not usually on guard duty on the windswept battlements. I was in the comfort of the great hall, which this place seems to lack.'

'No. This is an old castle. Very old. From the times of the Saxon kings. The time of Arthur. It is a very long time ago, indeed.'

'Gives me the chills,' said Jack, shivering. 'Like a place of ghosts.'

'Oh indeed, Master Tucker!' said Teague, pulling his cart alongside Jack's horse. 'Ghosts abound, no doubt.' He swiveled his head, scanning. 'I long to hear the tales of those ghosts. But alas, I can only find their tales in the treasure they leave behind. Oh, I have found all manner of strange things. Clay pots and woven mats, decayed by time and neglect. Even some rags of clothing. They could have been great tapestries. Or perhaps the cloak of a king.'

Or the strips from a latrine, Crispin mused. He shouldn't like to dig those up.

'And I've found rusted knives and swords and shields.'

'But rags and rusted swords aren't worth naught,' said Jack.

'Ah! But I have also found silver goblets, dented and ruined from the soil heaped upon them. Golden torques – that's jewelry for the neck, worn by warriors of old. Oh, yes. They tell tales, these objects.'

'And you sell those,' said Crispin. 'That which you do not surrender to the crown.'

'Of course. I have no need of them, and they fund my further explorations. Someday, I shall retire from this, with good coin in my purse. But the finding of Excalibur. That would be a grand prize indeed.'

'You'd keep it, then.'

'No, Master Crispin. I should find a wealthy patron to sell it to. It wouldn't do me proud at all to keep such a treasure. It belongs to a lord, quite properly. I am no lord, after all. Just a simple merchant.'

They passed through what might at one time have been a lychgate but was little more than weathered posts stuck in the ground and covered with moss. Crispin and Jack dismounted and tied their horses to the cart.

They entered through the west door and came to a rectangular space, with small windows of glass and plastered walls. It was so insignificant a space that it needed no pillars or columns. Just the framework above of roof trusses, holding up the slate roof.

The tile floor was damp and smelled of mildew.

Jack crossed himself, looking up to the cracked and weathered crucifix of the wooden rood screen. The shadowed chancel lay beyond it. A small stone tomb without adornment, stone rubbed raw through the passing years, sat in one corner. The altar in the sanctuary was sorry and sad without its altar cloth or candelabrum. Just another dim detail against the crumbling plaster.

'Master Teague,' Crispin began, 'how is it we are to explore the chapel without, well, destroying it? The building is made of stone. Even if we lift up these tiles on the floor, surely someone will notice.'

'We must be very careful, Master Crispin. And very judicious as to where we decide to— Oh! Look here.'

Crispin hurried over, joined by Jack. They looked where Teague pointed. Up on the wall on a keystone above an arched window was the vague outline of a chiseled sword. The stone was worn and smooth, and the sword seemed to have beams of light surrounding its blade. At least the damaged and pocked stone made it look that way.

'Bless me,' Teague breathed. 'And look.'

There was a shield painted on the tile below it. The arms were unknown to Crispin. There was a crown above a winged dragon. Crispin's own arms sported a dragon, for his ancestry was Welsh, but it wasn't like this one. The painting was rough and damaged with age. It couldn't rightly be identified except by the most experienced heralds.

'The Pendragon arms,' said Teague with awe.

'Are you certain of that?' Crispin got as close as he could, but the dragon could just as easily be a lion, or some other fanciful creature.

'Yes. I have seen this before. Master Guest!' He rubbed his hands before gesturing to the tiles around the base of the window. 'Beneath these tiles must lie the sword Excalibur!' The man danced about a bit, looking like a mastiff sniffing the tiles, touching them, spitting and rubbing along the worn designs. 'We must be careful. We'll use the pickax if need be, but it would be wise at first to use the chisel and carefully scrape away the mortar. And look here. You see this tile is different from the ones around it? As if it covers . . . a vault!'

Could the man be right? Crispin examined it for himself, and what Teague said was true. The tile was different, and could indeed be covering a later vault. 'But it might just as easily be the body of the last chaplain here.'

'Under a window? That doesn't seem likely, does it? Master Tucker, be so good as to fetch the pickax and chisels from the cart.'

Jack waited for Crispin's nod before hurrying outside. Crispin paced slowly before the window and then decided to check the one opposite, across the nave's aisle. There were carvings there as well, but not the same as the shining sword. Looked like a distorted angel.

But Teague's excitement was creeping upon him. What if Excalibur *did* reside beneath these tiles? Any knight would like to see such a thing, and he was no exception.

'Master Teague, according to the law, would not treasure found in a religious house belong to the Church?'

'Quibbling, Master Crispin. I have my charter.'

'From King Edward. Long dead now. If you have made no new charter with Richard, to whom do you make your payments to the crown?'

'The coroner of London, of course. He doesn't seem to vex himself about them.'

And doubtless does not pass them along to the king, Crispin considered. And why should he? What Richard doesn't know . . .

Jack returned with the chisel and hammer and studied them skeptically. Carantok Teague knelt beside him, showing him what was expected. Reluctantly, Crispin thought, Jack set to with cautious hammering on the chisel head, dislodging old mortar. Jack and Carantok slowly made their way around a single tile when it finally loosened. Heartened, Jack held it up proudly, showing Crispin.

Crispin supposed he was to stand by as guard. Well, it was better than getting his hands dirty, he decided. He rested said hand on his hilt and made his way down the dim nave to the door. He pushed it open with his shoulder and stood on the porch overlooking the green plain sloping away from him.

It seemed open and unsheltered. But Crispin well knew that a man on the moors or out in the vast wilderness would not necessarily stand out among the shrubs and rock outcroppings.

'What do you seek, Master Guest?'

Crispin jerked to the side, his heart pounding. He realized his sword was halfway from his scabbard when he slapped it back in place. 'Master Gwyls. You have a habit of appearing out of thin air.'

'Do I?' said the old caretaker. 'I did not mean to startle you.'

'And I was just now contemplating the fact that a man can hide easily in plain sight out here on these hills.'

'Oh, yes, indeed. For it is not as flat and as featureless as it first appears. There are many places for a canny man to hide.'

'Like you?'

'Master Guest, I was not hiding. I was going about my business. And as caretaker, I . . . er . . . *take care* of all. For instance, I noticed people up here at the chapel where there usually are none.'

Crispin surreptitiously closed the door. 'My man and our employer are doing some . . . research.'

A loud clang, a sound of something shattering, and Jack's muffled oaths rang out at just that moment. Crispin never changed expression, but he could feel his cheeks warm.

'Loud research,' said Marzhin, with something of a smile lighting his eye. 'Your employer, Master Guest,' he went on, looking down at his shuffling feet, 'digs holes. Like a rabbit. I have watched him for some time. He seems to be looking for something. Something in particular?'

'I do not wish to lie to you, sir. But I am not at liberty to discuss the details.'

'He disinters history, as you said before. Interesting.'

'Just so.'

Marzhin's milky blue eyes raked over Crispin as if reading his character with the mere movement of his lashes. He leaned heavily on his staff. 'Have a care, Master Guest. Sometimes digging up the past leads to trouble.'

'I wonder. Could that be why Roger Bennet was killed? Was more dug up than Saxon trinkets?'

Marzhin shrugged.

'And what do you know of him, Master Gwyls? Did you see Roger Bennet double back when he was supposed to be leaving Tintagel?'

'I think Tintagel has a way of getting under one's skin, sir. You might leave the grounds, but Tintagel never leaves you.'

'I have seen more beautiful castles.'

'I imagine you have. But . . . none quite so old, eh?'

'I have been on pilgrimage to the Holy Land, sir. With my Lord of Gaunt.'

'John of Gaunt's man, were you? And you've seen the Holy Land. Well, those are old places indeed. Nearly fourteen hundred years old. And more.'

'Those places were as vacant as these grounds, though they were dry and dusty, not lush and green. But they were just as lonely, just as inhabited by ghosts as this place is.'

'Ghosts. Yes.' He leaned forward on his staff, resting his temple against it. 'I've seen the ghosts. Maybe *they* killed our Roger Bennet.'

'I don't know that I believe in ghosts,' he said, but even as the words left his lips, he remembered a specter he thought he saw in Canterbury, so long ago now, when Jack was still a fresh-faced lad.

'Oh, there are ghosts, Master Guest. You can believe me on that. Perhaps they don't like your Carantok Teague taking their precious objects.'

'I do not think ghosts killed the man with a blow to the head. That is mortal mischief. Did you know the man well?'

He shrugged. 'I only knew of him. The caretakers do not mingle with the men-at-arms. The guards do not wish it, and we do not like to be where we are not welcomed. They are too rough for old men, anyway. Bennet was a man who took his lot unhappily. He did not choose to be at Tintagel. Though some see it as an honor' – he bowed slightly – 'others did not see it that way. He was a gambler and a dallier. He lost at both.'

'Simple jealousy, perhaps. A jealous husband or lover.'

'That certainly could be the case.'

Crispin's eyes couldn't help but sweep over the verdant hills and up to a gray sky that hung over the cliff edges to the sea like a tapestry. 'Can you do me a service, Master Gwyls? Can you alert me as to who comes into the castle?'

'Of course. But . . . have you considered that it might not be anyone outside the castle?'

'I am well aware, Master Gwyls. I must find the right time and place to talk to the men here in greater detail.'

'In that case, I wish you luck, Master Guest. In all your endeavors.'

He bowed. Throwing the end of the staff forward, he stepped off the chapel porch and strode away, punching the staff into the turf as he went.

Crispin watched him grow smaller into the distance. A mist was rolling down over the landscape, as if climbing up the cliffs from the sea. It made him mindful of the time. He didn't want to miss tonight's performance.

He opened the door and walked down the nave to gauge the progress of his companions. A pile of tiles sat beside them, and Jack had employed pickax as well as spade to dig a hole. Teague eagerly scrambled to his feet and approached Crispin. 'We have found a vault.'

Merely raising his brows in comment, Crispin peered over his shoulder into the hole Jack had excavated. With a smear of dirt on his face, Jack looked up at his master. 'Sir! Look here.' He lifted something from the hole and held it aloft.

A gold pendant in the shape of a dragon.

'It's got writing on it,' said Jack, screwing up his face to hold it close. '*Whosoever seeks the resting place of Calesvol must in all faith look deeper . . . but not here.*' He kept using his thumb to scrap away the dirt, and read it again, his lips moving silently over the Latin words. 'Then we are not in the right place. For this *Calesvol* isn't what we seek.'

'Merciful God and all His angels!' cried Teague, and then he danced a jig, lifting the hem of his long gown.

Crispin and Jack exchanged glances. 'Sir,' Crispin ventured, 'I take it these are *good* tidings?'

'Yes. Yes!' He bolted toward Jack and swept the dragon from his grasp, turning it over and over, first looking at the dragon side, and then reading the back. 'This is very good news.' He closed his eyes and pressed his lips to the golden pendant. 'Master Crispin, this is what we seek. Don't you see? *Calesvol* is the Cornish name for . . . Excalibur.'

NINE

Crispin ran his fingers over the cold metal, the carved dragon whose tail was wound about it, making a teardrop shape. On the other side, the pendant was flat and etched with the Latin letters. 'Then by these words, we are not digging in the correct place. Why would they have put this here?'

Teague snatched it back, breathing heavily and staring at it. It glimmered in the last faint glow of sunlight through the glass panes. 'Because I believe the sword *was* here at one time. Someone deemed it unsafe to remain. You see here the vault.'

There appeared a rectangular space that Jack had yet to fully unearth. It was constructed of stone. Too small for a body. But just right for a sword. Crispin's heart stuttered. Could this excitable man have been right all along? Was there truly a chance to find this sword of swords?

'And they left this here to . . . to what? If it were unsafe here and liable to be stolen, why would someone leave a clue as to its true whereabouts?'

'That is a puzzle.' Teague's round face fell to shadow in the dying light. 'It could mean that this clue is a ruse.'

'Though etched on gold . . .' said Jack.

'Ah, but Master Tucker,' said Teague, 'what better way to lure us to some other location, far from the sword. An expensive trifle this, but it would do the trick. *Will* do the trick, I daresay, for we have no other clues to follow.'

Jack's shoulders fell. 'Do you mean it's a lie all along?'

'That remains to be seen.' Teague's face turned dreamy. '*In the sanctum it abides, the undercurrents of time do guard, the hollow of Caliburnus, until the King rises again*,' he recited. 'Do you understand the meaning, Master Jack? The sword Excalibur lies in wait in the mysteries of the ages, waiting for Arthur to come again. He is the king that will arise and make the land whole again. For Arthur was more than a slayer of Saxons. With the magic of Merlin he shall be the great king once more.'

'How you weave fanciful tales out of history,' said Crispin.

'Not a bit of it, sir,' said Teague, hand to his heart. 'This is what so captures the hope and imagination of the telling of his tale. And did we not pass through plague times and these endless winters? It is all a sign.'

'Will stealing his sword from its hiding place bring him sooner, do you think?'

Teague frowned. 'You may well mock me—'

'That was not my intention, sir.' He did not like bringing out the sour expression on the usually merry merchant. 'I have always been a pragmatic man. I take history as it is written, not the fancies in the margins.'

Teague smiled again. Crispin felt relieved at it. 'I see your character, Master Crispin. You like the recitation of facts. It is your catechism. But do we not need both kinds of men, like you and like me? Else there would be no philosophers, no alchemists, no architects or masons to imagine building the great palaces and cathedrals. Oh yes, that takes imagination, too. We have our world because practical men teamed with dreamers.'

Crispin nodded and offered a smile. 'I concede it.' He glanced again toward the window. 'But our dreaming further will have to wait for the morning. It is growing late and soon to be dark. I do not wish to be on this road in the darkness.'

'Right you are, Master Crispin. But this calls for a celebration! We shall go to the inn and get ourselves some wine.'

'There is a performance of the players at the village green,' Crispin reminded him. He hoped his voice did not sound overly eager.

'Is there?' said Teague. 'Well then! Let us fix this place, and get us to the inn. We will see the players at nightfall!'

Jack repaired the floor with mud, sweeping it clean with a broom from Teague's wagon – and did an adequate job of it, Crispin noted with some pride – and they grabbed their mounts and followed Teague's wagon down the winding lane.

Looking up at the distant hill with its small stone church upon it, Jack tutted. 'I hope Roger Bennet's family will soon fetch him. That's a sad thing, him lying there all by himself, not even a monk for prayers and company.'

'Yes. A sad state of affairs,' said Crispin. 'And speaking of affairs, we might spend our time at the green asking – discreetly – if Bennet might have had other female companionship in the village.'

'I suppose a man has nothing but time at an outpost like this.'

'Except that he soon discovered how little time he actually had.'

'God caught up with him,' said Jack sagely. 'Or the Angel of Death, I suppose.'

'And there is still the problem of getting to this other village.'

'Do you think it *is* true, sir? That there *is* this other village?'

He shrugged. 'Sir Regis and some of the men in Treknow seem to think so. There is the woman Eseld. Perhaps she is a fabrication. Perhaps not. In any case, we need to be certain.'

Jack adjusted his seat on the horse. 'If we can convince a man to lead us.'

It was a slow amble through the gate, through the mainland ward, and then out onto the road to the village. They stabled the horses and got inside the warm inn, and settled in with their celebratory wine, though Teague kept his excitement from getting the better of him. No sense in alerting strangers that a great treasure was at hand.

Crispin cocked half an ear to the others at the inn, talking about tonight's performance. Even in crowded London such a thing would have gathered most of the populace, but in a small village, it would be as good as a market day. Everyone was certain to be there. A good chance for he and Jack to peruse the crowd, to ask some questions . . . before the revelers got too drunk.

There was no sign of Kat. No doubt she was with her fellow mummers. He had more questions for her. Casting a glance at Jack, he supposed he should make sure his apprentice was with him. To avoid any . . . conflicts of interest.

It seemed the inn also served as the local alehouse. Villagers sat with the inn's guests; there was talk all around him of the murder and the speculation about it. He listened hard to any clues. The man's conquests in the village were often mentioned.

Jack sidled closer to him and spoke quietly. 'Master Bennet seems to have been all over this parish.'

'You're listening, too.'

'Aye, sir. Maybe we should gather all the women in one place. It will save us time in questioning them.'

'That does not sound wise.'

'Oh. I see what you mean, sir.'

'Perhaps it is a simple case of a jealous woman.'

'And she killed him? Blind me. Then we will have to enquire of all his women.'

'You didn't get anything out of the milkmaid Janet?'

'I fear that I did not. She was so woebegone . . .'

'It might have been playacting.'

Jack frowned. 'God's blood! It seems I am as feeble around women as you are . . . Sir,' he quickly added.

Crispin didn't bother scowling. 'Kat told me she tried her wiles on you . . . and was unsuccessful.'

'I'd never, sir! For one, I'm a married man. And for another . . . well. She . . . she was with you, sir. I'd never . . . never . . .'

'I get your meaning, Jack,' he muttered.

Crispin rose, deciding to approach some of those in the inn now before they became lost in the darkness on the green. Jack seemed to know his intent and rose to follow him.

With his cup in hand and a smile on his face, Crispin approached the first group of men. He pretended to be tipsy and off balance. 'Did I hear you aright?' He leaned over conspiratorially and placed a hand unsteadily on their table. 'You were talking about that dead man.' He husked a whisper. 'And his *women*?'

The man looked Crispin over and glanced back at Jack . . . who suddenly had a sloppy grin on his face.

The man chuckled. 'Oh, he had women, right, lads?' He raised his cup to his companions and they all laughed and drank.

Crispin slid onto a vacant stool. 'More than one? In this little village?'

The man wiped his mouth and leaned toward Crispin. 'He had bollocks, that's a certainty. I know of Janet the milkmaid, Derwa the goose-girl, Mabyn the weaver . . . who am I forgetting, lads?'

'Gwendolyn,' said a man with a dusky blond beard. 'That's all I can think of.'

'And the woman Eseld from the village in the forest,' offered Crispin.

They stared at him, all laughter suddenly dropped from their faces. 'Eseld?' said a man with a blue cote-hardie, before men closest to him hushed him to silence.

He cleared his throat. 'Oh . . . er . . . well, no one goes there . . . to that village. Even Roger Bennet had more brains than to do so.'

'But I heard he had,' urged Crispin. 'A woman named Eseld.'

There was a bit of murmuring before all fell to stark silence.

'Aye,' said a man speaking at last. His hair as red as Jack's. 'I heard that Sir Roger carried on at that village. Strange, that place.

I shouldn't like to go to theirs. Might get swallowed up like a faery barrow.'

Crispin forgot to appear drunk when he asked, 'Would you be brave enough – for enough silver – to take us to that village?'

The man glanced at his companions. He looked like the ones earlier, who had declined to even speak of it, before he seemed to draw himself up. 'Aye. For the right amount I would.'

'And your name, sir?' asked Crispin.

'Kenver. Kenver Treeve.'

'Thank you, Master Treeve. I'll contact you on the morrow. Can I find you here?'

'As well as not. And who might you be?'

'I am Crispin Guest, in search of Roger Bennet's killer.' The room quieted at that. 'And what of these women of Roger Bennet,' he said to the others. 'Do they know of each other?'

Smiles slowly returned to the men's solemn faces. 'Oh, aye,' said the blond bearded fellow. 'They do now. There's been a bit of hair pulling. Wouldn't be surprised if one of them – whist!' He drew his finger over his throat like a knife blade.

The others laughed heartily at that. Blue Cote-hardie seemed to have recovered his tongue and took another drink. 'A man who can't master his women, well. I suppose they'll master him.'

'You think one of them murdered him?' asked Crispin.

Blue Cote-hardie settled back in his chair. 'I shouldn't be surprised.'

'Well,' said Crispin, buttoning his cloak, 'I hear the mummers are performing a play at dusk on the green. I wouldn't like to miss it.'

'That's true, lads,' said Kenver. 'Let's to it.'

The rest of them rose, and soon more men were donning their cloaks and heading toward the door. Crispin and Jack headed back toward Teague, who was buttoning his cloak over his chest. 'Let us all travel to the green,' said Teague. 'And then to bed, for early in the morning we must ferret out this clue.' He patted the pouch at his hip that held the gold dragon pendant. If he didn't find the sword, at least that gold would keep him for a while. Unless he turned it over to the coroner. Crispin snorted at the chance of that.

With a pink horizon hanging over the distant trees, the people of the village all seemed to be streaming from their houses and shops and heading toward the green. Crispin could see the light from many torches glowing ahead, and he was no less excited than the others.

He was glad of the cloudless night, for the many stars hung above them like a great dome.

Music filtered into the evening air, and once they turned the corner at an overarching oak, there was Kat with her mummer fellows, sitting on a bench and playing a tabor, beating on the drum to the music of a man playing a shawm and a woman sawing with her bow on a rebec.

Her glance seemed to home in on Crispin the moment he turned toward her, and he looked back unabashedly . . . a smile of remembrance blooming on his face.

The whole village had gathered. Kenver Treeve sidled up to him. He gestured with his head and pointed to a plump woman with dark hair. 'If you'd know it, Master Guest, yon is Gwendolyn. And there . . .' He pointed toward a fey-looking blonde woman. 'That's Derwa.'

Derwa seemed to have a sour look on her face, and she was standing next to an equally grumpy man. Could it be her husband who had learned of his wife's infidelity? Crispin made his way toward them and bowed. He surveyed the thin-boned woman, who seemed bird-like and fragile. 'Are you Derwa?'

The man stepped in front of her and even pushed her back. 'Who are you?'

He bowed again. 'I am Crispin Guest, Tracker of London. I investigate crimes.'

Mention of London seemed to cow the man and his tense muscles eased. 'You've come all the way from London?'

'I happened to be in the region when Roger Bennet was killed. May I speak to your wife on it?'

'She isn't my wife. And not likely to be anytime soon.' Instead of demurring to the man, Derwa lifted her head and tossed back her hair. It appeared that her fragility was only skin-deep.

'Then . . . if I may speak to you?'

The man didn't seem to want to leave, but after a pause, he stomped away. Jack stood at a distance, keeping an eye on all who passed, and a particular one on the man betrothed to Derwa.

Crispin faced her. 'When was the last time you saw Roger Bennet?'

She folded her arms and sniffed derisively. 'Monday last. Had I known he was carrying on with so many others, I wouldn't have given him my time at all.'

'Two days ago. Did he come to the village, or . . .'

'He rarely came to the village.' She stopped, shook her head, and kicked at the turf. 'No, as I understand it, that isn't true. He only told *me* he didn't come to the village. But, er . . .' She glanced about and spotted Gwendolyn. 'I have since learned that this was not so.'

'You met him at the castle. Where?'

'At the chapel. I should be ashamed to say so . . . but I'm not. I know Menhyr promised himself to me, but so did Roger. He had more money. But all his promises were lies.'

'Demoiselle. You last met him the day he died. You might have been the last person to have seen him alive.'

'Would that not be the murderer?'

Crispin said nothing, but kept his gaze steady.

'I did not kill him, if that is your thinking, sir. I had no reason to. But since learning of his other liaisons, I'd have thought hard about doing so.'

'I don't blame you, demoiselle. But dallying with two men . . . might leave you with none.'

Her arms remained tightly folded. 'Are we done?'

'When you left him at the chapel, did you see anyone else along the plains?'

'I don't recall seeing anyone. None but them caretakers. That one with the long beard and staff.'

'Master Gwyls?'

'I don't know none of their names. I don't take up with those from the castle. Not no more. Not ever again.'

She didn't seem to have any more to say, so he bowed, and she turned sharply away.

Jack whistled. 'That is one angry woman.'

'I suppose I don't blame her. Though she is just as guilty and faithless.'

'But is she telling the truth about only finding out about his liaisons *after* he died?'

'That is the crux of it.' When he turned again to follow her on the darkening green, he spotted Gwendolyn, who was staring at him. He decided to take advantage of the remaining light and go to her. When she seemed to sense that he was approaching, she threw the end of her cloak over her shoulder and turned to hurry away. Crispin trotted to catch up.

'Demoiselle!'

She stopped. He doubted anyone ever called her that. Likely

'wench!' was what they called out to her most times. She turned back to him with surprise on her features.

'You are Gwendolyn?'

'Who's asking?'

Her hair was a wild mass of curls. Brown, he thought, but it was difficult to tell by the easing of sunlight. She was a plump woman with a round face and a large bosom. Roger Bennet seemed to find himself the prettiest lasses in the village.

He bowed. 'I am Crispin Guest, Tracker of London. I investigate crimes.' She seemed as intimidated at mention of London as Derwa's betrothed had been. 'And I am investigating the death of Roger Bennet.'

'Him.' She snorted.

'I take it you were not aware of his other . . . erm . . . female companionship.'

'Companionship? Is that what they call whores these days?'

A woman came barreling out of the gloom. 'I heard what you said, you squealing pig!' she cried.

Before Crispin could speak, the woman laid hold of Gwendolyn, grabbing a fistful of her hair and slapping her face.

Gwendolyn screamed and, with clawed fingers, scratched them down the other woman's cheek. There was kicking and more hair-grabbing, and soon they were down on the turf, rolling about. A gathering of men formed a ring around them, and they all cheered and guffawed at the proceedings.

Crispin glanced helplessly at Jack and was about to intervene when a priest in a long black gown did it first.

'Gwendolyn! Mabyn! Stop this at once!' The young priest, whose tonsure shone bright in the torchlight, yanked at the backs of both their collars, pulling them apart. They panted and had their eyes fixed on each other, fingers curled, ready to go at each other like cats. He shoved one back and then the other. 'I know well what you are fighting over but it is only folly. And sin. Let it rest, like poor sinful Roger. Let his soul rest, and let yours seek counsel and prayers. You have all done wrong. Now you see where all this sin has gotten you. You see where it has gotten Roger.'

'She called me a whore!' screeched Mabyn.

'And so you are,' countered Gwendolyn.

Mabyn jolted toward her when Crispin grabbed her arm. 'None of that.'

'You are all whores,' said the priest with a snarl. 'You lay with men under the eyes of God without so much as a promise of wedlock.'

'He did promise to marry me,' said Gwendolyn.

'And me!' wailed Mabyn.

And Janet, thought Crispin. *And Derwa. What a churl.*

The priest seemed surprised. Maybe there weren't as many confessions taking place as there should have been. Surely Roger never confessed his sinful ways.

'That matters not,' he said, recovering. 'You must pray on it. Leave this place as penance. You do not deserve entertainments when you have behaved so shamelessly.'

Mabyn wrested her arm from the priest. 'You can't tell me what to do. No man will tell *me* what to do ever again!' But she stormed off anyway, leaving the green.

Jack sidled up to Crispin and whispered, 'That wench will find it hard to get a husband.'

Crispin wasn't so sure. He saw the light in many a man's eye in the circle. Some men relished the cultivating of a wilder woman.

Gwendolyn huffed a sigh. She straightened her cloak, made a half-hearted curtsey to the priest, and walked away, head held high. It seemed that Roger Bennet preferred a certain kind of woman.

So did Crispin, when it came down to it. He couldn't help but glance toward Kat, who was peering toward the proceedings from a distance, still keeping a beat on her drum, and scrunching her brow.

A man came forward on the makeshift stage and blew a strong note on a trumpet. Everyone suddenly turned toward him.

'We tell the tale of Arthur, King of all England,' he announced, and stepped to the far end of the stage. From behind a hanging tapestry, painted with images of angels and demons, a player stepped forth, garbed like a king with a crown on his head made to look like gold.

The people quieted and moved closer to the torchlit stage, their faces enrapt by what they saw before them.

This was unusual, thought Crispin. Usually such plays were about local saints or the mysteries of Christ and His Passion. Here was a secular tale, not unlike the Greek plays of old.

The player mimed the action as the man with the trumpet told the tale, of Arthur's bravery, his fighting skills against the Saxons

– and more players came out and fought him with wooden blades in something like a dance.

The tale wound around – bits and pieces of the history told out of order – until it came to Excalibur. A player wheeled out an anvil on a stone made of leather or painted canvas, with a wooden sword plunged into the top of it. With the musicians playing dramatically, Arthur approached the sword, even though the other 'knights' on the stage scorned him. But when he pulled it out to a great trumpet blast that stirred the sleeping birds from the trees, a shower of colorful ribbons cascaded from the stage, and the people cheered.

It ended as Arthur was borne away, mortally wounded on a wooden skiff. And as the players, dressed as grieving women, rolled the skiff through the curtain, the musicians played a mournful tune and the performance was at an end.

The villagers applauded and tossed coins into the baskets that other players brought through the crowd.

And it was over. Crispin couldn't help searching for Kat, but she had disappeared from the musicians' bench, likely helping her fellow mummers return all to the wagon for the night. There was to be a different play tomorrow night.

'I never seen the like,' said Jack, with eyes shining. 'It truly seemed like Excalibur. Especially when it glowed with fire. How'd they do that, Master Crispin? It was like magic.'

Teague had found them again and was smiling eagerly. 'Yes, it was thrilling, wasn't it? It makes it all the more exciting to find the sword, does it not, young Master Tucker?'

'Aye, sir, it does.'

'You seemed very keen on the performance yourself, Master Crispin.'

'Me?' Crispin straightened his cloak, and raised his chin. 'As much as any play, I suppose.'

'Come, sir. Even you surely felt the thrill of finding the true Excalibur. And not one of wood as we saw tonight. But the true blade.' He glanced about secretly, a wide grin on his face. 'And it is almost in our grasp!'

'Let us not get ahead of ourselves,' Crispin grumbled. 'The thing is yet to be found. It's stayed hidden all these centuries. We must not have been the first to search for it. And we may not be the last.'

'Oh, but I think we will be. I have such hopes.' He strode quickly ahead of them as Jack fell into step with Crispin.

'He's all fire, isn't he?'

'Yes. We might yet find the sword.'

'I hope we do,' said Jack, a quiver to his voice. 'I don't mind saying, sir, that them relics that we find give me the shivers. But this. This is different. It might even be . . . magical.'

'I don't believe in magic.'

'I do. In faery folk and the like. There's more than this around us, sir.' He waved his hand to encompass the world. 'There's God and His angels . . . and His relics. But there's more, too. Me mother told me as much when I was but a lad.'

Crispin didn't wish to dampen his apprentice's mood or his upbringing. He said nothing and walked with him back to the inn. Many had joined them with ale aplenty, but soon the innkeeper doused the lights. Those with rooms retreated to them, the villagers went home to their own beds, and the inn's servants positioned the benches before the fire and retired there.

Crispin and Teague shared the bigger bed, while Jack took the smaller. The excitable Carantok fell asleep almost immediately. *Must be a pure heart*, thought Crispin, for it hadn't taken Jack long either, snoring softly on his cot, long legs stretched out and stocking feet shooting out from the blankets past the edge of the bed.

Crispin sighed into the slightly smoky chamber and lay back. He was hopeful that the murderer would soon be found. Either a jealous woman or an angry betrothed was surely responsible. Simple.

He tried to reason out who it might be, but his treacherous thoughts kept creeping back to Kat. She was so close. Who knew where she spent the night? Was it on the wagon? In a room with all the players? All those . . . *male* players? True, there were some women as part of their troupe, but he knew Kat. She was an opportunist. She'd find the most important man in the troupe and . . .

He didn't want to think about it. Crispin had only been another opportunity. Of course, he'd used many a woman precisely like that. *The boot's on the other foot, eh?* He was certainly old enough to take it, but he'd never liked being made a fool of. *Perhaps it's only what you deserve*, he considered. He'd failed in keeping his oaths and honor. It was his lot to be used by others, even women.

Knowing all that didn't make the yearning for her any less. She was a beautiful woman with exceptional wit. And with the heart and courage of a man. For once, he lay in his bed and didn't think about Philippa Walcote, the mother of his bastard son.

He let his thoughts wander, replaying this most recent encounter, when he and Kat had been together in this very bed. It aroused him but he could do nothing about it now but squeeze at his groin to take some of the ache away.

Weariness finally overtook him and he drifted into sleep.

Crispin's eyes snapped open. A crushing weight on his chest; strong, taut hands encircled his neck and squeezed. Was he dreaming? But no. He realized in the dark that there *was* a figure above him. He thrashed, scratching at the wrists, but when that proved useless, he reached up into the shadowy face above him and plunged his thumbs into the eyes.

The man cried out. He fell away. Crispin gasped, sucking in air.

Jack awoke, shouted, and there was a scrambling at the open casement and a dark figure slipped out. Jack leapt and soared over the sill.

Crispin shot to the window while Teague woke belatedly and blearily.

'God blind me!' cried Jack from below, splashing and thrashing about.

Teague came to the casement with a lit candle and they both looked down.

Jack stood in a trough and wrung out his tunic. 'I'm sorry, master. I lost him.'

TEN

They bundled Jack in front of the fire in the inn's hall, and the innkeeper supplied more faggots to urge the flames. His wet clothes hung before the hearth and Crispin handed him some warmed wine. He took it gratefully and downed it, licking his lips as he handed back the goblet.

'Did you see anything that could identify the culprit?' said Crispin, touching at his sore neck.

'No, master. Nothing. A big figure is all. With a strong arm.' He rubbed at the side of his head.

'Someone doesn't want me investigating.'

'Then we *are* looking for a jealous husband or lover.'

'More than likely.'

'But Master Guest,' said Teague, 'how did they find you?'

'Master Crispin tells all and sundry where they can find him,' said Jack. 'So that witnesses can freely come to him. But sometimes . . . murderers do too.'

Teague pressed a hand to his mouth. 'That's appalling!'

'It's how I do business,' rasped Crispin, clearing his throat again.

'Sir,' said Jack, rising to refill the goblet and handing it to Crispin. 'You should drink the warm wine. It will help your throat.'

Crispin smiled his thanks and drank the heated brew. It did feel better.

After sending the innkeeper back to his bed, Crispin felt it was time to do the same. The servants who had been dislodged by their activity in the hall were already snoozing in the corners.

The three trudged up the stairs and back to their room. Jack made sure the door and window were barred. They settled in again to sleep.

The wine helped Crispin, and exhaustion did the rest. But when he awoke with the others the next morning, his anger at the night's proceedings returned. He didn't like the idea of someone coming into his chamber to murder him. Not one bit. And Jack was just as incensed, if not more so, that some knave had tried to kill his master while he lay sleeping.

'It's not to be borne,' grumbled Jack, dressing with a flourish of anger, slamming his knife in its sheath, shoving his belt strap through the buckle, wrestling his cloak over his shoulders.

Crispin watched his apprentice for a moment more before putting a steadying hand to his shoulder. 'Jack, calm yourself. A little anger is called for but it will blind you to the task at hand. You mustn't be diverted. We have a murderer to catch.'

Taking a deep breath, Jack steadied himself. 'You're right, sir. I'm letting my emotions get in the way of things. I shall try to be stoic. Like you, sir.'

Stoic like me. He wished the culprit was directly in front of him now. He'd show that man stoicism.

'Where do we look first, sir?'

Teague stopped fussing with his cloak and turned. 'Now hold, Master Jack. Though I understand the need to find a killer, I did not pay you to shirk your duties to me.'

'But . . . Master Teague. There's a murderer out there. And he tried to kill my master!'

'Yes, it's appalling to be sure. But I have a quest of my own. And limited time.'

Crispin stopped Jack's further complaint. 'He's right, Jack. We were hired by Master Teague to help him. He's already paid us half. I tell you what you should do: you go and help Master Teague as we promised, and I will continue the investigation.'

'But sir . . .'

'That sounds like an amenable solution, young Master Tucker,' Teague agreed.

Jack seemed obviously torn, but in the end he had to accede to both men's wishes.

'Come join us if you can, Master Crispin,' said Teague as he bore Jack away with him.

Crispin sighed. On his own once more. Now where to find Menhyr, Derwa's betrothed? He trotted down the stairs and looked over the hall. He headed toward one of the villagers from yesterday and gave Kenver Treeve a friendly salute. 'Good morn, sir.'

'Master Guest. You're from London, I hear tell.'

'Word travels. Yes, I am from London and I investigate crimes. Like murder. And I'd like to talk to Derwa's betrothed, Menhyr, before we venture to the outer village.'

'Menhyr Rouse is his name, and you've never met a sourer man what hasn't got a radish in his mouth.'

'You mean prior to this Roger Bennet affair?'

'Oh, aye. A sour man and a cheat is what he is.'

'But is he a murderer?'

'Oh, I see your meaning. Well, he gave slender Derwa the back of his hand, and rightly so. But murder? I suppose any man is capable.'

'No, not any man. Only some men.'

He looked Crispin over with a judicious eye. 'I suppose you would know. But Menhyr . . . I don't know. It don't seem likely to me.'

'Where can I find him?'

The man wiped at his nose. 'He has the stables down the lane. He's a smith.'

'I thank you.'

'Good luck with him, *sowsnek*. I don't envy you.'

Crispin left him with a bow and made his way into the cold September air. There was rain in the dark, heavy clouds in the distance, but he hoped it would hold off enough for him to make it to the stables he could see up the road with a dry cloak for once.

It wasn't long before he heard the clang of the smith at his work. The stables were at the brow of the hill – a stone structure with a thatched roof. Horses poked their already shaggy heads over the wattle fence to browse on the tall grasses on the other side.

Several village men sat on stools near the forge. Crispin assumed they were friends of Menhyr Rouse, though none of them spoke. Instead, they looked into the distance, at the sky, at the ground, while Menhyr hammered relentlessly at a glowing horseshoe, with sparks flying in all directions.

'Menhyr Rouse,' said Crispin, calling out over the striking of hammer on metal.

The three men on stools turned. Menhyr glanced over his shoulder and scowled. 'You again? What have I to do with you?'

Menhyr had muscled arms under his rolled-up sleeves, and massive hands. Crispin imagined them wrapped around his neck. And he saw scratches down the man's arms and dark bruises around his eyes. 'I would speak with you. Preferably alone.'

He shoved the horseshoe back into the glowing coals, hung the tongs on a hook above his forge, and leaned on his hammer against the anvil. 'You going to accuse me of murder?' He gestured toward his fellow villagers. 'They'll hear about it soon enough. Might as well do it while they sit.'

Sighing, Crispin widened his stance, ready for anything the man might mete out. 'Very well. Did you kill Roger Bennet?'

He laughed. The other men timidly laughed with him. 'You don't hold back, do you? Is this how you solve your crimes? You simply ask them and they answer you "yea"? That's how you work your miracles?'

'Let's put it another way, then. Where were you three days ago? Did you go up to the castle?'

'I might have. I might not have.'

Crispin turned to the smith's audience. 'Did Master Rouse go up to the castle on the day in question?'

They exchanged glances. One man in a gray cote-hardie and brown leather hood scratched his head over the leather. 'I believe he did, now that I think of it. Go up to the castle. Monday, wasn't it?'

Menhyr whipped his head toward the man. 'What you go and say a damn fool thing like that for, Tonkin Gover? You're a liar, is what you are.'

'Because it's the truth. No one would blame you for slaying that *emete* churl, Menhyr. I'd have done it m'self.'

'I didn't go to the castle!' he insisted.

'Oh, but you did,' said another man in a green tunic with sewn patches. 'Aye, it was three days gone now.'

'And so you too betray me, Myghal Kestel! Out with all of you!'

The three men grumbled as they rose, but seemingly mindful of Menhyr's temperament, ducked away quickly and trotted down the road, no doubt heading toward the inn where they'd share their tale.

'You haven't answered my question,' said Crispin.

Menhyr raised his hammer.

Drawing his sword, Crispin took a step back.

Brandishing the hammer, Menhyr moved closer. 'You come to my place and accuse me of murder.'

Crispin tightened his grip on the hilt. 'A man was slain, Rouse. A vile death. And you are lying to me about your whereabouts. Even your friends say so. Tell me now.'

'You think because you are from London and carry a sword that I have to obey you. Well, *emete*, I have a hammer and the where-withal to use it.'

Looking at his sword, Crispin was unsure if he could fend off a hammer blow. He'd have to deliver a mortal stroke first and he had no wish to do so. Against his better judgment, he slowly lowered his weapon. 'Master Rouse, I have no desire to exchange blows with you. Only to get at the truth. You were at the castle, that much is plain. What were you doing there?'

Menhyr breathed hard, flaring his nostrils and heaving his shoulders. His grip clenched over the hammer. 'Aye. I was there. Shoeing horses. And those whoresons at the castle saw me there. They can say when I arrived and when I left, right enough.'

'Did you see Roger Bennet?'

'No. But if I had, I would have killed him.' He smacked the hammer into his palm.

It was inevitable that Crispin would have to talk to the men-at-arms and now had more questions for them. If they could account for Rouse's comings and goings – and that he did not leave the stable area – he would be exonerated. But for now, he was on Crispin's list.

Deliberately, Crispin sheathed his sword, eyes on Menhyr the entire time. 'Very well, Master Rouse. I will talk with those in the castle to establish your statement. But if I find that you are lying to me . . .'

Menhyr raised his beard-stubbled chin. 'I am not. My betrothed may have been a faithless whore, but I am a man of honor.'

'So noted.' Crispin reached into his scrip and pulled out the brooch. 'Have you seen this before?'

The man merely swept his gaze over it. 'No.'

'Very well,' said Crispin with a nod. He left quickly. The tingle at the back of his head made him think a hammer might be whistling toward him. Everything in his being resisted looking back until he was well along the road, and he was glad he had, because when he did turn, Menhyr was still standing in his doorway, hammer in his hand but hanging at his side.

Now he needed to find out if Mabyn and Gwendolyn had men in their lives, or if they had ventured to the castle. Derwa had, but had the men-at-arms seen her?

It was becoming more evident that time could be saved if he simply talked to the men of the castle first. They may not have found true companionship with Roger Bennet either. They were just as suspect. But what of the village in the forest? Perhaps that would have to wait.

He hurried to the inn, apologized for the delay to Kenver Treeve, retrieved and saddled his horse, and urged it toward the castle.

ELEVEN

Jack saddled Seb, rubbed the sleek black neck of the beast, and calmed to his low nickering before following Carantok Teague and his cart. He worried a little about Master Crispin but the man could certainly take care of himself. He had done so for some forty-one years. He supposed he could leave his master for an afternoon.

Besides, he told himself, he was excited to find out if Teague could discover Excalibur. And as they neared the castle, his excitement increased.

They came to the mainland ward. Jack rose on his saddle, searching for the men-at-arms, but he saw no one. *Christ's blood! You'd think they'd be more aware since one of their own died.* But no. They didn't seem to care. Was living on this barren rock so soul-draining that they gave up all their Christian charity? Their love of their fellow man and his welfare? At the very least their responsibility as guardians? Well, he'd seen enough of the same in London, but it didn't seem that a small community such as this could be as heartless.

They rode single file through the narrow gate and into the island ward. 'Where to now, Master Teague?' Jack wrapped the leather reins around one hand as he'd seen Master Crispin do. 'It's useless to go back to the chapel, is it not?'

'Yes. Yes. The pendant . . .' He took it from his pouch and turned it over in his fingers. 'Clearly we were in the wrong place. But it did speak of some sort of burial. Perhaps not the chapel . . . but a graveyard instead.'

'Oh.' Jack swallowed hard. It had been a few years ago when he and Master Crispin were required to investigate corpses running loose in a graveyard of an abandoned church . . . but of course it was nothing of the kind. Still, it gave him the shivers to think about graveyards. He had no love of them.

'So . . . are there vaults there, do you think?'

'The chapel has no graveyard. Only the parish church on yon hill, and as far as I know, that church did not exist in Arthur's time, only this chapel. I imagine that this is much the same for you and Master Guest; investigating crimes. You do discover some intriguing things.'

'Aye, that we do. We've been to the palace in Westminster, we've been to Canterbury, and now, I daresay, we've got to do it here at the end of the world.'

'Hardly the end of the world, young man. You will find that the more you travel, the more you realize how amazing this wide world that God has given us is. I've seen heathen and Christian alike, working side by side. Incredible.'

'Were you relieved to get back home to England, sir? I should miss London. And, of course, me wife and children.'

'Ah, you are a family man, young Master Jack. Alas, I have none. No one to come home to. Not even a faithful dog. I envy you.'

'You envy me, sir? I haven't much at all. And you have all them gold pieces and such. That's more than the likes of me will ever see. Even Master Crispin . . . well. I shouldn't say. He used to be a wealthy man. A lord. I used to think it was such a waste the king throwing him out like rubbish. But he's done such good in London. He's . . . he saved me.'

Teague smiled, urging the horse to pull the cart up the hill toward the chapel. 'A servant who speaks well of his master, well . . . That is worth all the gold I have ever found. I wonder if your master knows what a faithful man he has in you.'

'He does sir,' said Jack, cheeks warming at the compliment. 'He's been good to me, and I daresay I've done him well too. We're closer than brothers, closer than father and son. I'll be a Tracker someday too. I hope I do him proud.'

'I'm certain you will, Master Tucker. I'm certain you will.'

The cart rambled over the stony road. Jack urged his horse up along the side of the cart and surpassed it, trotting the beast through what was left of the lychgate, dismounted, and tied his horse to it. 'Where to now, Master Teague?'

Teague pulled the cart to a stop and looked about eagerly. He jumped off and assessed the yard. 'The problem is, only churches have tombs and crypts – even ossuaries – below the foundations. We must search instead for some mound or mew associated with the chapel. *Sanctum*. Sanctuary. Hmm.'

Jack hadn't known how tense he had gotten thinking about the graves until he sagged in relief. That is, until Teague piped up with, 'Perhaps on the other side of the chapel! Let us go and see.'

Reluctantly, Jack followed the older man's quick strides and rounded the chapel with him. The stone was in sore need of repair, with some blocks without mortar. He wondered how the little chapel still stood. He scrutinized some low projections on the right side of the chapel porch tower. 'What is this, sir?'

'Hmm.' Teague looked it over, touching the stone wall above it, which seemed to be different stone. Jack suddenly saw it just as Teague pronounced, 'It looks very like a doorway that was closed up years ago. You see how the stone does not weave into the stone beside it as it does all along this wall. Yes. If you step back . . .' They both did, cocking their heads at the same time. 'Yes, the door was here, and they moved it there, building this fine porch tower.'

Jack nodded to himself. *Observation*, that was Master Crispin's motto. All Jack needed to do was look at it and learn a great deal.

But as Teague had postulated, once they got to the back of the chapel, they found a protrusion also built of stone at the ground level, and half the height of a man. 'Could it be a supporting structure? Like a buttress?' Jack asked.

Teague only made clucking, curious sounds.

'There don't seem to be any way into it, Master Teague. Not a doorway like the other side.'

'I think, Master Jack, that you are right. Perhaps from within the chapel.'

They marched around the stone structure once more, and again, walked up the few steps and pushed open the door.

'There doesn't seem to be any way through to it,' Teague was saying. 'If we go through . . .' Teague made a cursory look up and down the nave. 'That little carbuncle on the back of the chapel was nearly dead center.' He stroked his chin, glaring at the altar just beyond the rood screen. 'I wonder . . .' He went up the steps to the sanctuary under the rood screen arch and cautiously approached the stone altar poised against the back wall. It was made of stone like everything else in the chapel, and had an attempt at some crude carving on its legs, though it just might have been very old and worn away. Teague walked up to it and ran his hands along the top edge. Jack wasn't sure if it were proper for a layman to just touch the altar and he stopped himself time and again in a rebuke. It wasn't for him to tell his betters what to do in church matters. And hadn't Teague traveled all over the Continent and the Holy Land? Surely, he knew how to comport himself in a church.

Teague gripped the altar's table with both hands and yanked.

Or maybe not.

'Master Teague, er . . . is it quite proper to abuse an altar in God's house—'

But just as he said it, there was a click, a puff of dust, and the whole altar swung away from the wall as if on a hinge on one side.

'God blind me!' Jack muttered, crossing himself.

'You see, Master Jack,' said Teague, turning back to Jack with a grin, 'I have seen this before. Those masons of old were clever fellows. They never missed a trick. This could have been for a tomb or crypt of a priest or even a bishop. Tintagel was a grand castle in its day. The seat of Duke Gorlois, whose wife King Uther ravished in Duke Gorlois's guise with the magic of Merlin. Such a castle would need a grand tomb, but like so much of the past, it has been forgotten. Let us see.'

Behind the altar was a square hole, cold and devoid of light. 'Have you flint and steel, Master Tucker?' He pulled a short taper from the almost magical scrip hanging at his hip, its strap braced diagonally across his chest. 'Light the candle.'

Like a sorcerer, he is, thought Jack, and set about digging into his own pouch and pulled forth his tinderbox. He set the bits of fluff he kept for lighting fires on the altar's table, and saying a prayer of mercy, struck a spark, got a small flame and touched the candlewick to it. Once it was lit, he smothered the small fire, put his tinderbox away, and offered the candle to Teague.

'That's better,' said the man, and held it aloft before he plunged into the hole in the wall.

When Jack followed after, staying close to Teague and the small candle flame, he discovered there wasn't much room. He had to bend forward for the roof above him wasn't tall enough for a man to stand upright. 'Could this have been a tomb, sir?' asked Jack, eyes darting to every corner. 'You'd have to shove a body all folded up in here without so much as a by-your-leave.'

'It is strange, is it not?' There was no place to go, no secret passage. Only little better than a cupboard. But Teague scoured the walls, raising his candle, lowering it, to run his fingers over the stone. 'Aha!' he suddenly shouted, the sound echoing in the small space and startling Jack down to his socks. 'Look here!' He brought the candle close to the far wall and his fingers traced lightly etched letters. '*Whomsoever looks for Calesvol must go deeper.* Do you suppose it is telling us to dig here?'

'I don't know, sir. It is you who is versed in such, not me.'

'Go get the pickax and the spade.'

Jack happily complied. He trotted down the nave and out to the cart at the edge of the churchyard. Both wooly horses ignored him to nibble on the grasses beside the mossy stones. Jack grabbed the tools and ran back. *What would me mother have thought of this? I wonder. Your son digging up churches.* He hoped, in the end, she would have been proud of him for what else he had become: an apprentice to an important man in London. Still, in all his trials with Master Crispin, he hadn't imagined this.

The soil turned out to be softer than he thought, so he set the pickax aside and used the spade to dig deep into the dark earth. He prayed there would be no bones. He didn't think his pounding heart could take it. Instead he uncovered a small box made of iron. He pulled it free of the soil, brushed his hand over it as Teague brought the candle close. There was a lock, and he thought to perhaps pick it, but there didn't seem to be any point. Down came the spade and broke it off. He stepped aside so Teague could have the honors – and horrors. (Jack was having visions that it might be a human heart entombed as a curse, and this he did not wish to see.)

But when Teague lifted the rusty lid, inside were gold coins and gold jewelry. 'More treasure!' the man tittered. He dove in with his hand and pulled out a trinket, a bracelet in a pattern much like the brooch clutched in Roger's hand. 'More treasures of Tintagel,' he muttered, picking through the coins. The box was clearly not big enough for a sword. 'Marvelous. Marvelous.' He picked up a coin with the image of a king. 'Here you go, Master Jack. For your trouble.'

He gave the coin to Jack and he looked at it in his dirty palm.

'Master Teague,' he breathed. 'For me?'

'Of course. I always pay my employees.'

'But you've already paid us our half . . .'

He closed Jack's hand over the coin. 'But this is for you. Because you are loyal and hard-working. I see why Master Guest trusts you so much. You could easily have pocketed one for yourself.'

It was gold. A gold coin . . . and not a small one, either. He turned it over and over in his hand. The man with the crown had an inscription around him, too worn away to read. On the reverse was what looked like an angel holding a staff and an orb. 'I never had such a thing,' he breathed again. 'Oh! But isn't gold to go to the king?'

Teague chuckled. 'I tell you true, Master Jack, I am an honest man. And I surrender my trove to the coroner as prescribed by my charter. And though it is his duty to give it to the king as charged so by King Edward I all those years ago – you see, I know the law well – I have little doubt that it never gets there.'

'He steals it for himself?'

'Well . . . "steal" is a relative term. "Takes his fee", perhaps. In any case, it is his responsibility once he receives it. If, occasionally, a coin or two falls out of the trove I find . . . well . . . you see . . .'

'I get your meaning, sir.'

'If it doesn't sit well with you, you can always give it to the Church.'

Jack rubbed it between his fingers. 'Let's not be hasty, sir. I have three mouths to feed at home, and more on the way.'

He patted Jack's shoulder and closed the box. 'This is very valuable, Master Jack, and I am grateful for your digging it up for me. I am getting on, you see, and such things grow harder for me with time. But alas, it is not Excalibur.'

Jack's excitement diminished. Yes, the gold coin was of great value to Master Crispin and his retirement. But it wasn't the sword he had got his blood up to find. 'Should we try to make another hole, sir?'

'By all means, but I am beginning to think we have yielded all the secrets we can from the chapel.'

Jack did dig in another place but the space was so tight, there was little else they could do. And there were no other treasures to find.

'I have come to the conclusion,' said Teague, leaning on the pickax, 'that this vault has come to the end of its usefulness.'

'But where do we go now to find Excalibur?' Jack had gotten hot and sweaty in the tight space, digging as furiously as he had. He dug the spade in and wiped his face with his arm.

'Of that I am uncertain. I shall have to go back to my maps and papers. Though it is disappointing, it hasn't been useless. Look at what we have accomplished!'

Teague hefted the iron box and trudged back out into the nave, trailing a bit of soil with him. Jack looked around, gathered the tools, and followed him.

When Teague returned to replace the altar to what it was, it was as if they hadn't been behind it at all.

But something was amiss. He wasn't quite certain what it was, until he looked again at the altar slid back in its place. Yes, there were dirty footprints from their traveling back and forth from the sanctuary, down the nave, and out to the cart. But one set of footprints seemed to veer off in another direction. Jack's gaze rose to the arched window above. The glass was plain, not stained in colors as some churches had. And all the panes were intact. The window itself – which he had not known was a casement – was open the slightest amount.

And there was dirt on the sill.

TWELVE

Crispin entered the mainland ward and headed directly to the lodgings of the men-at-arms. He noted that there was no one in the gatehouse. *I have yet to believe there even is a porter*, he mused. No one on the battlements, no one in the courtyard. Surely someone should be there to greet the stranger. He'd never seen such lax discipline.

He dismounted, tied the horse, and proceeded inside. None was there. But he did hear someone in another room. He followed the sound and found the constable, Sir Regis, bending over a fire with a frying pan on a hob with smoking coals beneath it. He was frying sausages and drinking from a goblet. He did not turn when he heard Crispin's step. 'Did you bring the onions, Arno?'

'I am not Arno,' said Crispin, and the man stumbled to his feet, twisting around.

'Guest. What do you want?'

'I wanted to talk with your men. It will save time to ask them if they'd seen anyone enter the castle the day Roger was killed.'

He hacked a cough, rubbed his reddened nose, and sat back down at his stool, poking the sizzling sausages with a long fork. 'They are not here.'

'I can see that. Where are they?'

'I don't know.'

'That's very casual after there has been a murder of one of your own.'

Regis never turned. 'I know who you are, *Crispin Guest*. Don't lecture *me* on *my* responsibility. You're only here because I allow you to be. Don't be getting notions above your station.'

'My lord,' Crispin began, attempting to appease. 'I am only here because of the murder, which you charged me with solving.'

The man sighed, took a swig of his goblet and seemed to empty it before slowly turning toward him. 'Very well. What do you want to know?' He took up the jug sitting beside him and poured more ale into the goblet.

'First,' Crispin began, 'I wonder if this is a typical day, where there are no guards at the gate, no guards in the courtyard, and no one to challenge visitors.'

Regis snorted, stabbed a sausage, and brought it up from the pan. It was still dripping with grease; he blew on the end of it and delicately bit into it with bared teeth. He snapped off the piece and chewed thoughtfully. 'I tell you, Guest. We are out here in this cold, godforsaken wilderness, and not a soul in Westminster gives a damn for us. There was a time when Prince Edward sent his gold and his workmen here, but that day is dead. As dead as Edward. No one has spent so much as a farthing, and our pay is little enough as it is. If my men do not wish to man the gates when there is no threat from outside forces, then I do not command them to do so. They're all out taking a long shit, for all I know.'

He wanted to kick the man. Wanted to grab his coat and drag him to his feet and spit in his face. To take one's charge so haphazardly was unacceptable, as far as Crispin was concerned.

But he wasn't a knight anymore. Nor a lord. Hadn't been for a long time. He had no status, no name, no say in how this man chose to throw away his honor. He scowled instead and shoved his thumbs into his belt so that he wouldn't be tempted to punch him. 'My lord, whatever and however you execute your mission here is surely your business. Can any of your men recall with any certainty who came and went three days ago when Roger Bennet was killed? Can they recall at what time any of them arrived or left? For instance, the smith Menhyr Rouse claimed to be in the stables shoeing horses. Do you recall that?'

'I do,' he said, cheek bulging with sausage.

'And do you recall if he stayed only in the stable?'

'Yes. He had three horses to take care of, did his job in about four hours, and then left. Some of my men watched him. It was the most interesting thing that went on here. He never left the stable and he departed the castle about None.'

'Did you note anyone else coming into the castle?'

'No,' he said, chewing. 'But I was at the island.'

'Doing what?'

'None of your damn business.'

'Tell me, Sir Regis, do you approve of Carantok Teague's doings in the castle?'

Regis poked a second sizzling sausage with his now empty fork. 'I don't give a damn one way or the other. It's foolish. But I tell you, Guest, if *I* got hold of a gold trinket from the earth, I'd leave this place in an eye-blink.'

'Treasure is nothing to sneeze at.'

He chuckled. 'So he claims.'

'You have never seen any of it?'

He glanced lazily at Crispin. 'No. Have you?'

'Some of it.'

'Would you spend *your* time traipsing all over the kingdom digging in the ground?'

'I can't say that I would.'

Regis fell silent, blowing on the steaming sausage.

Crispin kicked at the floor with his boot, looking at the tip. 'Getting back to my earlier point, while you were doing . . . whatever it was you were doing on the island . . . did you note anyone arriving onto the island as well?'

'You'd only notice a rider,' he went on, eating the second sausage right off the fork. 'They are the only figures you can easily see. Tall enough. Nowhere to hide. Those rolling hills can hide a man on foot.'

'Yes, they can.'

Crispin waited, but Regis didn't seem to have more to add. 'I, er, suppose I can wait for the others . . .'

'Wait all you like. As long as it's in the outer room.'

Dismissed, Crispin crossed to the door and left through it. He sat by the fire for a time before his impatience took him to his feet and he paced, looking from fire to window. Where were these damnable men?

He couldn't wait any longer. He decided to hunt for them, and failing that, would meet up with Jack and Master Teague again.

He mounted his horse and moved slowly through the upper ward. There wasn't much to see. But when he turned at the shrill cry of a seagull, he noticed a figure up on the battlement. He was leaning there, looking out to the churning sea. The sounds of the waves crashing against the stony shore were loud here, the sound carrying up from below.

'You there!' called Crispin.

The man turned lazily toward him.

Crispin cupped a hand to his cheek and shouted, 'May I speak with you?'

The man nodded and slowly made his way down. When he

reached the courtyard, he sauntered toward Crispin. He was dark-haired with a trimmed beard and wore a leather tunic with metal studs. He walked up to the horse and even allowed it to nuzzle his hand. 'You're that man with Teague, aren't you? Crispin Guest, isn't it? I saw you when you found Roger.'

'Yes. And you are . . .?'

'Thomas Dunning. Guardian of this stunning castle.' He waved his arm dramatically, showing the courtyard beyond.

'How long have you been posted here?'

'Too damned long. Two years, if you must have a timeline. Why does a man of London find himself in the wilderness of Cornwall? I wouldn't wish that on any man. Even a one-time traitor.'

Ignoring the remark, Crispin pressed on. 'Three days ago, when Roger Bennet was supposed to be leaving the castle, did you see anyone enter?'

'I saw a woman. A comely thing, too. Blonde, willowy. I watched her for some time.'

'And did she come to the island?'

'Yes.'

'Did you see where she went from here?'

'No. I was watching the other one.'

'Another woman? Where?'

'Not certain if it was a woman. I caught sight of a figure in a cloak and hood, moving across the plain of the island. I was on the battlement and watched for a time. If they aren't on horseback, it's hard to keep them in sight. The land dips, you see. Outcroppings that look perfectly flat aren't. Sheep start to look like people. Hard to tell. It's an odd place. I don't care for it. I hate the smell of the sea.'

'So this person might have met up with Roger?'

'Don't know. Didn't see.'

'And the blonde?'

'Lost sight of her.'

'Did you see when she left?'

Thomas yawned and stretched. Crispin supposed he'd used up the man's interest. 'No. It's the hills, you see.'

'Would you—'

'That's all I know, Guest. I'm hungry.' He walked away, heading toward the men-at-arms' lodgings.

Crispin watched him go and threw his arms up in frustration. He wondered if either of the other men could have seen more. But since they seemed to be invisible – and he swept the courtyard with his gaze with an exasperated sigh – he clucked to the horse to move it along, clopping over the flag-stoned courtyard and beyond to the wilderness of the island.

He let the beast walk in a measured gait along the path, and on a whim, urged him downward toward the cliff edge. He wanted to look at the sea, to examine the beach below.

He dismounted when he reached the edge, leaving the reins trailing, and the horse got down to the business of gripping the grass with his big, square teeth and snapping it away from the turf, chewing.

Crispin looked out to the north and to the gray-blue water, churning in swells that seemed to meet the cloud-shrouded sky. Below was a cove of gray sand. They called it the Haven. Surely it was so to a sailor, for the land curved, making it a safe cove, and the waves proved gentler. He saw a stone wall far below that stretched over the shoals. He recalled Teague had called the wall the Iron Gate, where the soldiers of the fortress defended the Haven from the land.

The chalky cliff beneath him swept out like a foundation, and in one place there was a dark arched opening. He had heard there were caves here. This was likely one of them. The shore birds wheeled and spun overhead. Gulls, terns . . . even a kestrel darted from the cliff face and out over the shore. He watched them for a time before the cliff edge made him uneasy and he walked back to the horse. Once again, he looked upward to the hillocks of the island. There were the ruins of stone structures here and there. Duke Gorlois and then Uther Pendragon must have had a marvelous castle here once, with many outbuildings and prosperous trade. But there were only sheep grazing now. They moved in sluggish flocks up this hill and that. 'Sheep instead of soldiers,' he said to the wind. 'At least you could eat a sheep.'

He mounted again and suddenly felt a prickle at the back of his neck. He turned, eyes searching. Green, rock, sheep, low derelict building. And yet, he had the distinct feeling of being watched. The horse stamped as he turned it in a circle. High on the saddle, he felt he could see far, but it must have been his imagination.

Leaving his musings behind, he climbed the long trail to the chapel, a stone building with a simple porch at the west.

He found the cart in the distance and saw Jack and Carantok Teague milling about it. Jack looked up suddenly and saw him, too, and gave him a wave. Unconsciously, Crispin moved the horse quicker and arrived beside them.

'Master Crispin,' said Teague, somewhat out of breath. 'You have come most timely. Look here! Look at what we have found.'

The sword? He dismounted quickly and came alongside the cart. Teague was lavishing tenderness over some strongbox. 'Look!' he said, opening the lid. Gold, silver, and bronze coins, more jewelry. 'You are an accomplished hunter, Master Teague. I commend you. No wonder you have a charter from the king.'

'We've been searching about the outside of the chapel,' said Jack. 'But Master Teague found a secret place behind the altar.'

'*Behind* the altar? Master Teague, I am impressed.'

'Oh well . . .' Teague blushed a dark red and dithered at his gown. He was pleased with himself, and rightly so.

'How did the investigation go, sir?' asked Jack.

'The constable knows little. But one of the men-at-arms, a Thomas Dunning, seems to have seen Derwa come to the castle. He did not see her leave, but also saw another figure. Man or woman, he did not know.'

'Oh! That's something, isn't it.'

'It is. Whenever I can find the other men, I shall have to ask them, but they were nowhere to be found. Even the porter was absent from his post.'

Crispin felt that prickle again and suddenly turned. And yet, there was no one along the plain.

'They should be ashamed,' Jack was saying, as angry as Crispin was for their lack of discipline. 'And they don't care a whit that one of their own was killed.'

'It's curious. I should like to gather them, talk to them. Something is amiss here.'

Jack laid his spade in the cart. 'I thought it was a jealous husband what killed him.'

'That may well be, but the lassitude of these men in doing their duty . . . It does not sit well.'

Jack touched Crispin's sleeve and dragged him away from the fussing Carantok. 'Master,' he said quietly, 'while we were at our business and right under our noses, mind, I saw another set of muddy footprints in the chapel. Sir, it wasn't there before, I'm sure of it, for Master Teague and I with our digging had made the first set of footprints.'

'Another set? Show me.'

Teague was busy looking over his parchments and barely acknowledged Jack and Crispin enter the chapel. Jack pointed down to the floor. 'See here, sir. Now look. This set changes direction at the window.'

Crispin followed it, touched the mud at the sill, and pushed the window open wider to look out. There was a messy set of footprints below in the mud, as one would make jumping out of a window.

'When did this happen?'

'Not more than mere moments ago, sir. I don't mind saying it gives me the shivers that someone was right here watching us, almost breathing down our necks without us knowing. I dread to think what they could have done to us.'

A cold hand seemed to clutch at Crispin's heart. That certainly could have happened. And hadn't he felt the strangeness of someone watching him too?

Crispin stomped out of the chapel and circled it, looking for any indication of someone without. He could see no one along the plateau. But that did not mean that no one was there.

'I don't like this place, Jack. It is too strange.'

'Aye, sir. It is that.'

'Gentlemen!' said Teague.

Crispin and Jack exchanged a silent commiseration. Neither of them needed to say that they would not mention the incident to Carantok Teague. They rounded the chapel's corner. Jack's horse had gotten loose and had wandered down the hill. He trotted down to fetch the beast.

Crispin decided to take a look in the chapel once more. Strange that there should be such a hidden place for treasure, but he supposed Teague knew his own business well. Odd to go about the countryside – the world, even – in search of lost troves. Why would one lose treasure? But, he supposed, should something happen to Crispin or Jack – God forbid it – Isabel might not know of their own treasure that master and servant had carefully hidden away for their retirement. It might not be found for generations. Perhaps Teague had discovered such things on his travels. He made a note to himself to tell Isabel when they returned, just in case.

He made another circuit of its outer walls, another glance out to the swaying grasses of the plain, and then back to the front at the west door.

He stepped into the cold porch and looked up to the rafters. Spider webs and the casings of old insects hung there. A nest was tucked up in the corner with a few feathers dangling from the matted wad of grass, twigs, and wool. He pushed open the door and stood in the entry. He somehow felt the loneliness he hadn't in the deserted castle. A chapel, though small, was still a house of God, and when *that* was abandoned, there was no hope left. Still, there was a chaplain who came and went. He lived in the lower ward on the mainland. Perhaps *he* felt how lonely it was and did not wish to be an anchorite in such a wilderness.

The chapel was modest in its simplicity. Plaster walls, its paint chipped and faded, the plaster itself grayed from smoke, seemed the only color in the place. The window he had left open seemed to sway in the salty wind. And he told himself he should close it. He walked forward to do so, pulling it shut.

In the grayness of the nave, with its shadowed corners and gloomy ceiling, the worn and cracked rood screen shielding the chancel from the nave, a dark color of something at the foot of the altar caught Crispin's attention. He made his way past the open window, up the two steps of the sanctuary, and peered around the wooden screen that had gone unpolished for some time.

It took a moment for his mind to make sense of what he was seeing. For curled against the altar lay a man. Under him, like a rug, was a puddle of his own blood, very dark, and very still.

THIRTEEN

Jack pushed the heavy oak door to the chapel with his shoulder just in time to hear Master Crispin say, 'Good Christ,' and cross himself. 'Put everything aside for now, Jack. We have bigger problems.'

'What's that, sir?' Jack moved along the nave. His master knelt just behind the rood screen. 'What are you doing?'

'Thomas Dunning is here. One of the men-at-arms. And he is quite dead,' he pronounced.

Jack straightened. 'What?' He rushed up the steps and stood over his master, crossing himself. 'But how – what – we were only just here!'

'We are cursed, Master Guest. Cursed.' Carantok Teague was standing in the doorway, face white.

'Well, nothing has happened to us. I think, rather, that the men-at-arms at Tintagel might be cursed.'

'Oh, blessed saints!' wailed Teague.

Master Crispin didn't believe in curses, but Jack did. There was magic and faery folk and all manner of evil in the world. But if you prayed hard enough, the Almighty would protect you. He cast his glance toward the dead man. Well, perhaps some did not pray enough.

'It's my fault. It's all my fault. If I hadn't started digging here . . .'

'Master Teague, have you reason to believe you have created the circumstances where these seemingly unrelated murders—'

'Can't you see, Guest? It's all my fault. Because of me!'

Suddenly, the man was a gibbering fool and Master Crispin was forced to stride across the nave and grab him. He slapped him once to strike the hysteria from him. Teague stared at his master uncomprehendingly for a moment before he slumped in his arms. 'I'm sorry,' said Teague. When it looked like he was in his right mind again, Master Crispin released him.

'It is I who am sorry . . . for striking you.'

'No,' he said quietly, sliding down the wall. 'You did what you had to do. I had lost my head.'

'You are not responsible for this. Only the guilty party or parties are. You must not blame yourself. Instead, pray for God's mercy and that we are spared long enough to solve these crimes.'

'Yes. Yes, I will. And for you, Master Guest, for you are His emissary, doing His will. In my greed, I did not offer to pay your proper fee for your tracking business. And this I will. Never fear.'

Well, that was something at least, thought Jack. His master turned back to the corpse and bent over him.

'What do you see, Jack?' asked Master Crispin.

'He's a right proper mess. Someone stabbed him in the gut, sir. One . . . two times. Must have been able to get in close, for I do not see any marks of defense on him or under his nails.'

'Yes.'

'And he's warm, as you said, sir. But getting colder.'

'And it all happened so quickly. I had only just talked to this man. He must have followed me almost in my own footsteps and I never saw him. How could I have missed him?' Master Crispin flicked his eyes toward the window that had been open.

'God's blood! You think the murderer's out there?'

'Not only had Dunning shadowed me, but so did his murderer.'

Without waiting for his master to reply, Jack threw open the window, leapt up and out of the sill, and stood again where he and Master Crispin had stood mere moments ago. He could see no one. Maybe it *was* ghosts . . . or demons.

Jack heard a clatter and looked up. Instinct made him jump aside, just as the slate roof tiles skidded off the roof and shattered at his feet. His eye caught bits of mud up the side of the wall, as if someone had scaled it. 'God's blood!' Quick as a lizard, Jack leapt, fingers grabbing the sharp edge of the stone, climbing up the church with ease, footholds and handholds aplenty. On the roof in no time at all, he found more mud. He followed it over the spine of the roof to the other side, and when he looked out over the green plains, he saw a figure, running.

Jack scrambled back down, nearly leaping off the side of the roof, skidded around the corner of the chapel, and grabbed his horse's mane. He pulled himself up as he yelled at it to run. He'd barely made it into the saddle as the horse jolted into a gallop.

He couldn't find the reins and gave up and kept hold of the mane instead. Leaning so far forward his face was nearly beside the horse's, he urged Seb to full speed.

The dark figure, with cloak flying out behind him, came into view here and there as the landscape rose and fell. He'd almost caught up to him when he disappeared again down a ridge.

Jack plunged the horse down and the beast landed hard, knocking Jack's teeth in his head. Slowing the horse, he kept his ears sharp and his eyes open. He slid off the mount at a run and crouched low, stealthily making his way over the rocky mounds.

There! Something darted forward. He pounded ahead, kicking up turf and stones. Whoever it was seemed compact and agile, flitting from rock to rock like a bird. But Jack's longer stride served him well and he gained on him. He gathered himself and leapt, soaring forward with arms outstretched. He landed squarely on him, grabbing the bony shoulders and dragging him down, rolling down an embankment with his arms wound around the miscreant.

When they came to a stop at last, Jack was on top of the man and cocked back his arm to deliver a good punch—

'Stop, Master Tucker!' cried Kat, hands up over her face.

The hood fell away and her auburn hair spilled out around her, almost like the pool of blood he had just seen under Thomas Dunning. She was wearing a man's dark tunic and stockings.

Still straddling her, he sputtered, 'What . . . what are you doing, Mistress Pyke?'

'Get off me. I can't breathe.'

'You killed a man back there.'

'No, I didn't. I was hiding *from* the killer.'

'But you ran.'

'Of course I did! I didn't want him to catch me.'

Jack stared at the woman beneath him before she pushed at him. 'You are too heavy, Jack. Get off!' She shoved him hard and Jack finally took the hint and moved off her.

He sat back while she curled a leg under her – a very shapely leg in its men's hose – and held a hand to her chest. 'Whoo!' she breathed. 'That's better.'

Jack glanced over the plains. Nothing but sheep. 'You truly expect me to believe *you* didn't kill that man? There is no one else on this damned island.'

'Yes, I *do* expect you to believe me. I didn't even know who that man was. All I know is that he is dead.'

'So, who killed him, then?'

'I don't know. I didn't see him properly.'

'And where were you when all this transpired?'

She pulled her collar away from her throat. Her hair blew in curls around her face in the cold wind. She sighed. 'On the roof.'

'And what were you doing on the roof . . . and dressed disgracefully like that?'

'Spying on *you*. I wanted to see what treasure was being found. And it is much easier dressed as a man than flitting about on roofs in a gown.'

Jack frowned. 'I never heard you.'

'Of course not. I'm good at what I do.'

'Mistress Pyke!'

'Jack! I'm not lying! I *was* spying on you. And then that man showed up, creeping around the chapel, spying on you as well. And then he climbed up to the roof. I flattened myself so he wouldn't see me. Praise God he didn't. He must have been too distracted with watching what you were all doing.'

'Seems like an awful lot of people around this little chapel, and us not noticing.'

She shrugged. 'Can I help it if you're unobservant?'

Narrowing his eyes, he grabbed her arm and dragged her to her feet.

'Here now! No need to be so rough. I saw the other show up, the killer, I suppose. He came up from the other path.'

'What *other* path?'

She pushed her hair up off her face and pointed. 'Over there. The low side of the chapel.'

'I thought you said you didn't see anyone.'

'I *didn't*. I fear I never got a good look at him. He was wearing a cloak and a hood.'

'Did he see you?'

'No. This cloak is gray. It blends into most things, especially the slate roof. I was silent and still. And the wind masks the sounds.'

Jack listened. Yes, it was always windy on the island, it seemed.

Exasperated, he dragged her to the horse. 'You're going back with me. You can tell your wild tale to Master Crispin.'

She dug in her heels. 'Oh no, Jack, please! Crispin won't believe me either.'

'And well he shouldn't.'

'I beg of you. I don't think I can stand the thought of his disapproving frown.'

He tightened his grip on her arm. 'You either get on the horse with me or I'll toss you over the saddle on your belly. Which is it?'

With a sour expression, she relented. Jack held tight to the reins in case she got any ideas about escaping with the horse – and wouldn't that be a thing to face Master Crispin with? – before he mounted up behind her. He kicked the horse's flanks and they galloped awkwardly back. In truth, he didn't trust her and believed her lies even less . . . but he had a hard time truly believing she had killed Thomas Dunning. To what end would she have done it?

Master Crispin trotted forward to greet them and slowed when he recognized Kat.

'God's blood.'

'I didn't do it,' she insisted and slid off the horse. 'Crispin, I didn't kill that man. I swear by God and all His angels!'

'And what good are your protestations, Mistress Pyke?' he said tightly.

Jack could tell by the clenching of his master's jaw that he was holding his anger in check. But he wouldn't be able to hold it long. There was nothing worse in his master's eyes than a betrayal, and Kat Pyke was dressed in the very fabric of it. Still, Jack found himself wanting to defend her, God knew why. Absurd! He had no proof whatsoever that she was telling the truth. If she were, then where was the killer? He stretched his neck, searching for the hundredth time over the countryside. Of course, he had been focused on her. If another *had* done the crime, they could easily be hiding in any number of hollows or outcroppings over the whole of this stark island. And all they had to do was wait till nightfall and slip away under cover of darkness.

That is, if there *were* another.

Teague pushed Jack aside. The man stood with mouth hanging open. 'Mistress Pyke!' he gasped.

She flicked a glance at him, but her eyes seemed only for Master Crispin. 'Stand down, Carantok,' she said impatiently. 'I've no business left with you.'

The man sputtered and Jack laid a hand gently on his arm. 'Master Teague, sir,' he said softly. 'She and my master knew each other from a few years ago.'

'But she . . . she *used* me to . . .'

'Aye, sir. She did do that. Best to let it lie.'

And then he looked at his master.

FOURTEEN

Crispin felt his jaw crack as he clenched it. She lied. Again. And killed. *Again*. He had had his chance to turn her in to the sheriffs in London four years ago and she had cajoled him not to. Why had he not trusted his instincts?

He grabbed her arm and yanked her with him, stalking forward. 'I want to talk to you.'

'Why does everyone insist on grabbing my arm?' she muttered.

She struggled only a little as he took her to the other side of the chapel, away from Jack and Teague. He shoved her hard against the chapel wall.

'Ow! There's no need for—'

'*I* tell you when to speak and when to keep silent. Do you understand?'

She scanned his face, eyes flicking here and there. She had the sense to lower her face and at least have the appearance of humility for once.

'Tell me true or I shall beat it out of you. Did you kill that man?'

She raised her face, her mouth contorting to an uncharacteristic flat line. 'No.'

He drew back his arm to strike and she flinched slightly, recovered, and raised her chin higher.

His arm was drawn back, his hand open and ready to slap her . . . and he found he couldn't. He dropped the arm to his side. Kat's held breath released.

He shook his head at himself. 'You try me to the very edge, wench.'

'You . . . you told me to tell you true. I did. I did not kill that man.'

'Then who did?'

She sagged against the wall. 'I don't know.'

'It all happened in a matter of moments. Thomas Dunning wasn't there, and then he was, dead.'

'He followed you. I followed him. And the murderer . . . must have followed us all. Or was already there.'

'Why did you follow him?'

'I overheard you two talking. He rightly surmised you were seeking Carantok and his treasure.'

'And that is what you were after.'

'As you suspected all along.'

'Dammit, Kat! Why? Why must you . . . must you . . .'

She sighed, pulling her cloak about her. Though the chapel cut some of the wind, it did not shelter them completely from that and the salt spray. 'It is the way I make my living. Do I scorn the way you make yours?'

'I am not a thief.'

'Is your Carantok Teague a thief? If not, then I am doing what he is doing.'

He bit his tongue. If she was robbing from his troves, well . . . 'Tell me how you got here. To the castle. And I don't mean just now. I mean how you got to Cornwall in the first place.'

A lock of hair blew out of her hood and lashed against her lips until she took a finger and threaded it back beneath the hood. 'Are you certain you want to know?'

He was rethinking his not slapping her. 'Just tell me.'

'Well,' she said, 'it is a long tale.'

He crossed his arms over his chest. 'I have the time.'

'Very well. Let me think. I met Carantok Teague in some Cornish village inn over a month ago. The man was in his cups and talking much too loudly about his ventures. So . . . I sat beside him, shushed him a bit, and, with more wine, he told me more. And then we . . . you can guess the rest.'

Crispin scowled.

'He left early to get away from me and his embarrassment, I suppose. He was headed toward London – to fetch you, perhaps. Meantime, I set out for Tintagel. I got there in a few days on foot and I met a man from the castle in the inn in Treknow. I asked him if he knew about Carantok and he told me. He was most amused by him until one day he saw some of the man's cache. I convinced him to show me one of Carantok's "holes", as he called them.'

'Whom did you meet?'

'Some caretaker from the castle. An *old* man,' she said purposefully, for she knew what Crispin was thinking.

'And how did you come by the players?' he went on.

'Oh. Well, that constable sent me away. Said he'd throw me in the gatehouse cell if he saw me in the castle again. I tried to re-enter the castle by stealth but it's damnably hard to do. There's a sheer cliff on one side. I tried it from the beach side, from the cove they call the Haven, but that's fairly steep. The constable nearly caught me too many times for comfort. So I . . . gave up. I know it's uncharacteristic of me, but truly, it wasn't worth the hardship. I started out on the road again out of Cornwall. A few days later I ran into the players' wagon and cajoled my way into their company. I thought I could disguise myself and enter that way. I, er . . . convinced them to come here, in fact.'

So that was true too. He breathed deep for a moment. 'Did you know Roger was dead?'

'Never knew him.'

'If you're lying . . .'

'I'm *not*. Please believe me, Crispin. No one in the whole world believes me. If you stopped, then I don't know what I'd do.'

Her eyes grew glassy with tears. It was a good touch, he thought. Maybe even a bit of a tremble from her lips. Yes, there it was. As pathetic as could be. Any other man would instantly fall for it. But she was good at deception, this he knew. Still. Her earnest face could be very convincing. And appealing.

'*If* I believed you . . .' he said stiffly.

'You can. By all God's angels, you can. It's the truth this time.'

'*If* I believed you, what will you do now?'

'You mean . . .' She stepped closer, cautiously, taking one step and waiting, then another. 'If you let me go?'

'Yes,' he said quietly.

'I . . . I wouldn't go at all.'

He blew out a breath. 'You still want the treasure.'

'No! I want to help you solve the murders.'

'What? For God's sake, Kat.'

'No, I truly mean it. You've helped me before, now I can help you. Won't you let me? It's the least I can do.'

'I'd rather you left the area.'

'But I *want* to help.' She was standing right in front of him. How had she gotten so close?

'I don't trust you.'

'Yes, you do. Crispin, I would never betray *you*.'

'Ha!'

A genuine look of hurt passed over her face before she masked it. 'I won't. I want to help you and Jack. In gratitude for letting me go four years ago.'

He knew he was relenting. He knew Jack would mock him for it. He knew he would regret it.

'You do have certain . . . talents . . . that might prove useful.'

She raised an enquiring brow.

'Not *that* talent! Your skills at climbing, at being invisible, at . . . cajoling.'

'Oh.' She stepped ever closer until she rested her hand on his chest. He had forgotten how much shorter she was than him when he gazed down at her upturned face. 'Yes,' she said softly. 'I can do all of that. But the other . . . I reserve for you.'

He grasped her hand and gently pulled it away. 'That, er . . . we won't worry about.'

'Yes, Crispin,' she said with a knowing smile.

There was no question. He already regretted it.

FIFTEEN

When he came around the corner escorting Kat rather than manhandling her, he studiously ignored the expression on his apprentice's face. 'Mistress Pyke will help us with our investigations.'

'Oh, she *will*, will she?' said Jack.

'Yes,' he said curtly. 'First things first, Kat. You must put on a gown. You can't be seen wearing men's clothing. For that you will surely be arrested.'

'I've got it here. In my scrip,' she said.

'Then do so now.'

She began to disrobe when Crispin cleared his throat.

She chuckled. 'I'll go into the chapel porch, shall I?'

'Be quick about it.'

She trotted up the steps and disappeared within the porch, as Jack glowered at him.

'Master Crispin!' he rasped.

'Jack, I know what you're thinking.'

'I'll wager you don't.'

'I believe her when she said she did not kill him. She told me she followed him here as he followed you, Master Teague.'

'But we saw no one. Did we, Master Jack?'

'No, sir. Not a soul.'

'But as we've already established,' said Crispin, 'it is far too easy to hide on these plains. I have my suspicions that the murderer still lies in wait out there, not far from us.'

Jack looked about suspiciously, hand on his dagger hilt. 'That was a lot of people we didn't detect,' he said with a deep frown.

'I understand your skepticism, but the result is there in the chapel.' Just as he spoke, Kat stepped into the doorway, dressed in a woman's gown again. She pulled her hood up and looked at Crispin.

'We must talk to the constable and men-at-arms. It will be interesting to see if any of them are missing.'

'Master, should we take the body with us?'

Teague wore a horrified expression. He'd already been obliged to ferry one dead and rather ripe body. He'd certainly wouldn't be best pleased with a bloody one.

'No. I want Master Teague to get himself out of the castle and into Treknow with all haste. Our hunt for the . . .' He glanced at Kat. 'For the object is temporarily delayed.'

'Oh, but Master Guest!'

'It is delayed, sir. Please get into your cart and make haste.'

Grimly, he nodded and climbed up, slapping the reins on the horse's rump and rattling down the road.

'Shouldn't he be taking Mistress Pyke, sir? Back to the village?'

'No. She'll be with us.'

'I was afraid of that,' he muttered, mounting his horse.

Crispin mounted Tobias, then leaned over to offer Kat a hand. She hitched up her skirts, revealing that she had removed her men's hose, used Crispin's foot in the stirrup as a step, and propelled herself onto the horse behind him. He felt her arms reach around him before he dug his heels into the horse's flanks.

Teague was ahead but their horses would soon catch up. Crispin called to Jack to slow down. They made a more leisurely stride, allowing Teague to get farther ahead of them.

'Why did you send Master Teague ahead, sir?'

'I want him out of all this. I supposed that the murder of Roger Bennet was out of jealousy, but with the murder of Dunning, it doesn't make any sense. There's something more here, and it might have to do with treasure.'

'Many would kill for treasure,' said Kat, resting the side of her cheek on Crispin's back. 'Not me, of course.'

'No, of course not,' he said, not too convincingly. She jabbed at his side in retaliation.

'But I thought Master Teague was keeping it quiet, not discussing it with the others of the castle,' said Jack.

'We see by evidence of Mistress Pyke that he isn't entirely secretive. Sir Regis knew about it.'

'To be fair,' she said as they neared the island courtyard, 'Carantok talked mostly of history and the old warriors, and most men simply ignored him. They hadn't the cunning to understand the underlying meaning of what he was on about.'

'Just you,' said Crispin, liking the feel of her at his back.

'Just me,' she said with a smile in her voice.

Teague was through the courtyard and on his way out to the

mainland. Crispin signaled Jack and they headed toward the constable's lodgings.

He rode up to what Teague had said was once the great hall. Crispin looked up the stone walls to the holes that had once held up the heavy beams of the ceiling.

They halted and dismounted. Crispin couldn't help himself and assisted Kat by grasping her waist. She slid down him and offered a soft, 'Thank you,' that threatened to discomfit him, but he cleared his throat as well as his thoughts to get down to the business at hand. 'Kat, stay with the horses and try to be unobtrusive. Put your hood up. But, er, keep a sharp eye out, too.'

'Yes, Crispin.' Her smile and eyes were bright with adventure, and he had to admit, it caused a trill in his belly at her working *with* them rather than against them for a change.

He tied his reins to a post and pushed through the door. He was surprised to see the two remaining men-at-arms at various tasks. Their lodgings were down below on the mainland. Arno Leverton was polishing his sword and dagger, while Stephen Kettle was mending his stockings. Sir Regis was writing on some parchment.

They all looked up when he and Jack entered, somewhat surprised to see the both of them. 'Sir Regis, gentlemen, it is my sad task to inform you of another murder. Thomas Dunning.'

They jolted to their feet. 'What?' cried Regis, looking around, as if to put the lie to Crispin's words, searching for the lost man who was surely just hiding in the shadows. 'What are you talking about?'

'He was found dead. Just now in the chapel. Stabbed to death.' He did not mean for his eyes to travel to the man who was polishing his blades, but when his gaze went there, so did those of Regis and Stephen.

Arno pushed away from his sword and threw the rag down. 'What are you all staring at?'

'When did this happen?' asked Regis. 'I spoke to him no more than an hour ago.'

'As I said, just now. Who passed through the narrow gate to the inner ward, Sir Regis?'

'I did. Did anyone else?'

They stared at each other. No one would speak and incriminate themselves.

'If not any of you,' Crispin hurried to say, 'then did you note any other person? A caretaker? Anyone from the village?'

'We noted no one,' said Stephen. 'We were within these lodgings, for the most part.'

'For the most part?' Crispin repeated.

Stephen shrugged. 'A jaunt to the privy.'

'And was that all? Was any one of you gone longer than that?'

Arno, in his blue cote-hardie, lumbered toward him. 'Why are you questioning us? What gives you the right?'

'I am the Tracker of London, sir. I catch criminals and bring them to the king's justice.' He placed his hand on his sword hilt.

Arno kept coming till he stood directly before Crispin, all that breadth of him, and just as tall. 'I don't recognize any sort of "tracker". How do we know you are who you say you are?'

Crispin's fingers closed on his sword hilt. 'Be assured, sir, that I am. If you want proof . . .' He drew his sword and Arno jumped back. Regis had his sword out just as quickly, but Crispin raised his other hand in a gesture of appeasement. He merely tilted the blade so that the light could fall on the Latin inscription along it: *A donum a Henricus Lancastriae ad Crispinus Guest – habet Ius.* 'A gift from Henry Lancaster to Crispin Guest – He Has the Right'.

The three bent to stare at it before all straightening at the same time.

'I know that name,' said Stephen. 'I remember now. You were charged with treason, were you not? You should have found a traitor's death on the gallows.'

Crispin scowled and sheathed his sword before he was tempted to use it. 'Fortunately, I did not, and have served His Majesty in all loyalty instead.' He took a step back. 'With the death of another of your men, I suggest that you close the gates and check any who wish to enter.'

'You *suggest*,' said Stephen with a sneer.

Crispin felt obliged to take another step back. 'I wish to know who was missing in just this last hour.'

'You're no lord to make demands to us,' said Arno.

'I make a mere suggestion—'

They postured so close that Crispin was certain a fist was coming his way. Apparently, Jack thought the same thing, for he was suddenly in front of him, dagger in his hand, crouched forward and ready to spring.

'You, my lord,' said Jack to Arno. 'Surely you have heard of my master. And he is well-respected now in London, capturing many a murderer. Two of your own have been slain. Will you stand in the way of his finding that vile killer? Suspicion must rightly fall on those who hinder us.'

Regis stood a long moment without moving before he pushed himself away from the wall, lifting an admonishing hand toward Arno and Stephen. 'Enough. Let this man be. He is only doing as he has done in London. And he's right. Now Thomas has been slain.'

His words seemed to have made the men recall their dire circumstances. Arno unfisted his hand and stepped back.

Jack licked his lips and, with one deep breath, sheathed his knife. Crispin unconsciously sent a prayer of thanks heavenward for his prophetic insistence on buying Jack this new – and suddenly very useful – blade. 'Were any among you missing for more than an hour?' he asked, sheathing his sword once more.

Even though Stephen flashed him an angry look, the others grew thoughtful.

Arno shook his head. 'None of us, Master Guest.'

'There are no others in the castle besides the caretakers? No cooks, smiths, armorers . . .'

Regis straightened his cote-hardie. 'No. Just the caretaker, the porter, and the chaplain. I was in the stores, taking inventory.' He gestured toward the parchment he'd been writing on. 'I wasn't gone all that long. These two must have noticed my coming in from that door.' He pointed toward one of several doors at the other end of the hall. 'But I think it wise what Master Guest has said. Arno, go and guard the gate. Close it and lock it. But first, find that damned porter and the chaplain and send them here.'

Arno, not exactly happy to follow orders by Crispin, stalked out the door.

Crispin settled his thumbs in his belt. 'One of your men will need to get a cart to fetch his body from the chapel to the parish church.'

Regis no longer questioned him. He ordered Stephen to get a cart from the stable in the mainland ward. And just like that, they began to hurry to obey. Sometimes it took a lordly attitude to get things moving. But a steady hand and a steady head often did more good.

Regis stood before Crispin. A man in his position never liked demurring to a man of lower rank, and though this was technically so, Regis recognized in Crispin a man with experience at shouting orders and expecting them to be obeyed. 'What goes on here, Master Guest?' he said worriedly.

'I don't know. I thought I did, but with this second murder . . . It will take some thinking.'

'I give you the hospitality of the constable's lodgings. It isn't much, but there are rooms for you and your man on the upper floor.'

'Thank you, Sir Regis. It is appreciated. I, er, have another servant. A woman.' He gestured vaguely toward the entry.

Regis frowned and walked to the window. He pushed the shutter wider and looked out. 'You there! Come in here.'

The door opened and a humbled Kat stood before him, her hood low over her face. 'You are Master Guest's servant, then?'

Crispin could just see her cheeks redden prettily under the hood's shadow as she nodded.

Regis cocked his head. 'Do I know you?'

Vigorously, Kat shook her head.

He scratched his chin before shrugging. 'Go upstairs and prepare the rooms. The two rooms on the west side. Lay the fires and be quick about it.'

She kept her head down and curtseyed, but Crispin noted her whitened fists at her side. He'd hear about this soon enough.

He bowed to Sir Regis. 'Thank you, sir. I need to talk to the porter and the chaplain when they arrive. And then I expect I shall be forced to question those in the village.'

'What about that *druidae* village? Are you truly venturing there, Guest?'

'To further my enquiries. What is the word we are called in Treknow, Jack? *Emete?*'

Regis chuckled. 'That's their word for outsiders. It also means . . . *ants*. We are as pesky as ants to them.' He leaned in and took Crispin's arm, drawing him closer and speaking soberly. 'And it will be worse in the *druidae* village. They care as little when they crush us like ants. Have a care, Master Guest.'

'I shall.'

Regis offered a chair, and Crispin took it. The constable didn't sit with him at the long table, but set a foot on the hearth and leaned an arm on the mantel.

Jack stood off in the center of the room like a centurion.

They waited. Crispin let his eyes rove over the simple room of table and chairs, two coffers against a wall, a sideboard. There were doors leading, no doubt, to kitchen, buttery, and pantry. There was also an archway that he suspected led to a latrine. The hall itself was of a good size, for it was all built within the former great hall. It was tall enough for an upper story to be comfortably built as well.

He glanced at the stairs. He was sure that Kat was stalling. She had no wish to be under the eyes of the constable, who might recognize her in time.

This second death had been unnerving, not only because it had happened under their very noses, but because it didn't conform to what Crispin had originally thought. It seemed a simple case of jealousy when it had simply been Roger. He could have broken it down to the man – or woman – responsible. But Thomas's death had cast new light on it. He supposed it could still be jealousy of *two* men, but the timing of it was strange. Why kill the man when Crispin, Jack, and Carantok were so nearby? That was a dangerous enterprise. He could have been picked off at any other moment when he was alone in the castle. Why then? Why so . . . desperately?

He entertained for the span of a heartbeat that it might have been Kat after all. But that thought flitted away. He couldn't see her doing it at just that moment, if it were her at all. No, he eliminated her from his thoughts on the matter. It simply was not her.

There was a clatter on the porch and then two men walked in, followed by Sir Stephen and Sir Arno. One was a young man, probably Jack's age, and the other was in clerical garb, with a tonsure. Obviously, the latter was the chaplain, the former the porter.

They both bowed to Sir Regis, who didn't bother acknowledging it. The porter stepped forward first. 'Are you the gentleman to whom I should talk?' he asked of Crispin.

'Yes. You're the porter?'

'Yes, sir. Peter Shipley, sir.'

'And I am the chaplain here, Edward Allen.' The chaplain stayed where he was, merely studying Crispin.

'I asked the both of you here to enquire about the comings and goings in the castle. Another of your fellows has been murdered.'

'Yes,' said Shipley nervously. 'Sir Arno told us. I don't understand it. What would you wish to know from us, Master Guest?'

'I have come into this castle no less than three times, Master Shipley, and at none of those times was I ever greeted by a porter, let alone seen one. Can you account for that?'

His gaze flicked once toward Regis before resting again on

Crispin. 'Master Guest, I can only say that I was not required to greet visitors.'

'Not required? Then what, by all the saints, do you do in the gatehouse? Is that not the very nature of your job, man?'

'Er . . .'

'Master Guest,' said Regis with a sigh of impatience, 'I gave him that order. We are no place of royal residence. No one of any consequence ventures here. For as long as I have been here – and it has been many, *many* years – we have never entertained lords, sheriffs, or the clergy. It is a forgotten place, sir.'

'That it may be, but you now see where this lax behavior has gotten you.'

Regis scowled. '*You* aren't reprimanding *me*, are you, Guest?'

Crispin paused. 'No, Sir Regis. Merely pointing out . . . an oversight in protocol.'

The constable huffed and returned to his contemplation of the fire, perhaps thinking of his own better days and wishing for a servant – who will never come – to add more fuel to the hearth, for he seemed disinclined to lift the small bundle of sticks on the hearth to do the job himself.

'You are aware,' Crispin went on to the porter, 'of the recent murders?'

'Yes, Master Guest. I . . . I wish I could help you, sir. I wish I could say with certainty who has passed. But . . . I do not know.'

'I see. May I suggest – if it is permitted,' he said with a nod toward Regis, 'that you do so from this time hence?'

'Oh yes, sir. Very much, sir.'

He backed away until he was behind the chaplain.

'Father Allen?' said Crispin.

The chaplain stayed where he was, hands within his scapular.

'When was the last time you were at the chapel?'

'Oh, let me think.' He blinked heavenward. 'It must have been at least a sennight ago. Before all this unpleasant business.'

'You do not sing mass there?'

'Seldom,' he said.

'Can you think of any reason that either Roger Bennet or Thomas Dunning should have cause to be murdered?'

'Indeed no. I can't imagine.'

'Did these men use you as a confessor?'

'Yes, they did. As do some in the village of Treknow.'

'It seems to be well known in Treknow – at least now it is – that Roger Bennet was somewhat . . . free with his time with women. Has anyone—'

'Master Guest, I hope you do not intend for me to reveal what I have heard in the confessional, for the sacrament is sealed. I may not speak of it.'

Crispin did know, but hoped that the chaplain was freer with his talk. Sometimes an older man grew forgetful, but the chaplain was perhaps Crispin's age. 'I did not expect that you would tell me details,' he said sourly.

'I can tell you nothing. Either by hint or any other knowledge. Once it is confessed, it is not to *my* ears but those of God. I forget it the moment it is spoken.'

Do you now, he thought. That never seemed the case with his own confessors, who admonished him each time he was shriven that they had heard the same from him before. Come to think of it, it was mostly about women.

He shuffled in his seat.

'Those from Treknow and Prasgwig are owed my sealed lips on it.'

'Prasgwig? What is that? The village in the forest?'

The chaplain put fingers to his 'sealed' lips. 'Well. I . . . do see some of them from time to time.'

'God's teeth,' said Regis. 'I thought they were pagans.'

'Some of the villagers do seem to conform to older ways. I do not recognize some of their festivals as necessarily Christian. But there are many such traditions in small villages in the country. These are strange country ways in remote locations.'

'And they confess to you,' said Crispin. 'Recently?'

The man began to sweat with a bit of shine dotting his forehead. 'I . . . I cannot say, Master Guest . . .'

'Oh, come now, Father Allen. To merely remember if they came to you is surely not violating the *sub rosa*.'

His eyes darted between Regis and Crispin. 'Well . . . I . . .'

'For God's sake, tell the man,' said Regis, scratching his backside.

He lowered his face. 'I do hear their villagers. From time to time. And . . . one within the last sennight.'

'Did they confess to murder?'

He took a bracing breath. 'You know I cannot answer that question.'

'Man or woman?'

'Nor can I answer that one.' He took a few steps toward Sir Regis. 'My lord, I ask that I may leave you now. Master Guest has become impudent in his questions.'

He waved distractedly. 'Yes, yes, begone. But make sure you get that body out of the church.'

'And the chapel will need cleaning,' said Crispin. 'There was a great deal of blood.'

Appalled, the chaplain put a hand to his mouth and scurried out the door.

Looking around, the porter felt he was dismissed as well and took heel after him.

'Arno,' said Regis. 'See to the parchment on the table.'

Arno stepped forward to retrieve it. 'What's this?'

'A manifest. Of our stores. See to it. Make certain those villagers haven't cheated us. There isn't a thing to recommend this rock we live on.'

Arno stared at the parchment, and Crispin could swear that the man had begun to sweat.

'What's the matter?' said Regis, one side of his mouth curled up in a smug smile. 'Having trouble?'

Arno frowned. 'No trouble.'

'No?'

Arno looked up at Regis with flinty hatred in his eyes. 'No,' he hissed, and spun on his heel, taking the paper with him out the door.

Regis sighed. 'Did you get what you wanted, Guest?' He looked as if he would be pleased to see the back of Crispin as well.

'It was . . . helpful. Jack, go fetch K – our servant.'

Jack merely raised a brow and thumped up the stairs. 'My lord,' said Crispin. 'My servant must accompany us. May we borrow a horse for her use?'

'A horse for your female servant? Things must be done differently in London. Very well. Get one at the stables below.'

Crispin bowed to the constable who was not paying attention. Before he ventured forth, Crispin paused. 'If I may ask, how is it that you came to Tintagel, Sir Regis?'

'Must have angered some nobleman somewhere.' He rubbed at his shoulder, rolled it. 'I don't know. A man with few prospects must make due. I'm my father's third son and he had nothing to leave to me but a few coins and bolts of cloth. When this was offered, I took it, thinking that by my obedience I might find some compensation down the road. That never came, and I've been stuck here ever since. Six years.'

'I take it the pay—'

'The pay stinks. There are few opportunities for a man like me.'

'I suppose . . . Master Teague's doings might have intrigued you. Perhaps you thought to, er, confiscate some of the spoils—'

When Regis jerked from his chair, the blow to Crispin's jaw came in an explosion of stars and white pain, and he fell just as hard as if he had not been bracing for it.

He was on his arse, blinking as he looked up at the man rubbing his knuckles. 'Try it again, Guest. Call me a thief and see what next I mete out.'

Carefully rubbing his jaw, Crispin rose and kept well back from Regis. 'No, my lord, I don't think I will.'

'Good. Then get the hell out of my sight.'

He picked himself up, brushed down his coat, and left to stand outside with the horses.

It wasn't long until Kat and Jack joined him.

'Your servant, eh?' she said with a twisted mouth.

'I knew that would be the first thing you said. Come along. We're to get you a horse in the outer ward.'

She seemed surprised and it had the advantage of shutting her up. He helped her up behind him and they rode through across the land-bridge and under the gatehouse to the stables. He found the porter there who helped him find the tack and together they saddled Kat a gray mare called Chesten.

They all trotted through the courtyard – he noticed Kat kept her face well hidden by her hood – and they left the castle precincts, finding themselves at last on the open road toward the town.

'I think this is where we need to divide our strengths,' said Crispin. 'I have already talked to those parties that have an association with Roger Bennet in the village, but I think it wiser if *I* go to the village in the forest.'

'I don't like that, sir,' said Jack. 'By all accounts, it's a dangerous place. I don't care if the chaplain calls them Christian. That's not what the others say.'

'It is more dangerous, but they will likely talk to me instead of you.'

'But sir! Why not go together?'

'We are spending too much time. We don't know why Thomas

was killed and God knows who might be next. No, you go into Treknow, and I will go to . . . what did the chaplain call it? Prasgwig.' The uncomfortable name stumbled on his tongue.

'And what shall I do?' asked Kat.

Crispin and Jack stared at her. Crispin had completely forgotten about her. And he certainly didn't want to bring her with him to the outer village.

'Shall I go with Jack?'

Jack made some gesture at his throat. Clearly, he did not want her with him. Crispin felt the same. That meant . . .

'I suppose you should come with me.'

'But surely I can question people,' said Kat. 'It's not as if I can't learn their secrets like you can.'

Jack made some sort of sound in his throat.

As much as Crispin might wish to have her do that – *divide et impera* from *three* directions – he still couldn't bring himself to trust her completely.

'No. You'll come with me.'

'Now, Crispin—'

'Mistress Pyke, if you question every decision I make, then maybe it's best I leave you behind, trussed up in the constable's lodgings, where I will be sure you make no mischief.'

Slowly and deliberately, she folded the front of her hood back away from her face, but kept it snug against her cheeks. 'Whatever you say, Crispin.'

Jack gave him a wide-eyed look before he turned his horse and headed over the rutted lane toward Treknow.

She watched Jack ride and turned her face back toward Crispin, a smile curling the edges of her lips.

He cleared his throat, kicked the horse's flanks, and said, 'Follow me. And for God's sake, when we get there, keep your mouth shut.'

'Yes, Crispin,' she said again in that servile manner he could not trust.

They traveled first to the inn in Treknow. Kat waited with the horses while Crispin poked his head in. He couldn't hope that Kenver Treeve was still there waiting for him . . . but there he was. He offered the man a small pouch of coins, and by the look on his face, he didn't seem to have expected that amount. But he fetched his horse and soon joined them in the courtyard.

'It's a long way, Master Guest,' he said, first eyeing Kat and then turning toward the road that snaked over the countryside. 'There is a track into the forest but it soon dwindles. It's like a faery tale, them ones you always hear about when travelers are confounded along their way.'

Crispin never held much store for those superstitious tales . . . but the idea of it – this village hidden in the depth of the woods and those living there pagans – gave him pause.

'Is it dangerous, Master Treeve?'

'Well . . . it isn't altogether safe.'

They all fell silent and traveled quietly enough at first. It was a long way to the woods. They reached the outskirts of the forest, and Kat began to hum a tune and then to softly sing. At any other time, he might have enjoyed listening to her melodious voice, but not when he wanted to enter a dangerous village by stealth.

But it was Treeve who spoke. 'Wench, be quiet. These are rough men ahead of us.'

Crispin glanced back at her but by her demeanor he could tell that she wasn't taking it at all seriously.

'Master Treeve, you seem to be under the misapprehension that I am a babe straight from the womb. I have traveled far and dealt with men worse than these.'

'I've no doubt of that,' Treeve muttered. 'But just now, if you can humor us, lass?'

Her tittering laughter frightened a bird from a high branch. But she did keep silent at last.

The road narrowed, the forest seemed to close in and darken, and soon the road became no bigger than a deer path. If Treeve had not kept leading them further, he would have assumed they had lost their way.

The trees grew denser, and when they came to a bend in the road, Crispin pulled his mount up short.

Three men stood in their path, wearing rough tunics and aiming their taut bows and sharp arrows at him and his company.

'Where do you go?' asked the man to Crispin's left in a rough, Cornish accent. The full-bearded men all wore thick wool tunics and fur on their calves cross-gartered with leather thongs. Crispin had never seen the like. It was something from an old tapestry or painted on a church wall. Something from another time.

'I'm looking for a village in the wood. I am investigating a murder at the castle and need to talk to the gentle folk here.'

'And who be you?' he said, pulling back the bowstring just that much.

'I am Crispin Guest. I am called the Tracker of London. I investigate crimes.'

Though he kept his aim on Crispin, his eyes flicked toward his companions. 'From London, you say?'

'Yes. I merely come to speak with your villagers to ask if they have—'

'We don't speak to outsiders.'

Crispin bowed from his perch. 'I understand . . . and respect that. But a murder has been committed.'

'And you naturally blame us.'

'It concerns a woman in your midst. Someone named Eseld?'

The man turned his head to look at his companions this time, even lowering his bow slightly. When he turned toward Crispin again he gritted his teeth. 'What has this to do with her?'

'I will not know until I speak with her. Will you allow us to pass?'

The men conferred silently, only exchanging looks. The other two seemed to defer to the man who spoke to Crispin. He lowered his bow but the others kept theirs aimed. 'I will let you pass, Crispin Guest, but only so far. You will come to speak to our elder.'

Crispin didn't know what he expected, but once they'd cleared the trees he beheld a strange village. The people looked poorer than their brethren in Treknow, but still as industrious, bringing in a harvest on carts from the vast expanse of hilly farmland he saw beyond the village and the trees. The houses curved up the lane and the settlement looked to be almost as big as Treknow.

The villagers seemed to be decorating their huts with oak boughs and sheaves of wheat.

But as they cleared the forest, the villagers stopped in their tracks. Men with boughs in hand froze, staring. Even a stray dog that stood in the middle of the road halted and glared at them.

Crispin was struck by their clothes that were of a fashion that seemed to speak of another era, with houses more like huts, round with peaked roofs like a pavilion tent. There was a long house further up the lane with stone foundations. It all seemed so . . . primitive. Alien. Perhaps the rumors were right, that they *were* pagans. And just as the thought tickled at the back of his head, he saw something like a straw mannikin, some ten feet tall, standing on their village green. He'd seen harvest festivals before where a similar corn doll was made and burned. He supposed they were up to the same thing. But the thought suddenly made him shiver, of Julius Caesar's words on the *druidae*.

He glanced back at Kat. Maybe it wasn't such a good idea bringing her.

The villagers were still staring at them. They approached an old man sitting in a braided willow chair near a flaming brazier. He sagged in his age, staring into the fire with folds and pouches under his eyes, while small children sat around him on the ground. The children wore simple tunics, the boys with loose hose, cross-gartered at their calves.

The bowmen had lowered their bows at last and Crispin halted his horse.

'This is our village elder, Branok Trethewey of the village Prasgwig. My lord, this man calls himself Crispin Guest of London.'

The old man slowly raised his head and fastened his milky eyes on Crispin. His hair was white and long, braided at his temples, and his grizzled beard, just as white as his hair, fell to his chest. He looked Crispin over, didn't bother with Treeve, and hitched himself up in his creaking chair.

He cleared his throat with a gurgle, a cough, and finally spit on the ground. 'And what is a "Crispin Guest"?' he said in a rumbling, uneven voice.

Crispin bowed again. 'I am known as the Tracker of London.'

'This is far from London.'

'Indeed it is. I am hired to solve crimes. But in this instance, I was hired as a guard to my employer who has work at Tintagel. There was a murder there. Two murders. And now I find myself at my normal task of investigating.'

No one moved.

'If this happened at Tintagel,' asked the old man, 'why do you come here?'

'One of the murdered men was said to have . . . er . . . an acquaintance here in your village. Her name is Eseld.'

The old man raised his head to look around. 'Eseld? Is she here?'

Crispin had noticed how the crowd had gathered around them, noticed that they had converged behind them, cutting off any avenue of escape. He clutched tight to the horse's reins.

But now a woman in a simple dress came forth, a small child balanced on her hip. Her dark hair was plaited to one long braid, hanging down her back, and she sported the leavings of a bruise to her left eye, just yellowing. She bowed to the old man.

Branok Trethewey gestured toward Crispin. 'This *sowsnek* will speak to you.'

A few young men stepped forward, and argued with the old man in a foreign tongue. Several older men – each face carved in lines of age and dirt, with heavy dark beards, unkempt, untrimmed – dashed forward and interceded in their rough, barking language.

Silenced by the older men, the young men stepped back into the crowd, chastened, while the older men gathered nearer the elder like a fortress.

Trethewey turned his sagging eyes toward Crispin. 'It is not our way to allow *sowsnek* men to speak to our women. Our youth are strong in their traditions. While our older men' – he gestured toward his shield wall – 'wish to protect the word of their elder.' He folded his hands in his lap again. 'Eseld Gloyn, speak to the *sowsnek*.'

The woman glared at Crispin, her mouth fastened into a firm, immovable line. She lowered the child and pushed him toward another woman in the crowd, who took him up in her arms.

'Are you Eseld?'

She kept her mouth barred and only nodded.

'Are you acquainted with a man from the castle called Roger Bennet?'

She nodded again. She held her arms stiff at her sides and her hands fashioned into tight fists.

'He was murdered three days ago.' He watched her face for any indication of emotion. There was none. 'How did you know him?'

She slowly turned to Trethewey and spoke to him in what Crispin assumed was Cornish. He argued back at her in the same tongue, and she shouted, waving a fist. But when Trethewey rose unsteadily from his willow throne, she lowered her head, shaking it slightly from side to side.

Crispin couldn't help but survey the villagers, but their whispers ceased as abruptly as they had begun. 'Demoiselle, I ask again. How did you know Roger Bennet?'

'Must I answer this *emete*?' she hissed.

The old man nodded.

She lifted her chin and brazenly assessed Crispin down the ridge of her nose. 'I knew him. Ask my husband how I knew him. He were my lover. And a better one than the man who calls himself my *gour*.' She spit. 'I'm only sorry he's dead.'

The crowd erupted with calls and jeers, and there was a man roaring his displeasure from the back of the throng. Her husband, no doubt. What curious people, Crispin considered.

Crispin waited for the sounds to die down before he asked, 'When was the last time you saw him?'

She lifted her shoulder to him with indifference. 'A sennight. Maybe more.'

'And . . . what of your husband? Has he seen him of late?'

A burly man pushed his way forward. To her credit, the woman never flinched when he got right up to her, his shadow hovering over the woman like a Fury. 'I'm her husband, Jory Gloyn. And I never seen the scoundrel *marghek*. If I had, I would have cleaved him in two.'

'Interesting,' said Crispin, stalking closer. 'Or perhaps coshed him in the head?'

'Aye! I would have. Had I ever seen him.'

'Can anyone vouchsafe for your whereabouts Monday last? Did anyone see you go to the castle?'

He didn't answer at first, sweeping his eyes over Crispin's company . . . when they settled on Kat. 'What's she doing here?'

Crispin whipped his head toward Kat, and with an exasperated rasp asked, 'Why did you not say you have been here before?'

She shrugged. 'You didn't ask me.'

SIXTEEN

Jack rode into Treknow, passed it, and headed up the curve of the road toward the Penhall farm. He tied the horse to a post near the front door and knocked. A servant answered and bid him wait. Jack looked around at the manor house. It was nothing special. Just a larger version of where he and Master Crispin lived, but with a bigger great room below, several doors that must have led off to a kitchen, buttery, and pantry, and a wider staircase leading to a gallery of doors. The place was dingy and unkempt. It was a small village and the Penhalls must have made more with their dairy sales but did not come from nobility.

The man himself, Jowan Penhall, came down the steps. He wore a working man's clothes – a rough-spun tunic and simple chaperon hood. No necklaces, no rings, no ornaments at all, save for a simple dagger sheathed on his belt. Jack was certain that he worked right alongside what servants he had out with the cows, just as his daughter did. He admired that, for a man could become slothful and arrogant when he did not get his hands dirty in his own business.

'Master Tucker? Why have you returned? We are a mournful household.'

'Aye, sir, that I know. But . . . there were questions I was unable to ask last time. And now that the tidings are not so raw, I thought I could talk at length to you and your daughter.'

'I don't know that my daughter could be disposed . . .'

'Oh, but sir, she may have information that she doesn't know is useful. But *we* may speak first.'

'Well, it shall have to be on the run, for I must get to the work.'

'Of course, sir.'

Jack struggled, even with his long legs, to keep up with the man hastening through his house and out to a back entry. They came out to a wide yard with grass and large patches of mud and dung. Jack steered himself around those as best he could. Jowan Penhall didn't seem bothered by plowing through with his boots.

'Master Penhall, it's been three days since Roger Bennet was killed. Do you recall the last time you saw him?'

'I don't know. I have been busy here.'

'Then . . . when last was it that he came to the farm?'

'I can't be certain. He sometimes came and went before I ever heard he was here. He wanted to be alone with my daughter. Entirely inappropriate, but he was a knight, used to different ways.'

They came to a small storehouse where one woman was stirring a heavy iron kettle and another was pulling a wooden fork through the sluggish mixture in a big bowl. There were small wooden cylindrical forms – no bigger than two hands together – with an open-weave linen lying in them. Jack realized that they must be for cheese-making. Penhall inspected what the workers were doing.

'What are we making today?' he asked of the woman at the kettle.

'Spermyse,' said the woman. Her starched white veil was folded away from a face shiny from steam. 'We gathered the herbs early this morning.'

'Very good. The priest is fond of our herbed cheese and told me that he had run out.' He turned briefly to Jack. 'It's how we've grown from a humble farm to yon dwelling. We make cheese that is desired throughout Cornwall. My daughter shall have a fine dowry.'

'Much blessings on that, sir.'

The man moved on, leaving the storehouse and out to the fields where the cows grazed in the drizzle. Jack and Penhall put up their hoods. Beyond the fields, Jack spied the vast wood stretching out over the countryside. He knew his master was in the thick of it there and he murmured a prayer for him.

'Master Penhall, I must ask . . . did you know that Roger Bennet was . . . er, seeing other women in the village?'

He stopped and scowled at the ground. 'This was not known . . . until recently.'

'Aye, the village is in a bit of an uproar over it.'

'That my personal business should be talked about in the streets . . . Well. That is the way of it. He had promised to marry my daughter. But I have since learned he promised this many times.'

'This looks to be a fine farm, sir, with your cheese business and all. Were you in want of funds?'

His eyes narrowed. 'Why would you say such a thing?'

'When I last met you, you seemed to be mourning the fact that your daughter would not wed. But I interpreted some of your distress to be the loss of a joining of wealth?'

'That is very impudent of you. It's a lie. Look around you. We are very profitable. I only mourned for my daughter's sake.' He pushed his hood up off his head. 'If that is all, I have work to do.'

'Aye, sir. Where can I find your daughter?'

Penhall suddenly did not seem as jovial as he had been upon Jack's first meeting him a day ago. He waved his hand impatiently. 'Ask a servant.' He stalked away, stomping through manure.

Jack watched him go and considered. Any man would be irritated at the tidings of a betrothed behaving as disgracefully as Roger had. And being the butt of jests in his own village. He certainly had a right to his embarrassment.

Jack spotted a man carrying wooden buckets and trotted over to ask him. The man led Jack around the corner of a stone building where Janet and two other maids were putting buckets of milk on a handcart.

'Demoiselle,' said Jack with a bow. She startled and stared at him. The other maids stopped what they were doing and gave Jack admiring glances. 'I have come again to talk to you. May we speak? Alone?'

She put a finger to her mouth and gnawed on it. It was red and raw, obviously a habit. She dismissed the others. Both girls each picked up a handle of the cart and rolled it back toward the store-houses where the cheese was being made.

'You're Master Tucker, aren't you?'

'Yes, demoiselle. And when last we met your father imparted very distressing tidings regarding Sir Roger Bennet.'

Janet's eyes threatened to tear, but her frown seemed to stop them. 'Yes,' she said tersely.

'May I ask . . . when was the last time you saw him?'

'I don't know. Three days ago?'

'The day he was killed?'

She tossed her head and stalked away from him. 'I don't know. I suppose.'

'Did he come to the farm or did you go to him?'

She whirled back. 'Go to him? What do you take me for? A loose woman, like you see in the village? I don't run to any man.'

'No . . . of course not, demoiselle. Forgive me. I merely wish to get the facts right in me head.'

Janet seemed to calm slightly. 'This is such terrible business. And such lurid talk in the village. I *am* a maid.'

'I did not doubt it,' he said quickly, now suddenly doubting it all the more. 'And you were given to understand that you would wed him?'

'We did have an understanding. I don't believe the lies they tell in the village.'

'Well . . .' *Tread carefully here, Jack.* 'There were three women at least who claim to have been his lover. Why would they lie?'

'Because they are envious of me and my father's money. Just because we are more industrious than that lot, just because we have found a way to make our money, they throw vile lies at us. They've never liked us.'

'That is a shame,' he said, rubbing his beard in thought. 'They didn't seem as if they were lying. They were fighting among themselves . . .'

'Of course. They are a crude people.'

'Oh. Are your family not from the village?'

'Yes, but we found a way to better ourselves.' Janet pushed her veil back from her face with a dirty hand, leaving a smudge across her cheek. Jack couldn't help but stare at it. 'My father is going to be a knight. And they are jealous of that.'

'Oh. I didn't know.'

'Yes. His growing wealth makes it a certainty. He'll buy more land and have more servants. Soon, I will not have to be out with the cows any longer.'

'And Roger's family wealth would have made that happen all the sooner.'

'Of course it would have! And I have a big dowry. Surely Roger saw that too . . .' She gritted her teeth. Her hand clutched hard at her apron, fingers whitening. 'Is there anything else?'

'No, thank you, demoiselle.' Jack bowed but stopped before leaving. 'Well, there is something. Do you know Thomas Dunning, another knight at the castle?'

'Do you think I make it my business to meet all the knights up there?'

'No, demoiselle, but I thought—'

'I do not.'

'Very well. I bid you good day.'

She nodded to him like a noblewoman dismissing a servant and he turned on his heel. So the Penhalls had vain pretentions. He looked back at Janet. She was arranging her veil and her skirts like a lady, even though the hem of her dress was muddy with cow shit.

Jack couldn't blame her. Everyone wanted to better themselves and have fine servants to do their bidding. How would it be, he wondered, for his own wife Isabel to have a lady's maid to tend to her needs, comb her hair, dress her in fine clothes, with a wet nurse seeing to the babes? He would have done all he could to see that happen. Alas. Even when he inherited the tavern from Gilbert Langton, he'd not make enough to get her such a maid. It didn't matter to Isabel. She was happy with her lot; Jack and the children. And she was a miracle-worker, making the household what it was on their meager income. But a husband always wanted to make life better for his wife. This he could not deny. It was the very nature of being a man, he decided; protection, earning a decent wage. And a good father for his daughter, as Penhall surely wanted. And Jack wanted it too, for he was also father to a sweet young daughter who would someday need a dowry. 'Ah me.' He sighed, reaching the house again. It was best not to dwell on it. He was certain that he and Master Crispin would see to it that his family did not starve.

He passed through the house, poking around. He climbed the stairs only so far and just peeked below the gallery to see if any doors were open. No luck. Down the stairs again, unchallenged by any steward or servants, he stuck his head through a door and found a passage to the kitchens. There was a cook busy at a wide plank table, grinding herbs in a mortar. A boy was keeping the fire fed with small sticks, until he looked up and spied Jack. 'Oi! What do you want?'

The cook first glanced at the boy and then over her shoulder at Jack. 'You shouldn't talk to strangers like that, boy.' To Jack, she said, 'Good master, please tell me who you are and why you are here.'

'My apologies, demoiselle,' he said with a bow. He knew that kind of flattery always got servants to talk to him easily. When he looked up again, he smiled. Yes, she was flustered by his tone, his comportment, and by calling her 'demoiselle'. 'I am Jack Tucker, apprentice to the Tracker of London. I am investigating the death of Roger Bennet. Were you acquainted with the gentleman?'

'Oh aye. That was a sad, sad thing.'

'Indeed. When was the last time you saw him?'

'It was Monday. He dined here.'

'I see. He dined here in the company of Master Penhall and Mistress Janet?'

'Aye. He came often. The castle doesn't need defending, you see. And no one goes there but that funny man with the cart. I always thought castles were grand things, but that one is more like a crumbling hill, all by itself.'

'Have you ever been there?'

'Me? Oh no. Well . . . when I was a child, we used to go to it as close as we could. Children, you know.' She glanced at the boy by the fire, who must have been hers. 'You could climb the stone walls around it,' she said in a husky whisper. 'You could get mighty high. It's an easy climb for a squirrely child. You could look far out to sea, and also beyond the battlements into the courtyard. There's a narrow path up the side and around the battlements. Some of the braver boys used to go right up into the island castle from there. They'd tell tales of harrying the sheep.' She clucked her tongue and shook her head at the memories. 'We always thought the guards would chase us away but they never did. Even when there were workmen there. But the workmen soon left. If it weren't for the smoke from their hearths, you wouldn't think no one was there at all.'

'Hmm. When Roger was here on Monday, how did he seem?'

'You mean his character? Oh, he was always a jolly fellow. A fine gentleman. He laughed and loved his wine. I don't believe them lies they tell in the village.'

'About his seeing other women?'

'It's a shame what some people get up to when they want to tear another down. They don't like the Penhalls. They think they are above their stations, but they just work hard is all.'

'When did you find out about the stories they told about Roger?'

She came around her worktable and got in close. 'That was common talk for a long time.'

'Oh? Not just because he died?'

'Oh no. We all knew about it.'

'Are you certain it was just tales?'

'Well . . .' She glanced back at her boy until it looked like he was too busy to hear them. 'Maybe it was and maybe it wasn't. But don't tell the master, for Mistress Janet didn't know.'

'Did Master Penhall know?'

'I can't see how he couldn't. He went to the tavern like all the rest of them. The village isn't shy about poking a stick at a fellow to rouse him.'

'I see. Well, thank you, demoiselle.'

She curtseyed. 'God be with you, Master Tucker, in your quest.'

He nodded to her and left, leaving by the back door so that he could get around to his horse unmolested.

All the way back to the village, he chewed on his thoughts. Janet Penhall seemed terribly angry at the development that Roger was not as faithful as she had hoped. But could she truly have been unaware of talk of him? Surely she went into the village. She must have friends, and they must have told her.

If she knew ahead of time, then she was as good a suspect as anyone else.

And, of course, the both of them lied. The last time they both saw Bennet was in their very own hall . . . on Monday.

Master Crispin had told him about Menhyr Rouse who worked at the stables at the other end of town, but he thought he'd still save

him for later. Rouse sounded like a rough man and he'd rather see
to the women first. Jack knew he cut a fine figure and was not above
a little flirtation to get his way. Now it was just a matter of finding
Mabyn and Gwendolyn. He decided on the well. For if there was
one place you could be sure of a gathering in a village – besides
the tavern or alehouse – it was the village well.

It was at the edge of the green. He dismounted and, holding the
horse's lead, pulled it along to the stone well, where others had
gathered. Women were taking turns pulling the bucket up from its
depths and Jack hurried forward, letting the horse graze at the green.

'Demoiselles, allow me to help you.'

They all quieted in their chatter when Jack grabbed the rope
and began pulling it. They watched him for a time – and how
predatory were their eyes! It made him a bit uncomfortable, like
they were sizing up a pig hanging at the butcher, until he contented
himself with the idea that it would be easier to use his wiles to
get answers.

'You're with that man from London, aren't you?' asked a short
and round woman.

'Aye, that I am. I'm Jack Tucker.' He smiled and gave her a wink.
He saw the other women move in incrementally. *Like a cat on a
mouse*, he thought.

'Were you in London?' asked another with a long blonde plait,
balancing an empty bucket on her hip.

'I come from there. Lived there all me life.' He pulled up the
full bucket and looked around with it. Several offered theirs until
he just picked one. He filled it and then tossed the bucket back
down the hole. It filled, and he hoisted it up again, one hand over
the other, but taking his time.

'You're investigating Roger Bennet's death,' said another young
thing with a pretty smile and raven black hair.

'Yes, it's true. Who do *you* think killed him?'

She shook her head. 'I wouldn't know. I wouldn't want no one
to hang upon my saying.'

'But all good Christians want justice to be done,' said Jack.
'Murder is against God's law. It's the fifth commandment, isn't it?'

The women exchanged glances, nodding vigorously.

A woman with hair as red as Jack's piped up. 'I think Menhyr
Rouse did it. He was angry as a stuck boar when he heard about
Roger and Derwa.'

'Aye,' said the black-haired girl. 'It's true. And he's strong, too.' She said the last dreamily.

'Did he know about it before?' asked Jack, resting the full bucket on the edge of the well. 'Did not everyone know about it before Roger was slain?'

The short round woman held her empty bucket behind her back as she rocked on her heels. 'Oh well, when it comes down to it, we all knew.'

'It's true,' said the one with the blonde plait. 'And Menhyr knew, too. He was using Derwa to get money from the man. The priest did not approve of that.'

'Aye, it sounds unsavory,' said the short one.

Jack poured the water in the third bucket, and dunked the well bucket again. 'How was she getting money?'

'Oh, you know,' said the ginger girl. 'A girl wheedles and asks her lover for things. He gave her bits of jewelry. Menhyr promptly sold the things to travelers.'

Jack breathed a laugh. 'It sounds like this was no secret at all.'

'It wasn't,' laughed the ginger girl.

'Then do *you* think it was Menhyr Rouse?' he asked her.

Ginger Girl folded her lips. 'Could have been. But . . . those *druw* men. They're a rough sort, aren't they?'

There was some shushing and hands waved at her.

'Isla,' hissed the black-haired girl. 'It's bad luck to talk about . . . *them.*'

The others murmured, crossed themselves, and stopped talking altogether. Jack poured his last bucket and settled on the edge of the well. 'Why is it bad luck to talk about them men?'

'Because it is,' whispered the blonde plaited one. 'They're rough and pagan and frightening. We don't talk of them.'

The black-haired girl said, 'They've enticed many a maiden to them, and they were never seen again.'

'But they're just beyond the trees there. Only a couple of miles, eh?'

She shook her head and would say no more. It gave him the shivers.

'Do any of you know where Mabyn lives? Or Gwendolyn? I would talk with them.'

Glances passed from one to the other, fingers over tittering mouths. He wanted to rebuke them all for being such scolds, but he needed their information and so kept his face passive.

Ginger Girl pointed. 'Mabyn and Gwen are working at their looms, at the cottage up the hill by the broken tree.'

'They work together?'

'Aye.' She began to giggle and the others followed suit. 'They're sisters.'

What a world, he thought, and said his good days. He grabbed the horse's lead and tugged it along as he hiked up the road. It was little better than a track by the time he reached their hill and cottage. He heard the clack of a shuttle and the sound of two angry voices. The voices rose and then the sound of furniture clattered and something like crockery was smashed. A scream.

Jack ran to the door, tried the handle and found it barred. He rammed it with his shoulder . . . once . . . twice . . . and finally crashed through, splintering the door. He fell into the room and lay stunned for a moment. Until another scream rent the air and another piece of crockery flew over his head.

SEVENTEEN

'She's a troublemaker,' growled Gloyn to Crispin. 'And you're a troublemaker. What do you want?'

'I wish to talk of Roger Bennet . . . and Thomas Dunning,' said Crispin, sitting straight on his saddle.

'I have naught to say about Roger. And this other. I don't know him.'

'As I said,' said Crispin dismounting, 'I wish to talk to you. We can do it here in the street or go somewhere more private.'

As soon as his feet hit the turf, a fist crashed into his cheek. An explosion of stars accompanied it and he staggered back into the horse's flanks. A quick shake of his head, and he fastened his sight on Gloyn, rubbing his fist in his palm. The villagers gathered, closing a circle around them. Crispin took the chance that they only wanted to watch, and swung hard at Gloyn's face.

His knuckles smacked the man's nose with a satisfying crunch. Gloyn stumbled backwards but never could regain his balance. The crowd made room for him as he fell back on his rump and scowled, blood pulsing from his fractured nose.

'You broke it, you churl.'

'I'll break more than that,' said Crispin, standing over him, fists still balled and ready. 'I only want to talk, and I'll help you up if you agree to it.' Extending a hand to the man, he waited.

Gloyn glared at the offered hand until he finally took it. Crispin hauled him up, but no sooner had the man regained his feet than he swung at Crispin again, catching him at his ear.

The blow rang in his head like a belfry, but he reacted quickly and came up with his fist to the man's gut. Gloyn bent double, wheezing and coughing. Crispin wiped the sweat from his brow and blew out a breath. *Definitely getting too old for this*, he complained to his aching head and sore knuckles.

But Gloyn wasn't done. He kicked out, hitting Crispin's shin. It smarted enough that he hopped back, and the still out-of-breath Gloyn came at him, leaping with arms wide, ready to consume Crispin in a lethal embrace.

Ducking to the side, Crispin barely escaped, yet Gloyn came at him again with his fists raised. Crispin stretched an arm over his face to block the blow . . . but it never came. Gloyn seemed to freeze for a moment before he simply fell forward flat on his bloodied face.

Kat stood behind him, a rock in her hand. She tossed it aside and dusted her hands at a job well done.

'If you two *boys* are finished . . .'

'Kat . . .'

'Truly, Crispin, I can't sit here all day watching this spectacle.' She turned to the disappointed men in the gathered crowd. 'Well? Will no one drag him into the alehouse so that Master Guest may talk to him when he awakens?'

Two burly men stepped forward, each taking a foot, and dragged him down the lane and unhelpfully over the granite step.

Treeve turned to Kat. 'Is this always the way with Master Guest?'

She sighed. 'Always.'

Frowning, Crispin glared at her before shoving her aside and following the trail of Jory Gloyn's bloody nose.

The tavern was dark and close. The rafters formed a tall point in rough-hewn logs, blackened by soot. There was a hole at the top of the roof where the fire – sitting in the center of the floor amid a ring of stones – puffed gray clouds of smoke heavenward. The place smelled of damp wool, smoke, sweat, and dung. A goat with long, curving horns and tied to a table leg chewed on some scraps of kitchen leavings and glanced lazily at Crispin.

They set Gloyn in a chair and someone tossed a bucket of water at his face. He slowly came out of it, wiping his cheeks, eyes focusing blearily at his fellows around him. When he fixed his gaze on Crispin, he seemed to fully awaken. 'What?' he bellowed, trying to rise.

Crispin shoved him back down and leaned over him. 'Sit, damn you. I'm questioning you about two murders now, Gloyn.'

'Two? I told you. I never heard of that other.'

'You were angry that your wife carried on with Roger Bennet. Perhaps Dunning got in your way. You killed Bennet and then, days later, when you saw your chance, you dispatched Dunning.'

'No, he didn't.'

Crispin was going to kill her. He whirled and hovered darkly over her. 'Be still, Mistress Pyke.'

'Crispin, can you imagine this man stealthily dispatching Thomas Dunning, clambering over the rooftop of the chapel without a sound, then disappearing on the plains? *This* man?'

He turned again to Gloyn. He was a big man and moved like an ox. She was right. There was no possible way he could have performed the feats necessary to elude them by the chapel. Which touched a shiver down his back again that it might have been Kat all along. He cast that thought aside to menace Gloyn once more. Crispin noted that there were no scratches down his bare arms. 'Exactly what were your whereabouts three days ago? Can anyone vouchsafe for your time in the village . . . or did you leave it?'

'Aye,' said a man in the back of the crowd. 'He did leave the village.'

Men moved to reveal the short and wiry man standing by the doorway. He took in all the stares with a gloating raising of his chin. He pushed men aside to stand opposite Crispin. 'He left.'

'Did he? And who are you?'

'I am the proprietor and brewster of this house. Austol Kellow, and a respected name it is and has been for generations.'

'I have no doubt of that,' said Crispin. 'Then, Master Kellow, can you tell me when you saw Master Gloyn leave the village?'

'Oh, he was all stealthy-like, thinking no one was paying him any heed. But I seen him. I was opening the door in the morn, letting out the steam from my brewing in the back.' He thumbed behind him. 'He was heading out down the back lane toward the main road. I seen you, clear as day, Gloyn.'

'You're a liar and everyone knows it!'

'No one leaves the village. Not unless we go two by two. That's the rule.' The men around Kellow shushed him and Crispin studied all of their anxious demeanors. 'You can't call me a liar if I seen you,' said Kellow.

'You're still a liar, Kellow. And your ale tastes like piss.'

Kellow lunged for a stool and raised it over his head, stomping toward Gloyn. Two men rushed forward to hold him back.

'You're not allowed in here no more, Jory Gloyn,' rasped Kellow as someone wrestled the stool from his grasp. 'You find your ale elsewhere. Ha! And good luck to you!'

'Peace, gentlemen,' cautioned Crispin. If it were up to him, he'd let them at it. But he needed to know. 'And did you see him return, Master Kellow?'

'Oh, I seen him. It was late. And I saw blood on his hands.'

'You never did!' cried Gloyn. Crispin pushed him back down when he tried to rise.

'I did! I saw blood. And so did my servant, Cador. Where is that knave?'

Someone called out for the boy, and a skinny slip of a boy that reminded Crispin of Jack Tucker from twenty years ago came from the back, face smudged with soot. 'Oi?' he asked as he was pushed forward. 'What's happening?'

Kellow stood behind the boy protectively, pressing his hands to his shoulders. 'You tell him, boy. Tell the *emete* lord there what you saw with me three nights ago, when Jory Gloyn came stumbling home in the underbrush.'

'Oh!' he said, eyes suddenly wide. 'He had blood on his hands. It was near Compline but I saw it clear as day. Blood.'

Kellow smiled and gave a final nod. 'There! You see.'

Crispin turned again to Gloyn. 'Your own village folk accuse you, Gloyn. What have you to say?'

'They can all go to hell, the pompous arses.'

Crispin grabbed his arm and hauled him to his feet. 'You're coming with me, Gloyn, to face charges. The castle will hold you.'

Suddenly, the men closed ranks and blocked the door. 'You'll take him nowhere, *sowsnek*,' said one of the villagers. 'The rest of the crowd murmured their agreement.

'Will you bar the king's justice from doing its task?'

'The king is far from here in distant Westminster,' said one of
the men in a dun-colored tunic that hung below the man's baggy-
kneed hose. 'We don't have naught to do with him or him with us.'

'Justice must be done.'

'We'll do our own justice, if need be, not that of *sowsneks*.'

'I'm afraid I cannot allow that.'

'And who's to stop us?'

'I shall have to return with the king's men to seize him.'

They all looked around. Gloyn wrestled his arm away from
Crispin's grasp. 'It weren't no blood from Bennet.'

'Tell us another,' said Kellow.

'It weren't! It were . . . Ah, damn you to hell, Kellow! I . . . I
was poaching.'

The men laughed, cutting the tension.

Crispin thrust his fists at his hip. 'Poaching?'

'Aye. I took a sheep from the castle. I cut it up in one of the
hollows, wrapped the meat, and took it home. That's what you saw,
you son of a whore, Kellow.'

'No one believes your lying mouth, Gloyn.'

'Don't believe me, eh? Come on to my cottage and I'll show
you, then.'

Crispin sensed a change in the man's tone. And all at once he
didn't believe the man was lying. *God's blood. Is this all about
poaching damned sheep?*

'Very well,' Crispin said with a sigh. 'Let us see this meat.'
He grabbed the man's arm again and shoved him toward the
door. The men let him pass and followed Crispin to see for
themselves.

Soon, there followed an entourage like any feast day church
procession. All that was missing was the priest with his censer.
Some women from the village, carrying bound sheaves of wheat,
soon joined them, whispering to the menfolk and asking them what
was transpiring. They arrived at Gloyn's cottage – another round
hut, as were all the other houses in the village, with a pointed roof.
Eseld Gloyn had come out of the doorway and stood on the porch,
arms folded in front of her, glaring at the village as they approached,
a child with a dirty face clinging to her skirts.

Everyone stopped at the doorstep.

'Well?' she challenged.

'Madam,' said Crispin, 'if you please, I should like to see your pantry.'

'My what? What for?'

'Just show him!' growled Gloyn. He pushed past his wife and she ran after him. Crispin followed but couldn't very well stop the rest of the villagers from coming too, or at least as many as would fit.

They crossed through to a curtained alcove at the back of the hut. Jory cast the curtain aside and gestured to Crispin. 'See the joints . . . there and there.' It smelled strongly of blood with flies buzzing over his head, but even in the dim light he recognized two legs of mutton, hanging by the hocks from a low roof beam. They were obviously freshly done, but had hung for several days, a thin layer of white mold already on them. There were some small cylinders of cheese covered in cloths, and little else but some parsnips and onions in a basket. He withdrew and stood looking at Jory and then the rest of the village. 'I am satisfied,' he said to the guffaws of the men.

The crowd heaved Crispin suddenly out of the way and squeezed themselves into the narrow doorway to see the poached haunches for themselves. Men nodded their heads as they came out, allowing more in.

Jory Gloyn was a thief. He might have wanted to kill Bennet, but the blood from the corpse had not been smeared all over him. No, the killer had not touched the dead man except to strike him a mortal blow and shove him into the hole. Could Gloyn have done the deed and then poached a sheep to hide his guilt? Crispin doubted it. It sounded like more than the man was capable of conspiring.

In the end it didn't seem worth fighting a whole village for.

He'd leave it to these villagers to deal with his poaching. Could be he'd hang anyway. He was ready to leave when shouting rang out, and suddenly all the men crammed into the little cottage began yelling as well.

'You stole it!' cried Eseld, and then a slap.

'Get off me!' That was Kat!

Crispin leapt into the crowd of men, trying to get to the women in the courtyard. The men blocked his way, shouting, encouraging the two women to fight.

Crispin struggled against the tide of men like a fish swimming upstream. He pushed and boxed his way through and made it outside.

Kat was fully engaged with Eseld, hands around the Cornish woman's neck, while Eseld struggled on the ground.

The others seemed content to watch, but Crispin wasn't having it. He reached down and grabbed Kat by an earlobe. She released her captive immediately.

When she got to her feet, he let her go. She tried to swing at him but he captured her arms.

'She stole it from me!' cried Eseld, pointing a shaking finger at Kat.

'It's mine. It was given to me.'

Crispin pulled Kat back out of the way. 'What in God's name are you fighting over?'

'That!' said Eseld, pointing to Kat's chest.

Crispin looked. The horse brooch from Roger's dead hand . . . the brooch that had been in his pouch. He slapped a hand to the pouch and wasn't surprised not to find it there. 'You stole it from me.'

'It was mine.'

'What do you mean it was yours?'

Kat suddenly kept her mouth tightly shut.

Crispin grabbed her arm and squeezed. 'Kat. What. Do. You. Mean?'

She sighed and threw her head back. Her dress was torn, revealing a bit of her chemise, smudged with dirt. 'That brooch. Well . . . Roger . . . gave it . . . to me.'

EIGHTEEN

J ack fell to the floor, and looked up. Inside the dim cottage were two upright looms, both with the beginnings of a patterned cloth slowly being woven. The myriad long strands of warp strung up along the top bar were filled with the weft of the horizontal colored yarn. But the shuttles hung to the ground by their weft threads. The furniture was strewn about, and crockery sherds littered the floor.

Both women were rolling around, with clawed fingers in each other's hair.

Jack jumped up and reached down, grabbing for them. But a set of teeth chomped down on his arm.

'Ow! God's teeth and bones! Get up, you harpies.' He dove in a second time and pushed them apart, one with his foot, the other with his elbow. 'Halt your struggles at once!'

They pushed at him but, with finally the right leverage, he managed to keep them apart. 'Stop it!'

With heaving breaths, they stood back. Their dresses were torn, their hair disheveled. Jack gave each one a nasty eye. 'Look at the two of you. And do you think our Lord would gaze kindly upon the both of you? He'd turn His back, He would.' When he was certain they'd stay apart he looked down at his arm. At least the skin wasn't broken, but there were definitely teeth marks. He rubbed it and shook his sleeve back down.

'You should be ashamed of yourselves. Now what is all this?'

'It was her!' said Mabyn. 'It was all her fault.'

'It was not! It was you,' screamed Gwendolyn. She jerked toward Mabyn but Jack stuck his hand into her shoulder and shoved her back.

'None of that. Angels bless us. Behave like God's own, would you!' He wiped a hand over his sweaty brow. 'Now. One at a time. Mabyn. You tell me the grievance.'

She pointed a finger at Gwendolyn's face. 'She stole my Roger.'

'No!' cried Gwendolyn. 'You stole *my* Roger.'

'Now, now. By the looks of things, Roger was nobody's . . . *and* everybody's. He made promises to at least four women.'

Gwendolyn shook her head. 'That's not true.'

'I'm afraid it is, lass. And you well know it.' He took a breath. 'And . . . how long did you know it?'

She raised her sorrowful face.

'And don't try to tell me it was at his death,' said Jack, 'because everyone in the village seemed to know right well what Roger was about.'

She wiped a hand over her eyes, flicking it hard, as if angry at her own messy tears. 'I knew. But I didn't know it was me own sister.'

'Holy saints preserve us. The two of you . . . and Roger . . .' Well, there wasn't a thing new to him under the sun since he became Master Crispin's servant. Every foul thing, every detestable human sin came to light under his master's tight scrutiny. 'Two sisters fighting over a dead man. You two should be praying for forgiveness, not fighting.'

At last, the two of them seemed to sag. Gwendolyn found an overturned stool, righted it, and sat. 'He's right. He's dead. What's the use in fighting?'

'Because you are a miserable whore,' hissed Mabyn.

Gwendolyn sprang to her feet. 'And what does that make you?'

They seemed ready to charge each other again when Jack crouched with arms out between them. 'Leave it. The both of you are equally guilty. I'll wager you each knew the other was sporting with your man. So admit it and ask God for His mercy.'

They both shut their lips and turned their heads away.

'Oh, it's that way, is it?' Jack stuck his fists at his hips. 'I've never seen two women as sinful as the two of you. Won't even make the effort to be sorrowful. You're family. You need each other. And Roger is beyond your reaches now. You should be praying for him.' *He'll need it*, he ruminated.

Gwendolyn gave in first. She sat again and dropped her face in her hands. 'What's the use, Mabyn?' she sobbed.

Mabyn deflated. She stared at the floor and leaned against a loom. 'I knew he was trouble,' she said softly. 'I heard talk of him. I didn't want to believe it.'

'He was a terrible man,' said Gwendolyn with a wet snort. 'Look what he's brought two sisters to.'

'Aye.' She shuffled toward her sister and carefully put her arms around her.

Jack tensed, expecting at any moment he'd have to hurl himself on the two of them again. He waited . . . but nothing came of it. Only more sobbing on Gwendolyn's part as Mabyn rested her head on her sister's.

'Were either of you angry enough to do him harm?'

They looked up at Jack, frowns on their faces.

'Can anyone in the village vouchsafe for your whereabouts three days ago?'

Mabyn looked at her sister. 'Anyone in the village. We were here and at the well.'

'What about today? Do either of you know a Thomas Dunning?'

'The other knight at the castle?' said Gwendolyn. She shrugged. 'Told me to clear off a time or two. What of him?'

'He's dead. Murdered. Were you in the village all day? Can anyone say with certainty that you were?'

She slowly rose. 'Aye. Anyone. Ask them.'

'You can be sure that I shall.'

He gave them a stern look before he turned to leave.

'Why would anyone kill Thomas Dunning?' asked Mabyn.

Jack paused at the door and looked back. 'I do not know, demoiselle. It is less clear to me why he met such a sudden fate.'

He left after that and stood on the road, looking up toward the rest of the village. Why *was* Dunning slain? Did it have to do with Bennet's death or did it have no connection at all? *I wonder if Master Crispin is thinking the same thing*, he pondered.

Grabbing the horse's lead, he walked with him back down the lane toward the center of the village. The horse snuffled Jack's shoulder, blowing on his hair. He ducked out of its way and, instead, reached up to hug the beast's huge head and stroke its cheek. 'What do you think, Seb, old thing?' he asked the horse. 'Was it one of them villagers . . . or them in the castle?'

Some women were still at the well, and when he asked, it wasn't surprising that several of the women vowed that they saw both sisters in the village all day.

He walked with his horse past the inn and heard music coming through its doors. The players. He wondered how Master Crispin was doing at the pagan village. He wanted to know more about it . . . and he was feeling a bit parched. He turned into the innyard, left the horse with the stableman again and entered.

The woman player had returned and she sawed on her rebec while another played the shawm.

Gertrude, the innkeeper's wife, came over to him and brought him ale in a jug with a horn cup. He drank it slowly and watched the others who sang along with the musicians. After a time, they stopped to drink their own cups and the room settled down again to quiet murmuring.

Jack glanced over to the next table and noticed a villager with a dark beard. Jack rose, grabbed his jug, and sat with him, drinking quietly for a time, before he got up the courage to speak to him. 'It's a fair village you have here.'

The man smiled and raised his cup. Jack offered him more ale from his jug and the man gladly took some.

'Much thanks,' he said. 'You're from London with that other man investigating up at the castle.'

'Aye, I'm Jack Tucker.' He offered his hand and the other took it.

'Clemo,' said the man.

'Master Clemo. What do you make of them murders?'

'Murders? Two of them now?'

'Roger Bennet and another knight from the castle, Thomas Dunning.'

He crossed himself. 'Holy saints.'

Jack sipped his brew. 'Any ideas? Do you think it's some of the women in the village angry at being made a fool of?'

'That would be a sore thing, wouldn't it? Women taking to murdering men.'

'It's happened more often than you think.'

'You've seen a lot of it, have you? I shouldn't like to have a job like that.'

Jack settled back, holding his cup close to his chest. 'It's more interesting than any other vocation I could have had. Chasing down murderers. Catching thieves. It's thrilling to a man's heart, I can tell you. But you have to use your wiles more oft than not.'

He looked Jack over, appraising. 'Aye. I can see that. Well. Mabyn, Gwendolyn, Janet Penhall . . .' He scrubbed at the back of his neck, lifting his long hair out of the way. 'Those are some, er . . . *strong* women. I shouldn't like to get on the wrong side of them.'

'But murder?' Jack took another sip, gazing at the man from over the rim of his cup.

Clemo shrugged. 'Is not any man . . . or woman, for that matter . . . capable? I don't know. I don't know that I am fit to say.'

'It's just an opinion,' said Jack. He leaned forward, resting his elbows on the table. 'What do you know of Prasgwig?'

The man frowned. 'We don't talk about that place.'

'And why not? They are just over the hedge.'

'Farther than that . . . I hope.' Clemo leaned in too, speaking in low tones. 'They're pagan. Some believe they are descended from the *druw* with their *druwish* ways. You hear stories. They're brutes. Unchristian. If we could get up the courage, we'd burn them out.'

'What have they done to you and your village, sir?'

'They took some women. We never saw them again.'

'Have you gone to their village to find them?'

He shook his head. 'No one's brave enough. Men were killed. Do you think they murdered your knights?'

'All I know is my master is there right now, investigating, questioning.'

There was true fear in the man's eyes when he looked steadily at Jack. 'If I were you and that were *my* master, I'd go fetch him. Or you might not have a master to go fetch.'

A warm wash of fear flashed over his chest. 'Why?'

'Because they're pagans. They have strange ways. Not like us. They sacrifice to their gods in the old religions. They sacrifice humans. And it's end of harvest. That's one of their times.'

Jack staggered to his feet. 'Maybe I should go. Will you and your fellows come with me?'

Clemo shook his head. 'We don't stick our necks in nooses for *sowsneks*.'

'To hell with your *sowsneks*. We're all English under King Richard.'

The man stood toe to toe with Jack. 'That's where you're wrong. We're Cornish. This is our land.'

'But a Christian soul might be in trouble.'

He would only shake his head and walked away from Jack.

Jack watched him leave, swept his gaze over the men in the room who seemed to be looking his way. Had they kenned what he had been saying? None of them would help. Their expressions clearly said it all. England was England and Cornwall was another country, just like Wales or Scotland. He spit on the floor as they watched, tossed his chair aside, and strode out of the inn.

Grabbing his horse away from the stableman, he mounted and kicked Seb's sides, galloping toward the road to Prasgwig.

NINETEEN

Crispin grabbed Kat's arm and stalked away from the crowd. They tried to follow, but he shot them a glare that many took as a proper warning. When he was far enough away, he threw her forward. She stumbled but righted herself.

'You've been lying to me since we met. Want to try the truth this time?'

She straightened her clothes as best she could with their rips and dirt. 'About what?'

'You said you met a caretaker and he showed you Carantok Teague's "holes", as you called them. Whom did you meet? Tell me now or so help me . . .'

'Well . . . you won't like it.'

'*Who!*'

She winced. 'Roger Bennet.'

He wanted to punch something. Where was Gloyn's face when you needed it? Instead, he clutched his already bruised fist with his palm, rubbing it there. 'You told Jack you did not know him,' he growled.

'Well . . . that was a little fib. I didn't want you thinking I killed him.'

'*Did* you?'

'Now, you see, *that* is the very thing I wanted to avoid. For the hundredth time, I *didn't!*' She fisted her cloak, wadding up the material.

'But you met him and bedded him . . .'

She gave him a look that meant she knew exactly what he was thinking, that he was jealous of a dead man . . . and damn her, he was. He yanked the brooch from her chest, ripping more fabric, and stalked away, turning his back to her.

'That's my brooch!' She took a step toward it with an outstretched hand, but when he closed his fist over it, she stopped. 'He said he found it and was going to give it to me. If I . . .'

She didn't need to finish. He opened his palm and looked at it. 'It was found in his hand. His *dead* hand. Do you know where he got it?'

'From one of the "holes", he said. I was running out of money. He—'

'He was a seducer. He promised marriage to several women in this village as well as Treknow.'

'I didn't want to marry him, I just wanted to know where these "holes" were.'

With a sigh he stuffed the brooch back in his pouch.

Her eyes followed his every move. 'Aren't you . . . aren't you going to give that back to me? It is mine. It was promised to me.'

He gave her a filthy look.

She folded her arms. 'That looks like no.'

'The time for truth is now, Kat. There are two dead men and I haven't ruled you out as the murderer.'

'Crispin, I—'

'No more. I tell you now, Mistress Pyke, if you are guilty, I *will* hand you over to the hangman.'

Her features softened and she approached him, arms loose, eyes sincere. Ah, if only he could trust them. 'But I didn't, Crispin,' she said softly. She cast about her an aura of innocence. He knew it was all a fabrication. 'I never murdered those men or anyone. I'm completely innocent.' She closed her eyes and blew out a breath. 'You know what I mean. Innocent of murder. I'm not lying to you . . . about that.'

It was then that he noticed how quiet the crowds had become. When he turned, he shouldn't have been surprised to see that all eyes were on them. And all ears too, he reckoned.

The old man, the elder Branok Trethewey, was suddenly standing there, leaning heavily on a staff decorated with oak leaves and braided wheat sheaves. 'Master Guest,' he said in a wispy voice. 'It seems that your accusations are closer to home. That perhaps when you look for murderers, you need not go as far as fair Prasgwig.'

Crispin did not so much as glance at Kat standing behind him. 'You may yet be right, my Lord Trethewey. But surely you must see how I must dispel all possibilities. And there are guilty here, though perhaps not of murder.'

Trethewey squinted up at the sun. 'It is near the end of the day, Master Guest. We have Hærfest to celebrate this night, the end of the summer harvest and the beginning of autumn. It is best that all *sowsnek* leave our village. It is a private affair for only our own.'

Scanning the solemn faces of the villagers looking on, Crispin had no choice but to accede to their wishes. 'Very well,' he said. 'If there are any further developments – and I'm certain the good folk here would see justice done – I can be reached at the castle.' He bowed, grabbed Kat's wrist, and dragged her toward the horses.

Treeve was there, sitting on his horse while it nervously stamped. 'Shall we leave this place, Master Guest?' he asked nervously.

'There is no further business here. For now.'

They'd only just headed out of the village when Jack Tucker, like one of the Four Horsemen, charged out of the brush, dagger held high. He yanked on his horse's reins to skid him to a halt.

'Oh,' was all he said, mouth hanging open in something like surprise.

'What are you doing, Tucker?'

He glanced around and sheepishly sheathed his dagger. 'I . . . I was rescuing you.'

Crispin cocked his head. 'I see.' He clucked to the horse and moved it forward. Kat gave Jack an endearing smile. Treeve merely stared at him before Jack turned his horse around and followed a few paces behind.

Once they left the village and the forest and traveled down the winding road on the outskirts of Treknow with open meadow around them, Crispin, without turning to him, asked, 'What was all that about, Jack?'

'Well . . . I was told in the village, in Treknow, that you'd be killed there. That no one from Treknow ever went to their village. That they were brutish pagans, sir. And womenfolk went missing and never returned.'

'There is something odd about them.'

'Your man is right,' said Treeve. 'We were lucky. And if you don't mind, I won't be going there again. I think you can find your way back if you've still a mind to it.'

'Much thanks, Master Treeve.'

He nodded to Crispin, looked Jack over, and kicked in his heels. His horse galloped on ahead back toward Treknow.

'There, there, Jack. I appreciate your concern.'

Jack made more unintelligible grumbles before Crispin asked, 'What did you find out?'

Girding himself (and hiding his reddened face), Jack began. 'I first went to the Penhall farm and talked to both the father and the daughter. They were very different from the first time I talked with them when I gave them the tidings of Roger's death. Today, they both seemed rather haughty about it. And they knew. The whole village knew that Roger was an amorous devil. And they lied about the last time they saw him.'

Crispin couldn't help but flick a glance in Kat's direction. She discreetly said nothing.

'When was the last time they saw him?'

'Monday,' said Jack.

'I see. Go on.'

'Then I went to Mabyn and Gwendolyn. They're sisters, sir, and sore angry that the other was deceived. They got into a fierce fight. One even bit me.' He pushed up his sleeve to show him, shaking his head over it.

Crispin kept as straight a face as he could. 'Then what?'

'Well, sir, they got to talking and . . . I don't believe either one of them done it. And there's proof aplenty that they didn't leave the village. And why kill Thomas Dunning into the bargain? He don't seem to have aught to do with it. But I've got my suspicions of Jowan Penhall. He's got pretentions. Thinks he'll be a knight someday soon what with his lands and wealth.'

'He does, does he?' Crispin kept the envy from his voice.

'Aye, sir. And a man that disgraces his family like Roger did . . . well. I think he'd be angry enough to do something about it. And like I said, he lied about the last time he saw him.'

'That's an interesting notion. Then what of Dunning's demise?'

'Maybe Dunning saw him. That would assure that no one remembered it.'

'Yes, that fits well. We shall have to investigate further.'

'But sir, what of that man that broke into our chamber at the inn, the one that tried to kill you?'

'What?' asked Kat, the sound of genuine concern in her voice. 'Someone tried to kill you, Crispin?'

'A foolish attempt. It was Menhyr Rouse, I'm certain of it.'

Jack rubbed at his beard in thought. 'Why him?'

'Because he didn't like being threatened. And being the cuckold of the village.'

'The churl! He should be whipped for what he done.'

Crispin stared ahead. 'I don't need to bother with him. I think he's being punished enough. No harm done.'

'No harm done?'

'Tucker, if I am not vexed over it, why should you be?'

'Then who the hell – pardon me, demoiselle – killed Bennet and Dunning?'

'As you said, we must investigate the Penhalls further. Who knows? They could have plotted together, Janet standing as lookout.'

Jack shook his head and crossed himself. 'That's a sore thing.'

'Indeed.' He stretched, getting the kinks out of his back. 'I'm hungry. I hope we can get some food up at the castle.'

They skirted the edge of Treknow and Kat looked back anxiously.

'Do you crave the company of your players?' asked Crispin.

'Well . . . I did promise. They have another performance tonight. And they owe me money.'

Crispin ignored the temptation to let her go to them. 'I don't want you out of my sight, Mistress Pyke.'

She gave a pretty pout. 'But the money, Crispin.'

'You've only yourself to blame.'

'That's not very generous of you.'

He said nothing more, but couldn't help but notice Jack's brows lowering over his eyes.

Once they passed through the first narrow gate and to the mainland courtyard, Crispin turned on the saddle to look back at the entry. No porter in sight.

He threw himself from the horse and stomped up to the gatehouse. 'Porter!' he yelled. *The damn fools! What in blazes is wrong with their heads?*

Peter Shipley scrambled down the steps and met Crispin partway up them in the narrow stairwell.

'Master Guest, I am here.'

'But you were not *there*, Master Shipley,' he said, pointing down toward the courtyard. 'You do recall that you were ordered to greet all who entered.'

'But . . . I know *you*, sir.'

He ran a hand over his chin stubble. 'The *point*, Shipley, of your position as porter, is to greet each who enter and each who leave to make certain all is well . . . whether you know them or not.'

'Oh. It seems a waste of time for those that I know.'

'For instance, have any from the castle left it?'

'Not that I am aware of.'

And what is that *worth*, he thought harshly. 'You are not *aware* or you didn't *notice*?'

The man's face transitioned from curious to questioning. Was it possible he had no idea what his duties truly were?

'Erm . . . I am fairly certain?'

Crispin clasped the man's shoulders. 'Look, Shipley. You have an important task. It might mean the life or death for those who live in this castle. It must be known at all hours of the day or night who passes under that arch. And to that end, I want you to close the portcullis.'

'Close the portcullis? I don't know that I've ever—'

'Close the damn portcullis. *Now!*'

He jerked up at Crispin's tone and finally seemed to understand the gravity. 'Yes, my lord.'

He squeezed past Crispin, eyes flicking away in embarrassment, as he made his way up the stairs and to the portcullis windlass.

Crispin followed him to an arched doorway to a room, domed

by its vaulted ceiling. Two arrow slits let in dim light in front of the wooden windlass. At one end there was an iron ratchet and pawl. The windlass itself, a heavy beam cut to an octagonal shape, was mounted some three feet above the floor, and wrapped with heavy rope. The face of the portcullis – a grate of iron and wood – nearly blocked the arrow slits in its raised position. And the same heavy rope held it in place through block and tackle.

Shipley positioned himself at the pawl and released it from its ratchet, and began lowering the portcullis with the windlass. Crispin helped at the other end of the machine. The mechanism whined and squealed, shuddering as the portcullis gate slowly traveled through the tight space before its teeth met the holes in the stone-flagged entry.

When it was finally secure, the portcullis seemed to breathe a sigh as it once again found its useful place in the world.

Shipley ran his hand over his forehead. 'I don't rightly believe I've lowered that ever.'

Crispin gave him a sharp look. 'Get used to it.' He stomped down the stairs to the courtyard. He grabbed the reins from Jack and mounted again, turning the beast once more past the battlements toward the bridge to the inner courtyard.

When they reached the second gatehouse, he squinted angrily at that raised portcullis, but since there was only the one porter, that one wasn't likely to be lowered any time soon. It made no matter. The first one was sufficient for his purposes.

As they entered the courtyard, Crispin noticed Regis in a high window, looking down at them. He could not see the expression on his face, but the gaze was concentrated. Perhaps it was his imagination, since the man appeared mostly bored every time he'd encountered him.

The horses seemed to hurry their pace as they neared the make-shift stables. The three dismounted, and not seeing a stableman – for there was none – Crispin led the others in unsaddling the horses, freeing them from their tack, and securing them in stalls with hay.

They entered the great hall and went directly through a door that led to a roofed passageway to the kitchens. Jack took things in hand by pushing forward and resting his hands on his hips as he looked around at the disarray. 'What this needs is a good scullion.' He began cleaning up, shifting wattled crates and wooden bowls aside, and checking the sharpness of the knives.

Kat made herself busy by feeding the fire at the hearth, placing a trivet near the flames and shoving a hanging kettle out of the way.

Crispin checked the pantry for food. It was a narrow room with a window at the far end. He shivered at a draft and realized the window was open. He pulled it closed and looked about on the shelves and hooks. He grabbed an empty basket and began filling it with what he felt Jack could prepare; butter, a dead rabbit, an onion, and some leafy greens.

When he emerged and presented them to an admiring Jack, he nodded and asked Kat to fetch them ale or wine from the buttery.

After first setting a large iron pan on the trivet, Jack commenced skinning and cleaning the rabbit and chopping the onion. Kat returned with a jug and three cups betwixt her fingers. She poured generously and gave the first wooden goblet to Crispin, then one to Jack, and kept the third for herself.

She hovered near Jack until he told her what next to do. All the ingredients went into the pan and sizzled in the butter with a billow of steam wafting up into the hearth's flue.

Sitting back, Crispin drank his ale, watching his apprentice and his . . . and *Kat* create a meal. He almost felt like a lord again . . . except that he would never have been in the kitchens and fetching for his servants, though he had done his fair share of cooking for his lord, the Duke of Lancaster, when they were in the fields of battle.

'It will be ready very soon, sir,' said Jack.

Kat seemed to be keeping her head down and helping Jack where she could, staying quiet. Crispin knew she had begun life as a servant and had masqueraded as her betters. She had gotten so good at it that she seldom slipped into a lower accent, having mastered speaking with a palace tone, like Crispin. Why was he fascinated by such women? Was it some flaw in his character that he found most attractive women of low estate who climbed higher by sheer will and intellect? There was Philippa, of course, foremost in his thoughts and his heart. But there had also been, only briefly, Livith, a scullion. Then Julianne, a physician's daughter. And how could he ever forget Alyson of Bath? A merry woman, she had even asked *him* to marry *her*. Perhaps he should have. Though he would have been her sixth husband . . . or was that seventh? He smiled as he drank, remembering her. The smile faded when he recalled Anabel, the tailor's daughter. But the smile renewed again when his thoughts fell on sweet but lusty Avelyn, servant to a famed alchemist.

As for his noble betrothed of long ago . . . well. He thought he had loved her, but it was best not to think of her at all.

He sighed. There were ups and downs with such relationships, as brief as they were. But he never regretted them. Only Philippa. The one he should have married. The only other to have asked him . . . and the one to whom he should have said yes.

Kat brought the food on a platter and offered him a wooden bowl to serve him first. They didn't bother going to the great hall. The kitchens were good enough for them.

Kat watched him avidly as she spooned the meat and vegetables. For once, there was no artifice to her doings. She simply served him, served Jack, and herself last, as if they had been doing so all these years. They ate in silence, each with their own thoughts. When he raised his glance, she was watching him, but flicked her gaze away when he caught her.

Crispin finished scooping up the last from his bowl with a wooden spoon, set it aside, and took up his goblet. Kat jumped up to pour him more ale. 'Your thoughts on the matter are welcomed, Jack,' he said, belly full.

Jack cocked his head and picked at the bones in his bowl. 'Master Crispin, I tell you truly. I don't know. If you believe it isn't Jory Gloyn from Prasgwig – and there's never been a more guilty man in my estimation – then I've got naught on my mind. Though the Penhalls . . . They are a strange lot. I wouldn't put it past Jowan Penhall for the sake of his honor.'

'Where is your employer?' said Kat suddenly, wiping her lips daintily with the edge of the tablecloth.

Crispin had been so far into his thoughts that he nearly forgot about the man. He supposed he should have sent Kat for him to join their little feast. 'Yes, where is he?'

Jack sprang from his seat and trod across the floor to the door. Crispin could hear him march through the covered passage and up the stairs. He might have imagined hearing doors opening, some voices and other movements. But presently, Jack reappeared, somewhat out of breath.

'Master, Sir Regis tells me that Master Teague set out again to explore. Looking for . . .' He glanced at Kat. 'The . . . thing.'

'Oh, the *thing*,' she said with a smirking smile.

Crispin rose. 'It's best we go after him. Make certain there is no trouble.'

'Do you think there will be, sir?'

'I don't know. But I have a strange feeling about it all.'

He thought about what to do about Kat, but she wasn't likely to sit quietly in a room upstairs until they returned. She'd be off to her own mischief. Best that she come with them, even if she discovered what they were after. Better that she be safe.

That's what he told himself.

TWENTY

They saddled their horses again and headed out on the road toward the chapel. Crispin rose in his seat, searching the landscape for the little cart.

'There, sir!' cried Jack, pointing. Well past the chapel on its rise, Teague's cart stood out among the green plain. His shaggy horse browsed, unaware or indifferent to the sheep encroaching on the same pasture.

They rode out on the lane until it dissipated into a sheep track.

When they arrived at the cart, Crispin didn't see Teague anywhere. He hopped off Tobias and walked around the cart and horse. 'Master Teague! Where are you? Master Teague!'

The sea below was wide and blue. The view from the top of the mound showed him nearly the whole of it until its edge disappeared into the dusky distance. He felt the spray on his cheeks, heard the sound far below of the waves crashing against the shore, and sea birds, as always, winging and crying overhead.

'Master Guest, I am here!'

Teague seemed to pop out of the ground like a rabbit. Crispin wandered toward the mound and saw that the man was standing in a ditch. No. It was something like an entrance to a tunnel. 'Master Teague?' He rested his hand on his sword hilt. His relief that he was unharmed didn't affect his irritation. 'I thought I made it clear that you were to cease these investigations.'

'Oh, but I didn't see the harm. I was quite alone.'

'What makes you think so? There may be spies watching you even now.'

Teague closed his hand on the collar at his throat and swiveled about. 'Spies?'

'It may be, Master Teague. How can I protect you if you go on alone? We still don't know why those men of the castle were murdered.'

'But I thought it was because of Bennet's doings, or possibly a love triangle that was the reason. Have you not found the killer yet?'

Then Teague's eyes fell on Kat.

'What is *she* doing here?'

'It was unavoidable. I must keep my eye on her as well as you. Together, you are proving to be quite a handful.'

'I do apologize, Master Guest,' he said. 'But I couldn't resist. Remember what we discovered in the chapel? *In the sanctum it abides,*' he recited, '*the undercurrents of time do guard the hollow of Caliburnus, until the King rises again.* Well? You see?'

'See what?'

'What is here, Master Guest. Look. This hollow! In its *sanctum!*'

The idea of finding the sword Excalibur had never left him, and each mention of it pulsed his heart with renewed warmth. Teague gestured toward the tunnel, down the worn stone steps and into the dark hollow. 'But what is this place? Surely you did not dig it out.'

'No, come and see!'

He couldn't help but come around the mound and follow the eager man down the hallowed steps. The cold blast of wind from the sea whistled through the curved tunnel, for it was open on both sides, with an arched ceiling, hollowed out of the solid rock. 'But . . . this was here all this time?'

'Yes, Master Crispin. And I fear – if this be the place – we might be too late.' Teague laid his hand on the stone walls, fingers tracing strange markings.

He thought it was Jack at his elbow but it turned out to be Kat. 'What is it we are looking for?'

'You foolish woman,' said Teague, and then proceeded before Crispin could stop him. 'The sword Excalibur. It is *this* prize that we seek.'

She stared at Teague, looked at Crispin, and then burst into laughter.

'And this is why you must never take a woman with you on your adventures,' said Teague, with the sourest look Crispin had yet seen him wear. 'They think every one of your journeys is foolish and imprudent.'

She covered her mouth, but there was still laughter behind her hand. Her bright eyes were turned toward Crispin. 'I'm sorry. I did not mean to offend you, Carantok . . . but truly? I cannot see that such a thing can be found after so long a time.'

'Is that right?' said Jack, his hackles up. 'Then what about all them relics Master Crispin is always finding, eh? They're far older than King Arthur. And *they* are found.'

Kat put her fingers to her mouth, resting that elbow on her other arm. 'Well, you have the right of me, Jack. If the relics of our Lord can be found, why *not* this sword?'

It seemed that Jack suddenly realized what he had defended, and his triumphant expression was short-lived.

'Well that's done it,' grumbled Crispin.

'You're truly looking for Excalibur,' she breathed. And by her eyes, he knew what she was thinking.

'And certainly you must know that I will not allow you to run away with it.'

'Who? Me?'

'Yes, you. I know how that grasping little mind of yours thinks.'

'Grasping!'

'Peace, the two of you,' said Teague. 'I know Mistress Pyke has a nimble mind. Perhaps she can help us after all.'

'It's a mistake,' warned Crispin.

She pushed him hard out of the way and endeared herself to Teague. 'That is a very generous attitude, Carantok.'

He blushed and fumbled a bit before he straightened and put his hand on the strange markings on the tunnel's walls. 'These, my dear Master Crispin, are rudimentary Cornish.'

'Indeed.' Crispin stood over his shoulder and looked. They were very rudimentary, for he could barely discern the letters. It could almost be a mistake . . . or random figures, so worn were they.

'Merlin might have left this here.' Teague's fingers moved lovingly over them again. 'But this indicates that the sword . . . is not here. Nor was it. I do not know what this place was. It might have been a burial crypt.'

'Oi!' cried Jack, leaping out the doorway. 'They buried someone here?'

'It doesn't appear to be so. I see nothing to show it. No weapons, no jewelry. Of course, it might have been scavenged years ago. Though . . .' He walked toward one of the arched entrances and looked it over. 'It doesn't appear that this was sealed. And every burial mound I have ever found was sealed. To protect it.'

'Wait,' said Jack, moving toward him. 'You . . . you rob graves?'

'Pagan graves, Master Jack. Lost souls.'

'Still dead bodies, though,' he muttered.

'There is no dead here,' said Crispin to reassure him.

Kat moved toward the etched markings and ran her fingers over them, studying them intently. 'Merlin could have scratched this into the stone, you say?'

'Oh, it is very likely, Mistress Pyke. Oh, the stories these stones could tell!'

'Hmm. What was that quotation you said earlier, Carantok?'

'I found it very nearby. It goes like this: *In the sanctum it abides, the undercurrents of time do guard the hollow of Caliburnus, until the King rises again.*'

'What is "Caliburnus"?'

'It is another name for Excalibur.'

'Oh. That is very intriguing.' She gnawed on a finger and wandered out into the sunshine, looking north over the blue-green sea. 'Undercurrents of time.' She walked away from the tunnel and kept looking out to the sea. 'Until the King rises . . .' She turned and looked east. Crispin joined her and gazed outward too. They were surrounded by sea. And with its churning waves eating at that rocky coast, someday it might be a true island, cut off entirely from the mainland. Only a narrow land-bridge connected this part of Tintagel to the jagged coastline of Cornwall now. But it was crumbling, even as they watched it.

She turned back toward that mainland, eyes searching, mind working. He wished he could peer into that mind of hers. It was like a set of cogwheels; each tooth fitting into the next and turning every wheel, like a mill, moving ever forward.

'What is another word for "sanctum"?' she asked of the wind. Though Crispin assumed it was him she was asking.

He frowned, thinking. 'Refuge. Retreat.'

'Haven,' said Jack.

She whirled and stared at him. 'Haven,' she said. 'Haven.' Looking toward Crispin she then twitched her head at Teague. '*Haven*,' she said with emphasis.

Teague's expression slowly blossomed into amazement. 'By all the holy saints,' he breathed. 'She's right! Why have I never considered?' He walked in a circle, talking to himself, arguing, agreeing, lifting an arm into the sky toward the east. '*The King rises again . . .*'

'Master Teague,' said Jack with an exasperated breath. 'What are you talking about, sir?'

He whirled on Jack, grabbing his coat and hauling him in close, and in his excitement, dropping the honorifics. 'Don't you see, Jack? Haven!' He dragged him to the edge of the hill that seemed to drop away but was just high enough to look down far below to the sea. He pointed toward the small crescent of beach and even smaller and narrow place where the sea met the bit of shore. 'Down there. It is known as the *Haven*. It has always been thus known. And there are caves down there. Caves carved out by the sea! The *undercurrents of time*! Caves that have been explored countless centuries before. And nothing was ever found. But I have a hunch, an instinct where these things are concerned. And I think this is where we next need to explore.'

Jack pushed his hands off of him and yanked at his cote-hardie to take the wrinkles out. 'I get your meaning, Master Teague. There's no need to thrash me about, sir.'

'My apologies, Jack. But can't you see? We must go down there.'

'Hold, Master Teague,' said Crispin, raising a calming hand. 'Let us consider. As you say, the caves below have been gone through for centuries, as this place, this tunnel has. What makes you think anything could still be down there? And . . . much as I hate to think it, we assumed the murders were about Roger Bennet and his amorous ways. But maybe this is not true. Maybe it was all about the hoards of treasure you have unearthed. That would certainly account for the death of Thomas Dunning. Though just how, I'm still not certain. But with the two deaths, I am leaning toward this other reason. And the only reason worth killing for is treasure. Perhaps this puts *you* in peril, Master Teague.'

'Nonsense!' He waved his hand. 'If that were the case, shouldn't it have become a problem well before now? This isn't my first time here, Master Crispin. But I tell you what you can do. You leave the treasure hunting to me, and I shall leave the killer hunting to you, eh?'

Teague hurried away toward his cart, climbed on, and began busily turning it. Crispin sighed and looked toward the part of the castle they could see on the island, its crumbling walls, the portcullis that was still raised, and on to the sheep grazing along the hillside, the low huts of stone empty and devoid of human life.

If the murders were all about the treasure – and he wasn't certain if he was willing to rule out the other just yet – then those in the castle were still suspect too.

It reminded him that he had yet to speak with the other caretaker. Just where could he find *him*?

TWENTY-ONE

Crispin was torn. He wanted to go with Teague and venture down to the beach to see these caves . . . but there was still a murderer at large.

Jory Gloyn was a thief and no doubt the village was meting out its justice. But what of Menhyr Rouse? He had not yet exhausted his enquiry into *him*. And the Penhalls. He trusted Jack's work, but he wanted to talk to them himself, see them, test them. Any man who aspired to knighthood held dear his honor, and a man who dishonored his daughter might need to be dealt with.

As much as searching for Excalibur intrigued him, he knew that his responsibility lay with going back to Treknow. But what to do with Kat?

'Jack, you and Mistress Pyke should accompany Master Teague.'

Jack turned on his saddle. 'Eh? What are *you* going to do, then?'

'I'm going back to Treknow for more enquiries.'

'I'll go with you, sir. It is my place to be with you.'

'I need you to watch over Master Teague. And Mistress Pyke.'

'Aw, sir . . .'

'Jack. I need you to do this.'

His apprentice heaved a world-weary sigh. Crispin leaned over and patted his arm . . . and to speak confidentially. 'Do not be so enamored of Teague's doings that you ignore your surroundings. I haven't ruled out a plot from the remaining men in the castle. Nor do I trust . . .' He tilted his head toward Kat.

Jack nodded. 'Right, sir. You can rely on me.'

'As I always have done.' Kat was looking at him with a frown. She tucked a loose strand of hair back into her hood. 'I'm also relying on *you* to behave,' he said to her quietly. 'And don't vex Jack.'

'I can behave.'

'Please do. For me.'

'For you, anything.'

He gave her a rueful look that she was quick to smirk at before he turned Tobias and had him climb up the verge to overtake Teague's cart and head for the castle.

But even as he rode toward the stone structure, he noticed a lone figure out in the countryside. He aimed the horse in that direction. At first, he assumed it was Marzhin Gwyls, but as he neared, he realized it was a man he did not recognize. When the man spotted him, he froze, flapping hood turned toward Crispin.

He pulled Tobias to a halt when he was several yards away and slid off the saddle. 'Forgive me, sir. I did not mean to startle you.'

'You did not,' said the old man, for he appeared to be as old as Gwyls was. 'I saw you with that man Carantok Teague. Are you, too, a sanctioned treasure hunter?'

'No.' He bowed. 'I am Crispin Guest. I'm called the Tracker of London.'

'London? Oh yes. My fellows at the castle spoke of you. Strange that we would not have met till now.'

The man wore a long cloak over his merino gown, its hem spattered with mud and grass. His hood was made of leather, as was Crispin's own, but unlike Crispin's was lined with fox fur. His craggy face with its lines and creases told of decades of a life lived in service. He wore a short-cropped beard, white as the clouds in the distance hovering over the wide plains. The staff in his hand could have been mistaken for a crook, so tall was it, but he kept a firm grip, leaning on it heavily.

'Indeed,' said Crispin, tugging on Tobias's lead. The horse wanted to run, and who could blame it? The green land was as inviting to the beast as it was to Crispin. He remembered a childhood where he was happy to run in fields with only the sky above him.

'Are you by any chance the caretaker, John Palliser?'

The man bowed slightly. 'I am.'

'A happy coincidence, for I have need to talk to you.'

'About the murders.'

'Yes. Roger Bennet—'

'I must tell you truly, Master Guest, that word of his murder did not surprise me.'

'Oh? How so?'

The old man turned back his hood from his face and scanned the skies. 'Well, if you have been investigating – and I heard in the village that you are – then you must know he has made some enemies. Shall we walk? I was making my way back to the castle and I'm afraid these old legs aren't what they used to be.'

'Of course. Do you generally *walk* these grounds?'

'Occasionally I take a horse, but I find the walk invigorating. I was cleaning the chapel.'

Crispin looked back at it over his shoulder. It stood on a rise above a chalky cliff face.

'You should not have done that alone. Surely some wench from the village—'

'I believe there was an order not to allow those from the village through the narrow gate.' He had a bit of a twinkle in his eye when he flicked his gaze at Crispin. Crispin was about to apologize when the man made a light gesture with his hand. 'It makes no matter. It was a holy occupation. And, as I said, it is good for me to get out into the fresh air. And I do love the sound of the sea. To smell the spray, to watch the waves . . . Do *you* like the sea, Master Guest?'

'I am not particularly fond of it. I get the . . . the *vomitus marinus*.'

'Ah! That is a shame. The sea is such a powerful force, is it not?'

'Not as much as *vomitus marinus*.'

Palliser laughed. 'I take your point. You are an important man from London. It is natural that you would have undertaken sea voyages.'

'I used to. Many years ago, with my mentor, the Duke of Lancaster.'

'Ah yes,' he said slowly, glancing at Crispin from under the edge of his hood. It seemed he remembered his name at last. 'And now . . . you are here to investigate these murders. Who do you think has done these crimes, Master Guest?'

'That has still to be determined, Master Palliser. Who do *you* think could have done it?'

'Well, as I said, Roger was not a well-liked man.'

'Among those of you in the castle?'

'Let us just say that a boastful man doesn't always find the best place by the fire.'

'Did those in the castle dislike him that much?'

'I cannot say that any of our company disliked him quite *that* much. But there are private things between men that others know not of. It could have been a wager unpaid, that sort of thing.'

'Was he in the habit of not paying his wagers?'

'That was a mere example, Master Guest. I don't know if such a thing ever occurred.'

Crispin watched the sea for a time. It was difficult not to be caught up in its lapis depths, its changing color with the passing clouds. 'Tell me, Master Palliser. Being a caretaker seems to send you all over this island. Do you spend much time with the others?'

'Not a great deal, no. When a storm blows, we are at the hearth together, but oft-times retreat to our separate chambers.'

'What brought you to such a post?'

'I am a Cornish lord with no revenue. My lands were sold and I found myself at loose ends. When Prince Edward of Woodstock took to rebuilding Tintagel, I offered my services. And though little has been done, I have stayed. It is enough to live on. I have the whole of this island as my domain, and a guarantee of retirement in the nearby monastery.' He paused, looking out to sea. 'You knew His Grace Prince Edward.'

Crispin stood and looked with him. 'Yes. As brother to my mentor, we had cause to spend time with him at court.'

He offered a conciliatory smile. There was much in that gesture.

'You, er, mentioned that you and your fellows here retreat to your separate chambers. What do you do there?'

'Me? Well . . .' Palliser fussed a bit with his cloak, adjusting the buttons and pin. 'As it happens . . . I am writing a history of Tintagel. I will continue it through my retirement, which I hope may be soon.'

'Are you? That would seem to be a very worthy enterprise.'

'I'm glad you think so. Some of the others . . . well. I have been called the "Monk of Tintagel".'

'Another worthy occupation . . . but of course they mean it offensively.'

'Yes.' He stared ahead, but the edge of his mouth turned down in a frown.

'Was Roger one of those men?'

The frown snapped suddenly into a smile, and he turned his sparkling gray eyes at him. 'You are a fisherman, Master Guest. You cast your net wide.' He heaved a sigh. 'Roger was a mocking sort of man, but so are the others. I take no offense. I knew none of them were capable of such work, and, God forgive me, I take pride in it.'

'As well you should. I do wonder, however, if someone from the castle could get so angry with Roger that they took it upon themselves to . . . take care of the problem.'

'I shouldn't wonder. But then why dispatch Thomas Dunning, the opposite in almost every respect from Roger?'

'You've been thinking about this.'

'Of course. The nights are long, the hours filled with the howling of the wind and the crashing of the sea. It makes a man lying in the dark naturally think of dark things.'

'Can you think of any reason for killing Dunning?'

'I understand that you were there, Master Guest, along with that silly man, Carantok Teague.'

'I was there. And it all happened in a matter of moments. There seemed to be nowhere for the miscreant to have disappeared to.'

'The island is deceptive. It gives the impression of a flat surface when it is anything but that. The dips and rises are as unsubtle as the sea. Men have been known to hide there. And women, too. They smuggle themselves in to find comfort with our company. These old hills have seen their share of more than sheep swyving.'

'The gates,' rumbled Crispin, 'are always open.'

'Oh, it's not by the gates that they get in. There are paths on the south side of the island.' He pointed toward the island's edge. 'They clamber down to the beach from the village and climb up the side on goat paths. Without a full complement of men-at-arms here, there is no one to see them.'

Crispin huffed a laugh. For all the growling he did to the porter, it appeared it was all for naught.

'Men and women always find a way, don't they?' said Palliser.

'Then anyone could have come into the castle and killed Bennet and Dunning?'

'Not anyone, Master Guest. Only the killer, surely.'

'Or killers.' They walked along, the horse clacking the bit, pushing it over its teeth back and forth. 'You do not seem to approve of Carantok Teague's doings.'

'I don't know his doings.'

'Come now. He is not a secretive man when it comes to it. You must have an inkling as to what he is doing.'

'He's a treasure hunter, that much I know. But royal charter or not, I do not like it. It is somehow . . . unsavory to me. Rattling around in the graves of others, even pagan graves.'

'He claims that most of his digging are not graves.'

'And so King Arthur's contemporaries had the habit of burying their jewelry or weapons haphazardly? I've seen the holes, Master Guest. I have seen bones within, though he has tried to conceal them.'

'Is that so? I did not reckon that. Though he said as much just today.' He shook his head at himself. 'I believed him too quickly, then.'

'Your soul must be pure. You trust perhaps too easily.'

'I do have that fault, Master Palliser.'

'Fault? Why, it is a blessing, surely.'

'Not in the game I am playing.'

They were silent for a time.

'I do know you,' said Palliser as quietly as the wind would allow. 'That is, I know *of* you.'

'And?' asked Crispin. For once, it hadn't the angry suspicion behind it.

'And . . . I suspected that a man of your character wouldn't work for a man whom he believed lacked that same character.'

'I must judge quickly sometimes. I can rarely turn away commissions. I have a household to feed, after all.'

'I understand the expediency of the stomach. One reason why I took this post. But I have come to enjoy it. The others . . . do not seem to share in it. But after all, they are young men who must seek a wife or already have them too far away.'

'But getting back to Teague's work, can it be said that it made you angry, his digging these holes, finding what he has found?'

He wiped a hand down his scant beard. 'I did not mean to sound angry. It seems foolish, is all. Disturbing that which has long past us.'

'But you are writing a history. I would think that the things he has found would be of interest to you.'

'There is no one alive today to tell me what they are and to whom they belonged. I cannot use them.'

'But they are worth money, so he says.'

Palliser smiled and threw his staff forward with each step. He did not seem to lean on it as he did earlier. '*For the love of money is a root of all kinds of evil.*'

'It is honest labor of body and mind.'

'I do not begrudge him, Master Guest. And now here we are at the gatehouse. Where will you go now?'

Crispin tried to take the measure of the man. Was he too intelligent to be a killer? Or did it take a man of intellect to do the job? But also, was he fit enough to climb all over the chapel to do the deed? He took his walks over uneven and rocky ground, and though he had a staff, he did not appear to use it to support himself.

'You are wondering whether I might be a murderer or not.'

The pronouncement startled Crispin. He gave a lopsided smile. 'Are you?'

'No, praise God. I am no murderer. But . . . I am flattered you entertained it.'

'Well, I haven't yet ruled you out.'

He laughed and clapped Crispin on the shoulder. 'Good! Good.'

'Nor have I ruled out the other caretaker.'

He frowned in a quizzical fashion. 'No,' he said after a pause, 'these others here must be on your list if you are to do your proper job. And I know that you do. Your reputation, sir, precedes you.'

Crispin said nothing to that, and watched the man move ahead of him over the stone-flagged courtyard and eventually into the great hall. Under the arch of the gatehouse, Crispin mounted again, looking back to the island. He thought he felt a small portion of what kept Palliser and Gwyls so interested in the place. The 'ghosts', perhaps, but the land itself seemed to pulse with vitality. Perhaps that was what attracted Gorlois, that first Duke of Cornwall, to build this place.

Or perhaps it was magic, for Merlin knew this place as well.

Magic. He chuckled. Was he supposed to believe in that too?

TWENTY-TWO

Jack looked back once or twice toward where Master Crispin had disappeared under the gatehouse arch. Then he glanced slyly at Kat Pyke . . . who happened to be looking at him with a suspiciously bright smile. He had no liking for her. She was capricious, deceptive, and a seducer. No good could ever come of that. But he knew his master was depending on him to keep an eye on her.

He turned forward and set his sights ahead. Carantok Teague was a bundle of vigor, chatting away about what they would find and where they would find it. Jack only half-listened. These murders were vexing. If his master was right about Penhall, then what sort of danger might he be in? He itched to follow him, and at the same time he knew Master Crispin would rather pursue the sword. For once in his investigations, he knew the man *wanted* to find the thing. It wasn't some relic with frightening powers. It was something from nobility. Something magic. And Jack believed in that ancient craft with something of fear and a bit of awe. Faery mounds, pagan *druw*, standing stones . . . England was full of secrets and magic just simmering below the surface. He wasn't sure if he wanted to know about those things but they did intrigue his natural curiosity.

'Them caves must have been gone through many times before, Master Teague,' he said, finally getting his words in when the man paused for breath. 'Why would anything of value still be there? Unless it looked like that rusty thing you showed us earlier.'

'Now Master Jack, that is our conundrum.' They had finally passed under the gatehouse on the mainland and began on the long roundabout path down to the beach. 'If it is the true Excalibur, would it have revealed itself to unworthy men?'

'Er . . . are you saying, sir, that it has special powers about it?'

'As the sword that had been embedded in the stone, it certainly has to be singular and distinct in an extraordinary way, don't you agree?'

'I don't know, sir.'

'Nonsense!'

Jack frowned and reluctantly turned toward Kat. 'And I suppose you have to have your say about it, Mistress Pyke.'

'Of course I do. It's all absurd. There is no magic sword.'

'You sound like Master Crispin.'

She smiled. 'And a fine compliment that is. I agree with him. These were tales told long ago. Who knows if any of it is true?'

'Course it's true,' grumbled Jack, wishing she'd keep quiet. 'They're histories.'

'And do you believe every history is true? My former mistress believed all the trifling nonsense about her own family, when it was only cobbled together from many diverse tales. The family priest told me so.'

'And why would he tell you?'

'I have my ways, Jack.'

He rolled his eyes. 'I should have guessed as much. Is there no sin you won't stoop to?'

She raised her chin and turned her face away, clutching the reins. She didn't need to say.

The road was steep, but Teague seemed competent enough

controlling his horse that the cart didn't sway or seem to lose footing. The road pitched downward again and then leveled out above the pebbled shore over a foundation of boulders. But that was as far as the cart could go. The way was too narrow, too steep. They agreed to leave the cart and horses there and walk the rest of the way down.

The tide, bubbling and foaming, was coming in. It had already reached the mouth of the caves and was spilling into them with a roaring echo. 'Perhaps we should choose another time, Master Teague,' said Jack, glancing nervously toward the churning sea.

'Nonsense,' said Teague, huffing a little from the scramble over the rocks to get to the beach.

The cliff face where they stood was green and mossy from a cascading waterfall – freshwater, Jack surmised – spilling down the side and splashing upon the slick rock surface below, dissipating into the foamy edge of the encroaching sea. Two dark eyes in the cliff wall told of two caves. And, far above, the castle was invisible to the observer.

The roar of the waves constantly crashed on the shoreline and around a marooned rock, a rock covered with white bird droppings from the circling gulls and terns. Jack decided that he didn't much like the sea, with its constant roiling noise and smell of salt. He liked better the bustle of London and Westminster. Good, honest sounds of men and women living their lives, shouting their wares, with noisy carts, barking dogs, and the many church bells. Perhaps it was too lonely here. And the sea made it worse, with its dark energy and relentless carving away at the solid rock of the land's boundaries.

'Do we go into them caves, Master Teague?'

'Patience, my friend,' he said, poring over his maps and charts. Kat came up behind him and peered over his shoulder.

'What's all this rubbish? Is this what you've used to get Crispin and Jack to follow you into this godforsaken wilderness?'

He snatched them back, holding them against his chest. 'And just what is your expertise, demoiselle? I think we all know. And it isn't reading a map.'

'You'd be surprised at what I know.' She grabbed it back and flattened it. 'There now. Let's take a look. I see there are notes on the margins. You didn't make those because they look too old. Hmm. Perhaps you *have* got something here, Master Teague.' She patted him on the back, which seemed to annoy the normally good-natured man. 'My Latin isn't quite as good as Jack's, I'm afraid.'

'*Mine* is sufficient,' said Teague with a snort of impatience. He nudged her aside to retrieve the maps once more. 'One of these is called "Merlin's Cave". And that sounds very promising indeed. It is this one on the left.' He took up the pickax he had brought with him from the cart, rested it over his shoulder, and proceeded forward, keeping his dignity even as he slipped on the spray-glistened rocks and the rising tide flowed into the cave's entrance.

'Here now,' said Jack, uneasy with the sea surging over his boots. 'Are you certain this is safe?'

'I haven't the least idea,' he said, getting his good humor back. He was smiling again, and splashing toward the dark maw without a seeming care in the world.

Kat had brought a shovel and used it to steady her footing. 'Are you afraid, Jack?'

He gave her as fine a London sneer as he knew how to give. Lurching toward the cave, he fisted the pike he had grabbed from the cart and stomped after them.

When the waves receded, the rocks and pebbles slid under their feet with a clatter until the wave returned. They stood unsteadily as the waves rolled out again at the mouth of the cave. Jack blinked at the wind blowing in his face. 'Where is the wind coming from?'

'The cave opens from the other side, Master Jack. There is an opening through to the other beach.'

He didn't like the way it felt or the way it sounded, thundering in his ears as it did. He glanced back at Kat but her eyes were shining and she shifted her gaze from the walls to the ceiling and back again.

'Don't naught scare you?' he growled.

She laughed. 'Very little. But don't you find this intriguing, Jack? Crispin would.'

'We don't like *all* the same things,' he said, with a significant look in his eye . . . that she didn't miss either.

But she said nothing and moved farther in, lifting her skirts to climb over sharp, jutting rocks. The floor was wet and filling fast from the constant barrage from the sea and the tides. And as they turned the corner, there was the opening, like a wide arrow slit on the other side, well up ahead, bringing in light and more pools of water.

'It is said,' said Teague, 'that Merlin, taking the infant King Arthur away with him from the arms of his mother Igraine, that he passed through here and magically opened the other side to escape the knights sent after him when King Uther changed his mind. They didn't know it was open and he took a boat and stole away with Arthur. Such a thrilling tale.'

'Aye. But . . . where's the sword, then?'

'Patience, patience . . .' He strode forward through the water, using the pickax to steady himself on the slippery floor. He opened his map; as far as Jack could tell, it was merely an astrological chart with what looked like a plan of the island with marks at various spots where, he assumed, Teague had dug, and lines drawn over it like a sailing chart.

'According to this – and with that helpful rhyme on my charts – it should very well be here.'

Looking around, Jack scoffed. It didn't look to him that there was any place to stash gold or jewels, let alone a sword, and anyway, weren't they going to be underwater soon? The walls were curved, carved out by the sea itself. Some of them were smooth, and some jagged where pieces, no doubt, dropped off. But with the light from the other end, there didn't seem to be much else to the walls. No secret entrances. No deep niches to hide something. It was likely already gone if it ever was here.

He watched as the water rose up to his ankles. 'Then, where do we look?'

Teague surveyed the walls, consulted his charts, and raised his head again. 'I think we should check the walls. Make certain there are no secret niches or hidden doors.' Teague climbed over a rocky outcropping and stepped nimbly to one of the walls to examine it in the dim light.

Sighing, Jack moved to the opposite wall and tried to see. He ran his hands over the smooth stones, wondering what he was supposed to be searching for, when a shadow overtook him. 'What do *you* want?'

Kat stood beside him, searching the walls and not looking at him. 'Only to talk to you, Jack,' she said quietly. 'I don't know why you hate me so much. I don't think I've done any harm to you.'

'You are a seducer,' he whispered harshly, looking back at Teague, who didn't seem to hear them and was absorbed with his own investigation of the walls and crevices. 'You tried it with me, you succeeded with . . . him,' he said, thumbing toward Teague over his shoulder, 'and you done it with my master. I don't trust you or your motives. That's why I don't like you. You're a thief.'

'And so were you, once.'

'And I don't do it no more, do I.'

'Because Crispin took you in. Who do I have to take *me* in?'

'You'll find some fool, no doubt.'

'Jack, Jack. You don't have to be jealous of me.'

He whirled around and glared. 'I'm not jealous of the likes of you.'

'Aren't you? You and Crispin have a singular association . . . but so do Crispin and me.'

'A farthing a dozen is what he has with you. How many men have *you* bedded?' He presented his hand like a weapon and began counting them down on his fingers. 'My master, that man,' and he flicked his head toward an oblivious Teague, 'the dead man Roger Bennet . . . and how many others? You're nothing to my master. You don't deserve him.'

Her face had gone pale and her expression blanked. For a moment, Jack felt the prick of guilt clawing at his chest. But he sniffed, thought of all the trouble she'd caused, and the guilt flickered away.

'Well,' she said, looking away and back to searching the walls. 'You've certainly spoken your piece on the matter. I suppose it's too much to ask for Christian charity . . . and forgiveness.'

The guilt was back and he rolled his shoulders with the discomfort suddenly upon him. 'I . . . it's my job, see? To keep him safe. Who else will do it?'

'I wouldn't harm him for the world. You must know that.'

The squirming in his belly wouldn't cease. 'Aye, I know.'

'Then . . . can we call a truce, perhaps?'

She was holding out her hand to him. He decided – after all he had said, and perhaps rudely, too – that it would have been disingenuous not to take it. He pressed his hand in hers, gave it a shake, and released her.

Two blooms of pink burnished her cheeks. 'There. We are now comrades in arms.'

'Comrades up to our cods in seawater, more like,' he muttered.

Kat suddenly turned to say something when Jack took a step back. But there was nowhere to put his foot. His other foot slipped on the slick rock and he plunged into a jagged pool of dark water.

It wasn't deep but his bum and his chest were soaking in no time. He splashed about, trying to right himself. Kat leaned over the edge and reached out an arm to help him up. He yanked on it and she flew toward him. He put out his hands to catch her but she slipped past them and landed with a splash beside him.

She cried out and Teague was suddenly standing over the two of them.

'Master Jack! What are you doing?'

'Falling into the water, sir.' He finally braced himself on a jutting edge of rock and maneuvered himself to his knees. But when he gained that angle, the sun from the far opening of the cave shone on something in the pool. It was something wooden that was shoved under the outcropping, effectively hiding it in shadow.

'What's this?' Already wet from head to toe, he knelt and peered down beneath the rock crevice. Definitely something of wood, like a beam. A shipwreck? Surely not a whole ship in this strange little cave. Flotsam, perhaps, wedged under the stiff rock. Still, the strange look of it compelled him to grab it and yank. It wouldn't move.

'Let me help you.' Kat was at his side and she grasped it as well. Together, they pulled until Jack felt it move.

'Master Teague! Come help.'

'What is it, Master Jack. Oh!' He plunged into the water and got down to grab it when a mighty wave sluiced over them and pushed them all back.

Jack spit out the salty water with a grimace. 'Master Teague, if we stay, we'll all drown. I suggest returning when the tide is out.'

He could see Teague weighing it unhappily, but in the end – and with another crashing wave raising the water around them another few inches – he had to concede it. 'You're right. We mustn't stay. But . . .'

'Master Teague, it's already been here for hundreds of years. A few hours won't make any difference. And then my master can be here to help.'

'Of course. Let's get you out of there.' He lowered the pickax and Jack grabbed hold of it with one hand. With the other, he grasped Kat's skirts and dragged her with him. Sputtering, dripping wet, and shivering, they all made it out of the cave and were suddenly dismayed at how high the tide had come up on the beach. They waded carefully to the higher edge of the shoreline and hiked up to the waiting horses and cart.

Shivering, Teague suggested they return to the castle for dry clothes and the others agreed.

Jack looked back down once they were high enough on the bluffs. Merlin's Cave was halfway submerged, and so would they have been, had they stayed. 'God blind me,' he muttered.

TWENTY-THREE

C rispin reached the outskirts of Treknow and paused. He looked over the little town, considering all the characters in play. Penhalls first, he decided. It would be good to get this over with.

He followed the road as Jack had described – how it turned on a bend. The slate mines were to the left of him, past rolling hills of green, and to the right, he followed the path till a farmstead revealed itself beyond the verge of the road. A gatehouse . . . unoccupied . . . a large stone barn, and a two-story manor house with a wide walled courtyard with a well.

He approached, ducked slightly to pass under the gatehouse arch, and dismounted in the courtyard. There was no one to attend to his horse, so he tied it to a rose bush near the entrance, ascended the few granite steps, and knocked on the oaken door.

He waited. No one answered. He knocked again and waited again to no avail. He tried the handle. Locked. Straightening his belt, he strode along the side of the house until he saw a door ajar and peered inside. The kitchens. A woman with sleeves rolled up over her elbows was tending to a pot over the fire. A mound of chopped vegetables and herbs lay on her worktable.

'I beg your mercy, madam . . .'

She jumped back, hand on her chest. 'Oh, how you startled me! What is it, now?'

'I apologize for startling you. I am looking for your master, Jowan Penhall. But no one was at the front door.'

'By the saints, what is this house up to? I apologize to *you*, good sir, for having to come this way to find aught. Bless me. Can I offer you refreshment, sir? A cup of ale?'

'No, thank you. I am merely looking for Master Penhall.'

'Well, he hasn't gone into the village. You might seek him in the cheese hut, or out in the fields seeing to his cows.'

'Then I shall.' But before he turned away, he asked, 'Tell me, on that terrible day when Roger Bennet was killed, was your master here or in town?'

'And who might you be doing the asking?'

'Forgive me again. I am Crispin Guest. My apprentice Jack Tucker was here . . .'

'Oh, him. He was a most polite young man. He did you proud, sir. He asked much the same thing. Let me think.' She put a finger to her lips and thought, before the kettle boiled over. She made a screech and took up the hem of her apron to swing the arm it hung on away from the fire. She took up the wooden spoon balanced across the pot and stirred the contents. 'Where is my head today. I nearly spoiled the pottage. Now what was I saying? Oh, yes. Master Penhall *had* gone into the village.'

'To do what?'

She shook her head and frowned. 'I don't know, sir. I have little to do with the likes of that.'

'Could he have gone to the castle instead?'

She rested the spoon against her spotted apron. 'Well now. I suppose he could have. But I wouldn't know.'

'Would anyone here know?'

'Might be Kenal would know. He often escorts him as his footman. But he's more used to working with the cows.'

Crispin smiled and fixed his thumbs in his belt. 'Master Penhall seems to want a proper manor house and attendants.'

She cautiously glanced over his shoulder. 'I tell you true, Master Guest,' she loudly whispered, 'he has airs, he does. But you can't blame a man what wants to better himself. Nearly married his daughter to a knight, didn't he?'

'No, I can't blame a man.'

'Here I am talking to you of such. I was told about you.'

His smile faded.

'You were a knight yourself, weren't you?' she went on. 'Course, them that were born to it are different than them rising to meet it.'

'I understand that Sir Roger dined here Monday.'

'He did. I served a nice roasted pullet with a lovely currant sauce, and an elderflower cheese pie for afters. They made much of that.'

'It sounds delightful. But what happened after the meal?'

'After? Oh, might you be meaning the terrible row between Sir Roger and Mistress Janet?'

Crispin's expression never changed, but this was news to him.

'A terrible thing it was. Enough to char a Christian soul some of them words, I can tell you.'

'And what of Master Penhall? Did he know about Roger Bennet all that time ago . . . before Monday, about Roger's infidelities?'

'I shouldn't say. It isn't for servants to say.'

'But if you *were* to say?'

She smiled and shook the spoon at Crispin. 'You're a clever gentleman, aren't you? Well then, if I *were* to say, I'd say he did. And he wasn't best pleased. Angry like a storm he was when he first heard about it. Kenal told me that he threw the furniture and broke a pot. But he made Kenal promise not to tell Janet. Though the poor soul already knew. Everybody knew. She reckoned she'd marry him anyway. Noblemen are different from the rest of us.'

'Some are not so different,' he muttered. 'Thank you, madam.' He bowed, making her titter and throw her hand over her mouth.

He left and stood in the back courtyard, sizing up what must be the cheese hut. This great secret about Roger was no secret at all, it turned out. And Penhall was angry enough to turn over the furniture. Perhaps angry enough to kill . . . and he had the time to do it.

He strode to the cheese hut and opened the door. Just a woman tending to the cheeses.

Walking past the hut and the stone barn – and poking his head inside in passing just to make sure – he ventured around the corner of the barn and looked out to the hills. In the distance he saw the tangled forest where Prasgwig lay. But in the fields, cows grazed, heads bent downward toward the waving grasses. There were two men among them, standing with staffs. Crispin headed toward them.

They looked up when he neared and never moved from their spots. Crispin raised his hand in greeting. 'Do I have the pleasure of meeting Jowan Penhall?'

The leaner man stepped forward. Crispin studied him, deciding that such a man could be limber enough to climb up to a roof, if need be.

'I am Jowan Penhall.'

Crispin bowed. 'I am Crispin Guest, Tracker of London. I believe you met my apprentice, Jack Tucker.'

Penhall scowled. 'I met him. And I thought that was the end of it. I'm a busy man.'

Crispin made a show of admiring the cows and the manor house several hundred yards away. 'Yes, so I see. It is just that I need to get the details fixed in my mind.' He turned to the other man. 'Might you be Kenal?'

'Aye. Kenal Corneys.'

'Excellent. Well, I don't mean to trouble you for very long, Master Penhall.'

The man took a deep breath and let it out slowly. 'Well then?'

Crispin flicked a glance at Kenal. 'Perhaps . . . you might wish to speak with me . . . alone.'

His breathing had become heavier. He jerked his head at Kenal and the man took the hint, plodding forward toward the house, but looking back suspiciously.

'Say what you have to say, Guest, and leave us be.'

'Very well. Where were you the day Roger Bennet died?'

'I was here.'

'That's not quite true, is it? You weren't here on your estate the whole time.'

He stared at Crispin for a heartbeat before he licked his lips. 'That's right. I went into the village.'

'And did what?'

'How can I remember? It was three days ago and I'm a busy man.'

'You don't recall why you would go into the village?'

'I said so, didn't I.'

'And so it will be an easy thing for me to find witnesses who can attest to that.'

His eyes widened. The staff was lowered into both his hands, parallel to the ground. 'Why would I need witnesses?'

'Because, sir, I don't think you went into town. I think you went to the castle.'

'I didn't,' he said between gritted teeth.

'I believe I can find witnesses in the castle to tell me otherwise,' he lied.

Beads of sweat sprinkled his brow. He loosened and tightened his grip on the staff. Crispin was already measuring how far he'd have to step back to avoid it. 'I . . . I . . .'

Penhall swung. Crispin ducked, and girded himself for its return, but when he looked up, the man was running toward the house.

'God's blood,' he muttered, and took off after him.

Crispin pumped his arms, gaining on the man. What was he to do? Tackle him? He wasn't a lord, not exactly. He didn't think further of it as he leapt, hands grappling him and taking him down into the wet turf. They tumbled and rolled. Penhall struggled and punched, landing only a few, causing Crispin to grunt with the blows. He managed to roll atop the man and wrestle his wrists together over his chest.

'Cease your struggling, damn you. You murdered a man and must face the king's justice.'

'I murdered no one! Get off me!'

'Stop fighting me.'

And just as he said it, the man went limp. Tears sprang to his eyes. 'I murdered no one,' he whimpered. 'No one.'

'Two men were killed up in the castle.'

His wet eyes widened. '*Two* men?'

'Yes. Two men. Roger Bennet and Thomas Dunning, another knight.'

'I . . . I do not know this other man.'

Narrowing his eyes, Crispin got off Penhall and offered his hand to lift him up. Penhall took it and stood before him, head bowed.

'Penhall, God save you if you are lying to me. I can assure you, the hangman will seem a relief after the suffering I will mete out.'

He took a horrified step back. He glanced back at the staff, now lying some distance away, and clutched his hands together. 'I'm not lying, Master Guest. I swear by Almighty God.'

'Then you killed only Roger?'

'No, no! I swear. No one has died at my hand.'

'You were at the castle?'

'I . . .' He looked away. Kenal was long gone to the manor house and nothing but cows grazed along the hills. One looked up and lazily stared in their direction, jaws working on its cud. 'Yes. I was at the castle that day.'

'And what were you doing there?'

He panted, wiping the sweat from his brow, eyes searching the hills, the farm. 'Please, Master Guest. You must understand . . .'

'I understand murder and the hangman. There is no compromise between them.'

He clutched his fingers together and brought them up to his mouth in prayer. '*Jesu*, mercy! You don't understand. You'll never understand.'

Crispin folded his arms. 'Try me.'

The man wiped his face again, his moist eyes. 'Do you have children, Master Guest?'

He hesitated. 'One. A son.'

'Ah. A son. Perhaps a son is so much easier. He becomes a man and you need not fear for his future. But a girl . . . I have a daughter, Master Guest. Only the one. And she is most dear to me. A pearl, a blossom. She must find a husband to care for her, to inherit the land I leave behind. But finding the right man is a trial. And we found him . . . or so we thought.'

'Roger Bennet.'

'Yes. And he . . . he seemed eager to gain a place in our household. A knight, a man of property in his own right, though distantly in Kent. It was arranged that he and my daughter would wed, though we had not signed a bargain as yet. And then I discovered his nature. That he had many women in the village. But . . . he still agreed and I was willing to overlook it. And . . . and my daughter, too, for she had discovered it as well. But the last time he was here to supper, my daughter and he had a great argument. Such words! The whole household could hear it. There was no place for them to go to keep it quiet from the servants.' He wiped his face again, shaking his head.

'What did they argue over?'

'She insisted that he be faithful after they were wed. It isn't an unreasonable request from a wife to a husband. The scriptures tell us that adultery is a great sin. But . . . but he was a man and men . . .'

'I see. He refused her, then?'

'He did. And she sent him away. But her anger did not abate. She . . . she . . .' He began to weep, great beaded tears.

'*She* went to the castle.' Crispin rubbed his chin. 'And . . . you went after her?'

'Yes, yes!'

'Did she confess to you that she had killed him?'

'No. She would say nothing of it. But I weep for her, Master Guest. I weep! My only daughter! My only *child*!' he wailed. 'Can you not find it in your heart to leave us in peace? She was wronged. Surely there is a place in the king's justice for a woman wronged.'

'I'm afraid not, Master Penhall. Please take me to her now.'

'Please, Master Guest. I beg you.'

'Don't unman yourself, Penhall,' he hissed.

Penhall wiped his face with his sleeve, and attempted to stop his blubbering. Crispin felt for the man. Had not his own son stood accused of murder? Crispin hadn't had to make the choice of what he would have done, had it truly been so.

Penhall dragged himself toward the house and once he came indoors, he called up the staircase, 'Janet! Janet, my love, are you here?'

A door opened and footsteps tapped across the gallery before a lithe young woman peered down over the side. 'Father? What's amiss? Oh. Who is this gentleman?'

'Daughter, go to the solar. We will meet you there.' He turned to Crispin, hands imploring. 'At least listen to what she has to say. It might have been self-defense.'

'I will listen, Master Penhall. But you must prepare yourself for the worst.'

Penhall, still quietly weeping, led Crispin up the stairs, dragging his feet the whole way. When they reached the solar, he gave Crispin a last pleading look before opening the door.

The girl sat at the window, looking out, but when they entered, she turned. Pink-cheeked, wide-eyed, and plump in all the right places, she was the very image of fruitful womanhood. Little wonder she had caught Roger's eye. But some of the other women were equally comely. And, he had to remind himself, Kat had bedded Roger too. He couldn't help feeling he was glad that Roger was dead.

'Father, what is the matter?' She rose from her seat and reached for him, laying gentle hands to his chest, hands that were raw and red from work. They weren't as genteel as Penhall seemed to want them to be. His daughter was not a wealthy lady to sit at her embroidery. In fact, he saw nothing of the sort in the stark solar. No embroidery frame, no tapestry. Only a crude mural painted on the wall in washed-out colors. She was a working lass. In another day, Crispin would have scoffed. Now, he thought it a most useful occupation. After all, Isabel Tucker took in sewing to earn a penny or two, and she with three children to tend to and another on the way.

Her father couldn't answer her, so bereft was he. He enfolded her in his arms instead, and wept on her shoulder. She comforted him in puzzlement, looking at Crispin for help.

'Demoiselle, I am Crispin Guest, Tracker of London. You have met my apprentice, Jack Tucker.'

'Oh. Him. Yes.'

'I regret to say that I am here to arrest you for the murder of Roger Bennet.'

He expected many things. That she would hurl a curse at him, that she would rave, scream denials, throw crockery.

But all she did was scoff and huff in disgust. 'Don't be absurd,' she cast over her shoulder. 'Come, Father, sit down here.' She led him to the chair she had vacated in the window. He sat but would not be consoled.

She patted his shoulder. 'Come now, Father. You know it isn't as bad as all that.'

'Child,' he cried. 'He will take you away and hang you.'

She eyed Crispin up and down before throwing back her head and laughing.

Crispin shifted on his feet.

'No one is going to take me away. I didn't kill Roger.'

'But . . . Janet . . .'

'I didn't kill him, Father. Oh, I wanted to. And perhaps, had I found him, I could have . . . I was certainly ready to, with my bare hands. But I could not find him. And I wasn't going to search all over that island looking for him.'

His tear-wet face rose and he looked on at her with renewed strength. 'You didn't?'

'Of course not. The Devil take him. I pray that he has.'

'Demoiselle,' said Crispin sternly, 'your father is of the opinion that you did.'

'Father!'

'You would tell me nothing! I had to assume the worst.'

'By the saints! My own father!'

'Forgive me, daughter.'

They embraced again, and Penhall fell to weeping once more.

Resting a hand on the hilt of his sword – and wishing he could draw it – he sighed. 'Demoiselle, have you proof of your innocence?'

'Well . . .' She peered over her father's shaking shoulders at him. 'I asked a caretaker where Roger might be when I first arrived, and he told me that he hadn't seen him, and that he could be anywhere on the island or the mainland. He saw me turn around and head for home. And that is when my father arrived to fetch me.'

'The caretaker's name?'

'Oh . . . John something.'

'John Palliser.'

'Yes, that's it. Is that proof enough?'

He measured her carefully. There were few who could be as cool as this and lie. Kat Pyke could do it . . . but he doubted this one could. He'd ask Palliser to verify, but his gut already knew the answer. 'Do you know a Thomas Dunning?'

'No. Your apprentice already asked me.'

'He was murdered too. At the castle.'

'Surely if I didn't kill Roger, I'd not kill this other, whom I have never heard of.'

'Yes.' He rocked on his heels. 'Very well, Mistress Penhall, Master Penhall. I will assert your tale with John Palliser. And, for the time being, I shall leave you in peace.'

'Forgive me if I say it, Master Guest, but I and my father would be grateful if we never had to set eyes on you or your apprentice ever again.'

The feeling is mutual. But he said nothing aloud and bowed instead.

TWENTY-FOUR

Such a strange little village, thought Crispin. So many ills woven together in a most appalling tapestry.

He left it behind to return to the castle. The gentle gait of the horse helped him contemplate just who might have killed Bennet and Dunning. It seemed too coincidental to be two separate murders, and Dunning's would have little to do with a crime of passion. So many in the village wanted to kill Bennet. But Dunning was a strangely singular situation. Someone had been so desperate they had stolen across the plains, skulked on the roof of the chapel while Crispin and company had been inside it, and dispatched him then and there, in danger of discovery at any moment. Was it to hide the first murder? And if it were, why? Had Dunning seen something he shouldn't have? And if he had, why hadn't he come to Crispin to tell him? Who would have been so bold as to kill him when potential witnesses fairly swarmed the place?

Someone sure of themselves. Someone with a deep motive. Someone like . . . Kat.

How he hated to think it of her. But she had killed before. She had said it was self-defense, but that case had been so convoluted, and part of that had been her fault. She had enticed others to kill for her, though she claimed she hadn't. It wasn't something Crispin had been willing to prove. She was supposed to keep out of trouble if he let her go. He had done so in good faith. Well, that's what he got for trusting such a woman.

He was sour when he reached the castle. He found Jack and Teague decidedly wet and with their soaking clothes drying before the fire.

Then Kat appeared, wearing what looked like Jack's old things – chemise too long and hanging nearly to her ankles – while she arranged her wet clothes before the smoky hearth.

'What is all this?' he demanded. He couldn't help but feel it was her fault.

'We had a bit of a swim,' she said.

'What?'

'Nothing so prosaic,' said Teague, and he eagerly turned to Crispin. He was in just a chemise and sagging stockings. 'Adventure, Master Guest! Adventure! We think we found the Sword Excalibur!'

Crispin could scarce believe it, and he turned to Jack.

He nodded. 'It's true, sir. We think we found it in Merlin's Cave.'

Excitement thrummed in his chest. 'Then where is it?'

'Still there, sir,' said Jack, pulling a flannel over his wet curly hair. 'The tide was coming in on us. We could have drowned.'

'Nonsense,' said Teague. 'But it was stuck fast in a secluded pool. Looked like a beam of wood left from a shipwreck.'

'What makes you think it wasn't?'

'Master Guest! No, no. It felt hollow. Like a box. Didn't it, Jack?'

Jack screwed up his mouth, thinking. 'Aye. I have to admit that it did.'

'Well . . .' Crispin forgot about murder, forgot about the Penhalls and Jory Gloyn and Menhyr Rouse. 'When does the tide go out?'

'Not till the evening,' said Teague. 'We should ready torches to go back out there. Are you with us, Master Crispin?'

'Yes, of course.'

'God grant us success in our mission!' he crowed.

'And what of your own mission?' asked Jack. 'Where's Penhall?'

Crispin sighed. He poured himself some ale into a cup and drank.

'It seems Penhall went to the castle to fetch his daughter, afraid *she* was committing murder.'

'Oh. And did she?'

'No. At least I'm fairly certain she didn't. I'll need to corroborate her story with John Palliser, but I'm fairly certain he will.'

'Then we're out of suspects again?'

'Not entirely. I'll have to think about it.' His gaze slid unintentionally toward Kat.

'In the meantime, I think I'll prepare us some repast,' said Jack. 'I don't mind saying that was hungry work.'

'And did you behave yourself, Mistress Pyke?' asked Crispin, now intentionally gazing at her, particularly her bare legs.

'I always behave myself. Didn't I, Jack?'

Jack grunted and left to take care of their meal.

Like the last time, they eventually wandered into the kitchens to eat their food. Teague spoke animatedly about the soon-to-be-discovered Excalibur, while Jack listened intently to him. Kat, on the other hand, kept shooting Crispin surreptitious glances while Crispin himself brooded. He didn't want Kat to be guilty. That was foremost in his mind. But he couldn't let her get away with it a second time. No, he'd take his stand on that. No matter how fond of her he was, it couldn't be allowed.

When they were finished, Jack and Kat cleaned the pots and bowls and set them aside to dry. Jack leaned into the window and looked up at the sky. 'When should we venture forth again, Master Teague? Do you think the tide is out sufficiently?'

'Would you prefer to go down to the beach and wait, Master Teague?' asked Crispin, trying not to sound too eager.

'I think that would be most expeditious. Let us find something to bring us light.'

Jack found two metal cages on pikes, with fuel in them enough to stay lit for their purposes. He lit one from the kitchen fire, and saved the other for when they got to the cove.

They found clothes to change into – Kat was in her men's clothes again, since she said her other gown was at the troupe's wagon – and they set out.

Instead of taking all the horses, they hitched up the cart horse, and climbed onto the cart themselves. Crispin sat beside Teague, while Jack and Kat sat in the back of the cart over the canvas-covered tools and crates.

They tried to be quiet, but once they were outside the castle gates, Jack leaned over toward Crispin. 'I can't believe it wasn't Jowan Penhall, sir.'

'They have an alibi. At least one I must make certain of from John Palliser.'

'By the sound of it, Roger Bennet was a right piece of work.'

'He was a terrible man,' said Teague.

Crispin stared. Carantok Teague had said very little about the dead man all this time. 'And why do you say that, Master Teague?'

'Oh . . . he was thoroughly unpleasant. He liked to tease, to harry me. I caught him spying on me once, and I had to divulge what I was doing. I even . . .' His voice trailed off, perhaps realizing what he was saying.

'You even what?' asked Crispin.

He muttered to himself, cursing, when he suddenly sighed and seemed to surrender something. 'I had to bribe him to keep silent.'

'My brooch!' cried Kat.

'*My* brooch,' said Teague with some irritation. 'Well . . . *he* found it and considered it payment. Taunted me with that, too.'

'Well, well,' said Crispin. 'What a creature he was.'

'And that's not the half of it,' said Teague. He was warmed up now and suddenly seemed bubbling over to talk about him. 'He harried the other men. And poor John Palliser. Did you know he was writing a history of Tintagel, a most scholarly pursuit?'

'Yes, he'd told me.'

'Did he tell you that Bennet stole his manuscript and, while reading it aloud to his fellows, began tossing pages into the fire?'

Crispin couldn't help but grit his teeth at the burning of a book. 'The churl.'

'Yes. And when Palliser arrived and caught Bennet at it, he flew into a rage. Said he'd kill him if he ever set foot in his chamber again. He managed to snatch the remaining pages of the manuscript, but I saw his face. Oh, he was in a right rage and quite devastated at the loss. All those pages. He would have to write them again. And all because a drunken Roger Bennet was bored. I can't for the life of me even blame his murderer.' He crossed himself quickly after that, but his mouth was set. He had no love for Roger Bennet.

'Have you any similar tales of Thomas Dunning?'

Teague maneuvered the cart over the steep path down to the shore. They would soon arrive at the place where they would have to leave the cart. 'That's the strange thing. For Dunning seemed to keep to himself. I didn't know him very well. He always had little to say. I can't imagine who would have killed him, or why.'

'It is a puzzle,' said Crispin.

'None of the men seem to want to be here,' said Jack.

Crispin adjusted his seat. The cart wasn't nearly as comfortable as his horse. 'John Palliser seemed to want to be here. He didn't mind it. He told me he came with Prince Edward and stayed on, expecting to retire soon to the local monastery.'

'Then he's the only one.'

Crispin turned. 'Mistress Pyke, how did Roger Bennet seem to you?'

'Carantok has the right of it. He was a thoroughly unpleasant gentleman, and I've met a fair few.'

'He schemed?'

'He schemed, he gambled, he coerced. He wasn't above extortion, I'm certain of that.'

'Then why did you . . .' But he couldn't complete the thought. She rescued him.

'He had knowledge I needed. He told me about Carantok's holes.'

It was Teague's turn to swing round. 'The scoundrel! And he spied on me to do it.'

'My brooch. He said he got it from one of your holes.'

'He never. I didn't see any such thing in my diggings. He must have stolen it elsewhere.'

'I concede it,' said Crispin. 'Bennet was a terrible man. But it doesn't explain Dunning.'

'It seems that it should have been the other way round,' said Jack. 'That maybe Dunning caught Bennet in the act and extorted him to keep mum. But then he would have been killed first, not second.'

Crispin sat back thoughtfully. 'I see what you mean. Bennet would have murdered him to keep him silent.'

Teague pulled on the reins and brought the cart to a halt. 'This is as far as we go.' He jumped off the side and moved to the back in time to help Kat off. She leapt nimbly to the ground, only touching Teague's fingers to do so. The man looked away from her deliberately, and instead took up a pickax. 'Just in case,' he said.

By now the sky was decidedly darker, and by the moonlight,

Crispin could see that the tide had receded enough along the shore. The cave would still be damp but not underwater.

Jack carefully lit the other torch and handed one to Crispin. With both torches in hand, he and Jack led the others toward the dark hole in the chalky cliff face.

The roar of the sea seemed to grow louder in the cave, like a hand cupped to an ear. It caught the noise and echoed it back. Everywhere was the smell of the salty ocean and damp. When he brought the torch in under the arch of stone, it reflected with flickering light on the roof and the slick walls.

'It was here, sir,' said Jack, splashing forward. 'In this pool.' Jack's torch lit the dark water. Its surface glittered with the fire's reflection.

'I'll hold that,' said Kat, taking the torch from him.

Crispin's blood was tingling through his body. There was no feeling akin to this except for that of awaiting a joust to begin. His sight seemed sharper, his ears keener.

Jack splashed forward and knelt, reaching down beneath a jutting shelf of rock. He struggled and Crispin shoved his torch at Teague, who barely had time to drop his pickax and grab it before Crispin plunged into the pool to help Jack.

His fingers found the wet wood, smoothed from the churning tide and time. Its surface felt uneven, like a timber floating on the sea for years, and he felt slightly disappointed that it might turn out to be nothing . . . when it moved. He and Jack exchanged a fleeting glance, when they set to again. Digging in with both hands, they pulled in tandem. It scraped along the rough surface and finally slid out. It was indeed a coffer of some size, and heavy. The uneven surface he had mistaken for driftwood were instead carvings that had lost their definition from their waterlogged state.

They carried it out of the cave and to the pebbled beach, setting it down. A long coffer, long enough for a sword, Crispin noted. With a slight arch to the top of it and a mechanism that was at first puzzling.

'I don't see a lock, sir,' said Jack, peering at all the edges, but edges there were and even a seam running along the sides. It opened, but how?

Teague was fairly vibrating with excitement. 'I think we should take it back to the castle. It is cold here and we need more light.'

They all agreed, and he and Jack carried it back along the beach and up the steep trail to the awaiting cart.

Kat's smile and the light in her eyes under the torch-glow gave him pause. She was as excited as the rest of them. And though she might not believe in Excalibur, she was as enthralled by the hunt as he was.

She raised her eyes to his and they shared an electric moment.

But it was gone again as they scrambled onto the cart and hurried back up the path to the dark castle above.

The porter had been there to open the gate for them, and Crispin called to him, telling him he could close the portcullis for the night. Shipley stared down at Crispin with a puzzled expression and, after a moment, disappeared to comply.

They heard the sound of the windlass creaking and whining and the solid thud of the portcullis's teeth hitting the stone behind them. Navigating over the land-bridge in the dark was more harrowing than Crispin cared to repeat, but he and Jack leaned their torches on either side of the cart to illuminate the narrow path, and an oblivious Carantok Teague managed without a fuss.

They brought the coffer to Teague's chamber, covered with one of his canvas cloths to hide it. They needn't have worried, since they saw neither Sir Regis nor the other two men-at-arms.

They lit the fires, lit as many candles and oil lamps as they could, while Teague examined the coffer and its mysterious and invisible locking mechanism.

'Have you seen the like before, Master Teague?' Jack bent over, hands on knees, to study it.

'Something like it before in the Holy Land. But not quite as puzzling as this.'

'I can break into it,' said Jack and Kat at the same time. They exchanged glances.

Crispin took Teague by the shoulder and gently guided him back. 'I'd leave it to these two professionals.'

'I thought you weren't thieving anymore, Jack,' said Kat in a lilting voice.

'I don't. But . . . there are occasions when me master and me must—'

'Never mind,' she said, squatting in front of it.

Jack reached over the coffer. 'I've seen tricks where you have to release secreted catches on the side . . .'

Jack's arms were long enough to be able to reach both sides at once. He fiddled at the edges but eventually pushed away with an exasperated huff.

'Or,' said Kat, running her fingers along the front, 'there are sometimes hidden panels that you must compress to reveal the mechanism.' Her slender fingers moved smoothly along the wood.

'Damn,' she whispered, after working on it for some time with no result.

'I once opened a small jewelry casket by rocking it from side to side,' said Jack. 'Here, help me,' he said to her, the first civil thing Crispin had heard him say to her. They each took a side of it and, on Jack's instructions, carefully lifted one side and then the other. 'There was a weight in it, you see, a ball. And by rocking it just so . . .' But that proved as useless as the rest.

Kat frowned. 'Stupid, sarding box!' She slammed her fist on the top of it and they all heard a spring and a click.

The seam of the coffer widened and the lid suddenly stood ajar.

'Or that,' she said in whispered awe.

By rights, Carantok Teague should have opened it, but Crispin didn't think when he instinctively moved forward, grasped the lid, and pulled it open.

An embroidered silken cloth lay on top, each colorful thread bright as if sewn only yesterday. There were knights and horses and a great battle. And in the distance, a bearded man in a long gown and a staff observing it all.

Gently grasping the cloth and pulling it away, Crispin glimpsed first the wire-wrapped grip, a shining silver crossguard molded into an elegant arc, and a pommel with a carved dragon in a circle, much like the piece found in the chapel.

He yanked the cloth aside, letting it drop to the floor.

A perfect blade glimmered in the firelight, resting in a nest of velvet. The blade was polished, without a nick or scratch. It had to be his imagination that it almost seemed to glow.

He reached out to touch it, to grasp the handle and curled his fingers around it. When he lifted it from its coffer and raised it upward, he felt its perfect balance, its grace of shape and line, its weight that felt so right in his hand. He could slay a dragon with it. He could slay a hundred men and never tire.

'It's magnificent,' he whispered.

He swung it back and forth. He'd seldom seen so perfect a weapon. It felt right in his hand. When he swung it a few more times, he knew how graceful the blade was, how cunning it could be. In his mind rushed the many encounters he could have had with it, how the outcomes of those long-ago days could have been different with *this* blade under his control. He didn't remember closing his eyes, but he could imagine and then *saw* Arthur pull it from the stone. The king bore it up and showed it to the crowd who hailed him. The scene shifted and Crispin saw Arthur in battle with it, mowing down his enemies. And then the scene shifted again, and Crispin himself was in a great hall, shining with candles everywhere, and he was kneeling, and felt the flat of the blade gently tap his shoulder as Arthur himself knighted him.

'God blind me,' breathed Jack. 'That's it, isn't it?'

'If it isn't,' said Teague, 'then I can't imagine what it is.'

Crispin's eyes snapped open. The images in his mind fell away, like a dream fading . . . but so much not like a dream at all. His heart hammered wildly in his chest, and he could barely draw breath. When he felt more himself again, he turned toward Teague and reluctantly presented it to his employer. 'Your prize, Master Teague.' But even as it slipped through his fingers, a sharp pang stabbed at his heart. And then a hollowness that he hadn't felt since losing his knighthood squeezed his vitals. *By all the saints, it's only a sword*, he told himself. But he couldn't help but feel . . . it was more than that. The visions in his mind were surely more than reality.

Teague generously allowed both Jack and Kat to touch it, but Jack kept looking at Crispin, as if he expected him to burst into tears. Or rage against someone. He turned from Jack, because there *was* something beginning to bloom inside of him. Loss. Pain. Sorrow.

He tried to smile at his apprentice, but it came out a weak grimace instead.

Teague stroked it, studied the pommel, ran his hand along the length of the still-sharpened blade. 'I think it best we return it to its coffer,' he said softly after a time. He set it inside its velvet cushion, laid the discarded cloth over it and closed the lid. He got Jack to help him slide it under his bed. And then they all stood in front of the bed, looking at it.

Had no one else experienced what Crispin felt? They had marveled at the blade, but they hadn't *seen*.

Kat moved first, and she, too, was looking at Crispin with some concern. 'I say we've had a long day and must retreat to our beds,' she said.

Annoyed by her expression, he agreed with a grunt and turned away, stomping toward his chamber. Jack would share his chamber, and Kat would take the other separate chamber. He stared at the bed, sitting in its corner. Felt like kicking it, throwing the bolster over itself, hurling the sheets to the floor.

Why am I so angry? Not angry, exactly. Frustrated, perhaps. But why even that? What had he expected? He had held the sword of swords, and it had been a marvelous thing. Miraculous, even. But it wasn't his, anymore than it was Teague's. Maybe that was it. That it didn't belong to Teague either. Who, then, should have the sword? Not him. He wasn't worthy. He wouldn't even have been allowed at the Round Table, what with his committing treason and all.

And there it was again. His past, slapping him in the face. He had meant it to be honorable. It was honorable, wanting his mentor to be king over that whelp of a boy, over Richard . . . who had not wanted to execute his own mentor – Crispin – but was being forced to by his many handlers. The fact that Richard had admitted to him that it had been a relief when Lancaster stepped forward to plead for Crispin's life . . .

He ran his hand over his face. 'Can you not simply rejoice in seeing such an object?' he muttered to himself.

A cleared throat in the doorway made him jerk back and whirl around. Jack. And Kat.

'What is it?'

Jack rubbed his beard and then dropped his hand away. 'It seems foolish to house Mistress Pyke in the next room . . . when she'd end up here anyway.'

'Tucker!'

'I'm not wrong.' Standing behind Kat, he grasped her by her shoulders and gently propelled her forward into the room. 'You know I'm right.' He ducked quickly away before Crispin could say more.

She wore an apologetic smile. 'He is right, you know.'

Crispin surrendered with a sigh and sat on the edge of the bed. 'Is that your will? To be in here with me?'

She moved cautiously into the room and stood before him, hands demurely placed in front of her. 'It is.' She gazed at him for a moment before crouching and taking his hands. 'You know it is. Even as peevish as you are.'

He lifted her hand almost unconsciously and kissed it. Still holding it, he gently pulled, and she stumbled forward. He caught her and drew her into his lap. 'Peevish, eh?'

'Grumpy, even.'

'Mmm,' he murmured, looking her over. He couldn't help but lean in to kiss her.

She offered her lips and then her smooth neck, and he drew her closer to nuzzle it, to nose his way down to the flesh at her chemise's neckline. His hands found the softness of her breasts, the curve of a hip. But his mouth wanted more kisses and found her lips again.

She smiled, making a sound like a purr, and gathered him close. He soon forgot about the sword.

Something woke him. A sound. A scrape along stone. But suddenly he was wide awake. He looked down beside him, but Kat was not there. He stumbled from the bed and tripped over something on the floor.

Grabbing his chemise from where it lay at the foot of the bed, he pulled it on. As his eyes adjusted to the dark, he saw that he had tripped on one of her shoes. He did not find the other. 'Kat?' he husked in the dark.

A yell. Crispin fell on his belt and grabbed the dagger, pulling it from its scabbard. Scrambling into the corridor, he suddenly ran into Carantok Teague in his nightgown. 'It's gone! God have mercy, it's gone!'

Jack stumbled into the corridor half-dressed, hair messy, face still slack from being awakened so suddenly. 'What's amiss?'

'The sword!' cried Teague. 'It's gone!'

Jack swiveled around, seeing just the three of them. 'Where's Kat Pyke?'

Crispin gritted his teeth. 'She's gone too.'

TWENTY-FIVE

He couldn't have been that stupid. He simply could not have been.

Barefoot, Crispin paced the floor, wiping his hand down his beard-stubbled face. He should have known she would steal it. Would have wagered money on it, in fact.

'Where do you suppose she is?' asked Jack, leaning against the wall. He glanced at Teague through the doorway of Crispin's room, sitting on Crispin's bed, his head in his hands.

'Far from here,' he growled. It was all his fault. Jack had warned him, but he hadn't listened, hadn't wanted to.

Jack took several steps into his chamber and picked up the lone shoe. 'She left this.'

'Foolish of her,' he said from the corridor, where he continued to pace. 'It's cold and damp out.'

'Aye.' Jack took it with him and left the chamber, re-entering his own. Crispin could hear him rumbling around, opening coffers. He stuck his head out the door. 'The rest of her things are still here.'

'What would she need with them? She had something of great value to sell. And she was in a hurry.'

'Aye,' he muttered uncertainly. Scratching his head, he stared at the shoe. 'But, as you say, it's cold and wet out. Could a person not slow down enough to retrieve one shoe?'

Crispin looked at the dagger still in his hand, walked to where he had discarded his belt in his chamber, and shoved it in its scabbard. 'What are you saying?'

Jack stood a moment in the doorway, clutching the shoe, staring at nothing, or so Crispin thought. But when Jack cocked his head to glare at the floor, the man froze for only a heartbeat before Jack ran to the corridor to retrieve the oil lamp in its niche.

'Sir,' he said, crouching. He held the little clay lamp near the floor, moving it about, leaving a dim halo of light here and there.

Teague still sat on the bed, cradling his head, moaning softly.

Crispin stopped pacing the chamber and turned. Jack seemed engrossed with examining something on the floor. With a sigh, Crispin crouched alongside him.

Dots of mud. Muddy . . . footsteps?

He grabbed the shoe from Jack's hand. No mud.

He bolted upright and followed the mud out of the chamber where the steps left a faint trail, and then down the stairwell.

'Those aren't her footsteps, sir,' said Jack, stating the obvious.

Crispin stared into the gloom of the floor below. 'She was abducted?'

'She lost her shoe . . . or left it on purpose.'

'How did I not hear it?'

'Sometimes you sleep deeply, sir, when . . . when you are content.'

'God's blood!'

But now Teague was awakened from his mourning and staggered to the doorway. '*She* took the sword!'

'I don't think so, Master Teague,' said Crispin over his shoulder. He grabbed another oil lamp from further down the corridor and ventured into Teague's chamber. He knelt at the bed and moved the lamp about. No muddy prints. This was someone else. They *could* be working in tandem . . . but he didn't sense it in his gut.

'It wasn't her. She was abducted. And the sword taken at the same time.'

'This is impossible!' cried Teague.

'Improbable . . . but not impossible. Jack, get dressed.'

'Aye, sir!' He hurried to his own coffer in Crispin's chamber and dug out his clothes.

Crispin dressed quickly, and was surprised to find Teague dressed as well and waiting outside his chamber.

Footsteps on the stairwell. Crispin shoved Teague behind him and drew his sword. But it was only the sleepy face of Sir Regis, bearing a candle on a tin holder. 'What goes on here?'

'My . . . my servant has been abducted.'

Regis glanced at Jack and then seemed to remember. 'The girl? What, by the mass, is going on? Who stole her?'

'I don't know. Someone in the village . . .'

'God's wounds,' said Regis quietly. 'It's Hærfest.'

'Harvest? What has that to do with—'

'Those damned pagans. Hærfest. Treknow and any other village celebrate the end of the season. But those *druw* in Prasgwig . . . It's happened before. They stole women from the village and they never returned. The fool men of Treknow tried to get them back, but they were killed. They steal women for their damned rituals.'

'But why her? Why come all the way to the castle just for her? Why not go to the village?'

'Maybe she caught their eye somehow. You didn't take her with you, by any chance?'

He cursed himself. Not only had he, but she'd already been there before. And that brooch . . .

He slapped his hand to his scrip . . . No. It wasn't there. *Damn her!*

'We must go to Prasgwig to rescue her. Will you come, Sir Regis?'

'I want nothing to do with those people.'

'Sir Regis, a woman under your care here, in the castle, was taken. Is it not your responsibility to help us?'

Regis sneered. He looked as if he was opening his mouth for a stinging retort . . . when he suddenly drooped. 'Very well,' he grunted. 'Await me in the courtyard.'

He retreated to his chamber below, and Crispin and the others wasted no time buttoning their cloaks and donning hoods as they went, bustling down to the courtyard.

They saddled their horses, preparing an extra one for Regis when he appeared.

'Grab that torch,' he said to Jack, and mounted.

Jack leaned down from his mount and grabbed the torch from the entrance to the lodgings.

Regis led the way. 'Let's go.'

The horses clattered over the flagged stone and, when they got to the portcullis on the mainland, Regis whistled up to the tower. 'Ho! Shipley, damn you! Open the sarding gate!'

A figure appeared at the topmost window. 'Sir Regis?'

'Open the gate, you imbecile!'

The head ducked away again, and they heard the slow grind of metal and creaking wood as the windlass bore up the heavy gate.

When it was high enough, Crispin called up to Shipley. 'Did anyone come to this gate? A group of men?'

Shipley, though sleepy, shook his head. 'No, my lord.'

'They must have come up from the beach.'

Regis stared at him uncomprehendingly.

'I was told that some got into the castle by taking a route along the beach and climbing up the battlements.'

Sir Regis glared up at the raised portcullis. He must be thinking what Crispin was thinking; why lower the gate at all.

They wasted no more time and galloped through, weaving their way down the treacherous and narrow paths toward where the roads diverged. Crispin didn't relish going through those woods at night. If the villagers posted archers on watch, there was a very good chance of ending up dead.

None of that mattered. None of this was to be borne. They'd rescue Kat and then search for the sword. God knew who had taken that.

They rode over the meadows and plains, finally reached the

shadowed edge of the forest, and plunged in. The torch was a sorry sun. Though it did illuminate the road ahead, its light painted the over-arching boughs only in slashes of gray on black. It seemed to make the woods appear even more fearsome in its scant glow, for as soon as the forest around them was briefly illuminated, it would fall quickly away to darkness again, only to light another arc and then another.

When the path narrowed, they paused. Crispin looked about and remembered a tree stump just there when it became a deer path. Under the hoofbeats, birds, frightened by their ride, tore from the branches and hiding leaves, screaming into the night above them.

Was it his imagination, or was it getting lighter up ahead? It was still late in the night, not early enough for dawn to be breaking. No, it was light from something like a great bonfire. He motioned for Jack to put out the torch, and the man dumped the cage upside down, and crushed it into the dirt. He held the cage on its pike like a lance, ready to use it as a weapon.

Crispin smiled grimly. He eased his sword from the scabbard. Regis did likewise. They rode slowly toward the light that was bright enough to illuminate their way.

As they got closer, Crispin was certain that it was a bonfire, with the flickering light spilling onto the heights of the trees, with the music of pipes and drums and people merry-making ahead. He was grateful that there were no guards along the road. Perhaps they were all at their Hærfest celebrations.

Crispin signaled for them to dismount, and to loosely tie their horses there. On foot, he led them toward the village, keeping low and nearest the darker edges of the trees. He noticed that Regis was pleased enough to allow him to lead. He supposed the man wasn't interested in doing more than absolutely required.

They came to the edge of the woods but the nearest hut was some yards away out in the open. Crispin measured the merry-makers and darted forward along a wattled fence and hid behind the cottage. He waited for the others to join him, one by one, Teague being last, his eyes wide like bezants. Crispin ran for the next cottage, hiding in the shadows. A hog nearly the size of a cow rumbled, nipping at him through the fence. He jumped back and warned the others by signaling. They all avoided the hog by skirting past the fence as far from it as they could go, and slipped toward the stone foundations of a longhouse almost opposite the village green.

Crispin clung to the wall and peered around the corner with one eye. Jack was right above him.

That large corn mannikin stood where he'd seen it before, its form highlighted in gold from the leaping fire. His gaze passed over it, stopped, and looked again. A struggling figure was tied to it.

Jack tapped him on the shoulder and pointed. He realized it was Kat.

What the devil . . .? And devilry it was. The villagers danced near the bonfire, wearing masks made of leaves and braided sheaves on their faces. Only their eyes glittered from time to time from the depths of their eyeholes.

'What manner of—'

Jack clamped his large hand over Teague's mouth. His eyes widened above Jack's fingers, and Crispin turned to him with a digit over his own lips, and a glare stern enough to silence any further protests. Jack slowly released him and Teague nodded, acknowledging that he understood.

Crispin adjusted his grip on his sword. There was only the four of them, and only two swords between them. Jack had the snuffed torch and Teague, he presumed, had a dagger. That didn't seem particularly good odds.

He glanced back at Regis, eyes darting here and there, but he didn't seem to be a fount of ideas.

Jack's mustache was suddenly tickling his ear, and then his whisper. 'We'll have to make a dash for the other side of that green behind the corn man. If we went the long way round . . .'

Crispin nodded. It was their only chance. They'd stick to the shadows and make their way there, untie her, and try to steal away while no one was looking.

Was there even a chance of that?

There was no alternative. The only thing they had on their side was surprise. Crispin motioned for them to follow, and he moved along the huts that fell into darkness far from the bonfire.

They worked their way along the trees on the other side of the green and then crossed the green along the shadow of the corn mannikin. Crispin held his hand up to pause and listen. No one seemed to have sounded the alarm. He waited one more heartbeat before he dropped to the ground and crawled around the mannikin toward the struggling figure, bathed in firelight. When he was certain he remained in shadow, he slowly rose to stand beside her. 'Kat,' he whispered into her ear. She froze. 'I'm going to cut your bonds. Make no sudden moves. Only move when I tell you to.'

She didn't so much as flick an eyelash. Her breathing evened over the gag covering her mouth, and she stood straight and still. Crispin leaned into the straw, seeking the shadows, and sawed on her bindings with his knife. She was smart enough to leave her hands behind her, even as the ropes were cut free.

'Now slowly,' said Crispin to her ear. 'Sidestep toward me. Very, very slowly.'

He marveled at her coolness, how she moved incrementally toward him, sliding against the straw at her back, stopping when someone appeared to be looking her way, and proceeding again when they weren't. At the edge of the mannikin's leg, she slipped behind it, yanked off her gag, and kissed him soundly. 'I knew it!' she hissed. 'I knew you'd come.'

'Foolish woman.' He grabbed her arm. 'Make for the woods.'

They all ran together toward the trees on the other side of the green. No sooner had Crispin stepped over the line of green to woods, the music stopped and people began to shout. He led his troupe farther into the brush and the sheltering darkness, turned, crouched, and waited.

The men scattered on the green, into the village, and to the end of the road.

So far, they hadn't looked in their direction. But the horses were clear on the other side of the green in those woods, far from where they hid. He began to wonder if they shouldn't just abandon the horses and set out on their own . . . when something poked the back of his head.

'Stand up, *sowsnek*,' said the man behind him.

The arrow poised at his head insisted, and Crispin slowly stood.

TWENTY-SIX

The man with the bow ticked his head toward the green. 'Make your way there, all of you.'

Kat's fingers dug into Crispin's coat, holding on tight as they walked back across the wet grass.

'You shan't get away with it,' said Crispin over his shoulder. 'The men from the village—'

'The men from the village are all *mogh*,' said the man. 'They squeal and make their noise but they never do aught. And put your hands up away from your blades, *emete*.'

Hands raised, they marched back to the gathering at the mannikin. An old man leaning on a staff came forward. His face was masked by a configuration of leaves, like the leaf-faced men found carved out of stone in many a church. But it was easy to see that it was Trethewey.

'Why have you come to disrupt what is ours alone, Crispin Guest?'

'Because you have stolen away one of my people, my lord. We cannot sit back and do nothing when our friends are captured.'

'She is our Hærfest sacrifice. It is so ordained.'

'By whom? The Lord Jesus Christ does not demand human sacrifice.'

'What is ordained is far older than your Christ.'

'I knew it,' hissed Jack.

'You would have murdered Mistress Pyke?' said Crispin.

'It is as our gods ordained.'

'What is she to you? Could not any one of you gladly sacrifice yourself if you must do this thing?'

Another man rushed forward. He, too, was masked, and he raised his fist. Crispin faced him down. 'She is a robber of our sacred dead,' said the man. 'That brooch was from a burial.'

Crispin turned to her. 'Well?'

'Roger gave it to me. I don't know where he got it. He said he got it from one of . . . from the other holes.'

He had to trust that she was telling the truth. This time, he believed her.

'Mistress Pyke claims that the murdered man from the castle stole it.'

'And if he is dead, she is the next best thing.'

'Nonsense. You celebrate your pagan ways on your own, and leave Christians out of it. She's coming with us. And we are leaving.'

He heard the sound of a bowstring pulled back at his ear. 'Think again, *sowsnek*.'

He waited a breath that seemed like an eternity. And then Crispin whirled, grabbed the bow, and yanked. The arrow pinged off to the side into the straw mannikin. Crispin swung the bow hard, slamming the archer in the head. Once he went down, he swung it at the surprised villager with the leaf mask, and he, too, was knocked to the side.

Regis drew his sword.

'Jack!' cried Crispin. 'Take my sword!'

Amazed for only a moment, Jack lunged forward and wrenched Crispin's sword from its scabbard, holding the blade aloft as Crispin had taught him to do.

The villagers all stepped back while the bonfire painted their faces with jumping shards of gold.

Crispin was aware of their precarious situation. The three of them could not hold off an entire village. At any moment, they'd be rushed.

Out of the crowd, a screaming woman hurled herself forward with knife raised. Crispin dropped the bow and grabbed her, disarming her. She hooked his neck with her arm and pulled herself close. 'Hold the knife on me,' she hissed to his ear. 'Hold me hostage, or you'll never leave alive.'

He pushed her back and looked into her face. Eseld. But he quickly did as she said, whirling her around and holding the blade to her throat. 'Hurt any of us and we kill this woman!' he cried.

Some gasped. And a masked Jory Gloyn pushed his way forward. 'Eseld!' Apparently, by the crack in his voice, all had been forgiven.

Trethewey raised his hand for his more zealous men to stop. 'She is brave for attacking these *sowsnek*. We must respect her.'

'You have back your brooch,' said Crispin. 'Allow us to leave or I will kill this woman.'

They moved back, but Crispin wasn't satisfied. How dare they come into his chamber to steal Kat and threaten her? How dare they threaten him?

'Jack,' he barked. 'Do some damage.'

With a grim smile, Jack seized a flaming log from the bonfire and threw it at the mannikin. The flames roared and surged up the figure. He and Regis seemed to have had the same idea, for they both stood at the flaming mannikin's legs, and pushed. The burning straw man teetered and smoked. The villagers screamed. Slowly, the straw man fell toward them and their thatched houses. When it slammed down, it exploded with a great fiery crash, catching the thatch, and sending a roaring fireball and sparks into the air.

Crispin and his company ran. Ducking into the woods, they stumbled and rushed toward their horses. When they reached them, they could see more glowing light and sparks light the night.

Crispin turned to his erstwhile 'captive'. 'Eseld, you saved us. Why?'

'If they weren't going to kill her, they would have kept her. Like they kept me all them years ago.'

His eyes tracked all over her face, trying to discern the emotion there. But it was blank. 'Come with us, back to Treknow.'

'No. I have a child here. It's been too long. I'm as pagan as them now. I can't go back.'

'Bring your child. You don't have to stay.'

'I do. It's too late for me.' She stepped back from Crispin. Her stark face was still blank. He could not tell if she were happy with her lot or simply resigned. When she turned and ran back to the village, he decided it didn't matter.

Kat had mounted on Crispin's horse and reached out a hand to him. 'Crispin, come on!'

He looked back at Eseld, but she had disappeared into the darkness.

'Crispin!' Kat insisted.

Without another thought, he grabbed Tobias's mane and swung up. They kicked in their heels and tore through the woods, their path lit by the conflagration behind them.

They reached the castle, called for Shipley to open the gate and close it after them, and made it back to the great hall on the island. John Palliser, and the two men-at-arms, were waiting for them when they arrived.

'What by the mass happened to you?' asked the caretaker. 'And what's happened to the sky?'

Crispin looked out the window toward the distant woods and saw that the sky was still lit with the fires. 'Hærfest,' he said.

'Good God,' said Palliser, crossing himself.

'Those goddamned pagans!' Regis tossed his cloak aside and slammed it to the floor. 'Someone build a damn fire!'

Jack hurried to comply since it didn't look as if anyone else would.

Regis stomped toward the sideboard, poured himself some ale, and knocked it back. He poured more and threw himself into a chair with a belch. 'That was a hell of a thing, Guest. And all for a sarding servant?' But then he finally looked at Kat, who didn't have a cloak and hood and could no longer hide her face. He nearly leapt from the chair. 'You! I thought I told you . . . I should have let them burn you.'

She sidled next to Crispin, and then hung on his coat and edged behind him.

'Will someone tell us?' cried Palliser.

'The pagans in Prasgwig – and indeed they are, as we now have proof of it,' said Crispin, 'abducted our servant girl and threatened to burn her as their sacrifice.'

'And we burned them down,' said Jack in a rush. He was still breathing hard. There was a smudge of soot on his cheek.

'Holy Mother of God,' said Palliser. He went to the window and looked out. The sky was still lit up with flames. For all Crispin knew, the whole forest was aflame. He hoped the village burned down to cinders.

'Then . . . did *they* murder Bennet and Dunning?' asked Palliser, still staring out the window.

'No,' said Crispin. He went to the sideboard. He didn't realize he was holding Kat's hand until he noticed he had dragged her with him. He let her go as he reached for the jug, but she grabbed it first and poured for him, handing him the cup with a grateful smile.

He took it to wash the smoke from his throat, and leaned heavily with one hand on the sideboard as he drank. He hadn't noticed setting the cup down, nor when Kat refilled it, but he took it thankfully and walked to the fire to stand before it.

'At least, I don't think it was them,' he continued, drinking again.

'Then who did, master?' asked Jack.

Crispin wiped his lips and lowered his cup. 'Master Palliser, just how angry were you that Roger Bennet maliciously burned your book?'

Palliser's face was white. He stood still for a moment before he carefully walked to a bench and sat. 'I was extremely angry,' he said in a steady voice. 'But not enough to kill, Master Guest.'

'And can you prove where you were Monday?'

He said nothing. The room fell silent. Just the crackling of flames in the hearth and the blowing of the wind outside.

Someone cleared their throat.

Everyone turned toward Arno. He hesitated, touched his coat that had been so hastily donned that he hadn't buttoned it. 'I . . . was with him.'

Crispin sipped. 'And so?'

'He . . . he was teaching me . . . to read.'

Regis threw up his arms and laughed. 'For the love of—'

'I didn't want to say,' Arno went on angrily. 'You're always carrying on about it, mocking me,' he said to Regis, who turned his nose up at him and continued to drink. 'But it isn't a fair thing if you want to arrest Master Palliser for murder. He couldn't have done it. We worked all day. He's a good man.'

Palliser lowered his head and folded his hands.

'You're a fool, Guest,' said Regis, slumping in his high-backed chair. 'You're grasping at straws. I daresay you might never find the killer. And who cares, anyway? We are forgotten by God, forgotten by the saints, forgotten by the law. Who gives a damn whether a killer was climbing chapel roofs and dispatching our men in holes? We are damned nonetheless.'

Crispin slowly lowered his cup. 'Sometimes I grasp at straws, Sir Regis. And sometimes . . .' He turned toward the man, lounging in his chair like a king on his throne. 'And sometimes I listen when someone lets slip a word or two. For instance, I don't believe I ever told you that the killer was stalking us on the roof of the chapel.'

Regis stared at Crispin for a long moment, the ale glistening on his mustache. He swept his glance toward Arno and then Stephen before he began to chuckle. He pointed a finger at Crispin. 'I see you, Crispin Guest. You think you are a damned clever man, don't you? You think I can be caught out just because you say so. But that stain won't wash. You're a traitor. You'll always be a traitor.'

'That may be true, but I am not a cold-blooded killer.'

Regis's easy smile suddenly faltered. His cup flew toward Crispin, who ducked in time. When he looked up, Regis was standing with his blade drawn.

Tossing his own cup away, Crispin drew his sword.

Everyone moved back to the edges of the room.

'Regis!' cried Stephen. 'Tell him it isn't so.'

'He can't,' said Arno. 'Because he's guilty, the bastard.'

Regis aimed his sword high over his head toward Crispin. 'Do you know what I hate the most, Guest? I hate that man.' The sword suddenly pointed toward an unusually quiet Carantok Teague.

'Me?' said Teague. 'What have I ever done to offend you, sir?'

'Your presence offends me. Your digging holes and hauling out
the prizes of the dead offends me. Your stupid face and your
damned charter offend me. I dug my own holes when you left.
And I found gold trinkets. I was collecting enough to get off this
goddamned rock. Until Roger found *my* trove.'

He and Crispin circled one another, even as Regis sneered at
Teague.

'So on Monday he confronted me when I was looking in that
hole you covered up. He knew what I was doing and he wanted
part of it too. So I bashed in his sorry head with a rock. As any
one of you should have done ages ago.'

Arno stepped forward boldly. 'But what of Thomas? He'd
done nothing.'

'Oh, you think so? You think he was innocent little Thomas? He
saw what I had done and vowed to say nothing . . . if I paid him
enough. He threatened to tell Guest. I suppose I could have just killed
you, Guest, except I was tired of paying ransom for my own hoard.'

'Greed,' Crispin sneered. 'You killed them both for greed.'

'What else is left me here? You sniveling cowards. You complain
and do nothing and rot here. I will not. I'm leaving.'

Crispin stepped closer, keeping his blade steady. 'I beg to differ.'

'You think *you* can stop me?' He looked Crispin up and down.
'How often do you practice with that?' He gestured toward Crispin's
sword. 'And you're older than I am. Well. We shall see.'

Regis lunged forward and slammed his blade toward Crispin's
neck and shoulder, but Crispin was ready, and blocked it with his
own with a loud clang of steel on steel.

Regis stepped back and laughed. 'You'll tire. You're *old*, Guest.
All I need to do is wait until you're tired.'

Crispin was thinking the same thing. 'Then we'd best not wait.'
He swung low, aiming for the man's legs. Regis deflected the sword
with his blade. He smiled and sent forth a volley of overhands,
uppercuts, and two-handed slices, sending sparks into the air around
them. Crispin parried all of them, but without getting in any offensive
strikes of his own.

Crispin took two steps back, breathing hard.

'You're winded already,' said Regis, moving the sword tip like
a snake waiting to strike. He rolled the sword over his wrist, showing
off his prowess. 'Good.' Suddenly, he grabbed the blade with two
hands and swung the pommel toward Crispin like a club.

Arching away, Crispin slid *his* hands to his sword blade and used the crossguard like a crosier, hooked Regis's ankle, and yanked.

The man flipped back onto his arse. But before Crispin could readjust his grip to club downward, Regis scrambled to his feet.

'That gives you one, Guest. I'll not let you get another.'

Starkly aware that he wore no armor, Crispin knew that any kind of blow to his person was likely to be debilitating. He had no mail to deflect a blade, no steel plate to protect vulnerable limbs and torso. *I could use Excalibur about now.*

'I know what you're thinking, Guest,' said Regis, circling.

'I'll wager you don't.' Crispin matched him move for move.

'You're thinking you're not wearing armor. Any strike will be . . . well. Could be your last. Aren't you?'

'You do like the sound of your own voice, don't you? Then tell me this. After killing Dunning, how did you get back to the hall before we did?'

He chuckled. 'You were all watching that bitch run away. I went the other way, down the cliff path. It's dangerous, but much faster. The same way your pagans got *in*, I daresay.'

'And you slipped in by the pantry window. I found it open. So when the others saw you come in, it was by the pantry, where you claimed you were doing an inventory.'

'Yes, it was terribly clever.'

'And yet you still couldn't help talking, and fouled yourself.'

Regis's smile turned to a sneer. He raised his arm to strike, but Crispin swung upward underhanded and felt the blade pass through muscle.

Regis stumbled. His upper arm bled, bubbling up through his sleeve. He roared a curse and tried to grab his arm with the sword hand.

Crispin rushed in again and cocked back his arm, but Regis blocked it.

'A *little* blood, Guest. No more than that.'

But it *was* more than that. The sleeve was soaked in red in no time at all, and Regis gritted his teeth, wheezing his breath through them as he continued stalking Crispin. 'I must pay you in kind for that, Guest.'

Running forward, he swung. The blade came at him more quickly than Crispin had anticipated. The steel flashed. It took a heartbeat for the searing pain to register. Crispin staggered back, flicking a glance at his left shoulder, his coat growing as red as Regis's sleeve.

He heard Kat gasp somewhere behind him.

It was only a slice, not a gash. Painful, but nothing a needle and thread couldn't fix. But it did hurt like hellfire.

He inhaled sharply through his nostrils, smelling the stench of blood. He hoped it was Regis's, though he suspected it was his own.

Regis didn't wait. He stomped forward, raising his sword. Crispin stepped up to meet him, and blocked the blade, smashing it aside. Before he could jab, Regis knocked *his* sword aside.

And so it went. Advance, chop down, smack aside, turn, block, undercut, reach over, spin.

They both stepped back to catch their breath. His shoulder ached and every now and then twinged, as the cut opened each time he used the blade two-handed.

Crispin took a deep breath and abruptly charged, with a roar searing from his lungs. He chopped mercilessly at a surprised Regis, who backed away with each strong stroke of Crispin's sword. Regis leapt back, and with his left hand he drew his dagger. Sword in one hand and dagger in the other, he stormed forward. Crispin came up to meet him, blocked the sword, grabbed his left wrist with the dagger, and turned it, plunging it into Regis's thigh.

Regis hollered and staggered back, wrenching it out to a hot flow of blood; he couldn't hold the knife in his blood-slickened fingers. It clanged to the floor, and Crispin gripped his sword with both hands, giving Regis no time to adjust his stance.

With strength Crispin hadn't expected, Regis bared his teeth and knocked each charge away until he swatted underhanded and across, catching the crossguard of Crispin's sword.

Crispin felt the sword leave his grip, watched helplessly as it sailed in an arc away from him, and clattered to the floor. Then the pommel of Regis's sword slammed his chin and he fell back.

Regis staggered forward, sword raised high. 'On to Hell, Guest!'

Crispin gritted his teeth. There was little else to do. He couldn't even roll away. There was no time for a prayer. Just to cringe at the inevitable blow.

Regis paused, sword raised, glinting a little red at the sharpened edge with Crispin's own blood. He seemed to be suspended in time, like an insect in amber. And then for a little more, before he jerked up his head, and dropped to the ground like a stone.

Crispin blinked. *What . . . what . . .?*

He finally noticed Kat revealed, standing behind where Regis had been, a heavy log in her hand. She threw it angrily at the unmoving Regis, swiped at the strands of hair in her face, and pushed them out of her eyes.

Breathing heavily, she sneered first at Regis and then at Crispin. 'Men!' she spit.

TWENTY-SEVEN

Arno and Stephen dispatched a still-groggy Regis to a cell in the gatehouse.

Crispin shouted after them, 'And see that the authorities – the sheriff of the county, at least – is told of the pagans.' There was no sense in allowing them to further harass the people of Treknow. The Church authorities should be made aware, too, he thought, but the men-at-arms had already left.

He sat on a stool in front of the fire in the great hall, bare-chested, while Jack and Kat competed to help him with his injury. Kat carefully bathed his wound, as Jack readied needle and thread.

Kat tried to snatch it from his hand. 'I'll do it.'

Jack held it away from her. 'I can do it. I've done it hundreds of times before.'

'Hardly hundreds,' Crispin muttered.

'But I'm a woman. I can do a finely wrought stitch that won't look like some ham-handed apprentice shored it up like a ship's rigging.'

Jack sputtered, apparently unable to come back at her with a rejoinder.

'If someone doesn't do it in the next few moments, I will do it myself!'

They both stared at Crispin until Jack relented and grudgingly handed it to Kat.

'I hope you have done this before,' said Crispin, girding himself.

'I did sew up a goose with its dressing once. How much different could it be?'

She jabbed in the needle and Crispin tensed and hissed. 'The difference is, Mistress Pyke, the damned goose was dead.'

'It's going to hurt no matter what. There's no use in crying about it.'

He curled his fingers into his knees as each stroke of the needle entered his flesh and pulled it taut with thread, grunting each time.

'Almost done, Master Guest,' she said, keeping her shadow out of the way of her stitches.

'She's right,' said Jack, standing watch over the proceedings. 'She does have a better stitch than me.'

'If it was only my cote-hardie, I wouldn't care,' he hissed.

'There. All done. You can stop being a baby about it.' She reached up and kissed his cheek, returning the remaining thread and needle to Jack, who stowed it away in his pouch.

He glanced sidelong at it, tested it by moving his arm, and felt each twinge of the needle and sword edge all over again. She wrapped the arm over the stitches in torn pieces of linen and then helped him ease into his chemise before handing him a cup of wine.

He drank it gratefully, even though it wasn't very good wine. 'Thank you for saving my life,' he said quietly.

'It wasn't all that hopeless.' She smiled.

'I'm afraid it was. I'm not as young nor as agile as I used to be.'

She looked at him steadily, solemnly, before the enormity of it seemed to fall away. 'The fight had gone on long enough,' she said matter-of-factly, straightening out his chemise and tsking at the slash and blood on the sleeve. 'We'll have to wash this.'

'It can wait. Master Palliser.' The caretaker moved to stand over him. 'Forgive me for accusing you, sir.'

He bowed. 'All is forgiven, Master Guest. Routing Sir Regis was almost as satisfying as hearing that Roger was dead. Almost.'

Crispin gave a lopsided grin and cocked his head in an answering bow.

'And now, Master Teague.'

'I am here, Master Guest. I have never seen the like. You are a warrior, sir, like the knights of old.'

'And I am feeling every bit like an ancient knight. But that's not what I wish to talk about. You, sir, assured me that you were not robbing graves.'

For the second time in the same evening, Carantok Teague seemed to have been struck dumb.

'Well? Did you lie to me? Regis is a turd, but there have been others mentioning that they saw bones in the "holes" you've dug. And you admitted as much earlier.'

He licked his lips. 'Master Guest, I can assure you that if graves they were, they were not Christian graves.'

'Dammit, man. They were still graves and forbidden to rob.'

'I was not robbing them. I object to that characterization. I was liberating ancient objects from pagan burials.'

Crispin drummed his fingers on his knee. 'No matter how you wish to define it, it comes to the same thing. You will cease this at once.'

Teague blustered, pulling himself up and placing a hand on his heart. 'Forgive me, Master Guest, but my business is my own.'

'No, sir, the law is everyone's business. You will cease it at once or I shall be forced to declare you to the coroner.'

'But . . . but Master Guest!'

'I am adamant on this. The things you find that are not found in burials . . . well. That is for you to keep, I suppose. But no more burial mounds. I want your oath on that, sir.'

Teague wore a sour expression, and he seemed to plead with Kat and Jack, but they remained stoic. Even Palliser said nothing. He sighed. 'Very well, Master Guest. I so swear. That has severely curtailed my plans, I'll have you know.'

'I don't care. And you will pay me in full upon our return to London.'

'Oh. Yes, of course . . . But wait. What about the—' He caught sight of Palliser and bit his lip. 'What about the stolen object?' he whispered.

'Oh, that. I will do my best to recover it before we leave, Master Teague.'

'Well . . . see that you do. That was our sole purpose for coming here, you will recall.'

'I do, and I shall do my best. But in the morning. I think the night has been full enough.'

'But . . . won't the trail be cold? Won't they have escaped completely into the night and out of Cornwall?'

Crispin groaned as he rose. Since his blood had cooled, his muscles, unused to such work, now made themselves known. 'I said, Master Teague, that I shall continue this on the morrow. Good night.'

'Oh. Well. Good night, then.'

Crispin walked past the man, Jack on one side of him, Kat on the other. He made his way slowly up the stairs and leaned on Kat as he got to his chamber. Jack hovered in the doorway. 'Then . . . I'll say good night too. Kat can see to you. I suppose.'

'Thank you, Jack.' He eased himself onto the edge of the bed as Jack closed the door behind him.

'Let's get you comfortable, Crispin.'

'I'm not an invalid.'

'Of course not.' She pulled the sheets aside so he could slide his legs in.

'Then why are you treating me like one?'

She looked at him for a silent moment and suddenly reached over and squeezed his shoulder. He gasped through his teeth. 'How's the shoulder?' she said, with a less-than-innocent smile.

'Damn you,' he mumbled.

'Then shut it and let me help you.'

He did, and, grudgingly, he admitted he was grateful for her ministrations. He lay propped against the pillows as he watched her disrobe. No, he decided. There were compensations after all.

'Are you done ogling me?' she said, climbing into bed beside him, on the side of his good arm.

He watched her with half-lidded eyes. 'I'm far from dead, demoiselle.'

She chuckled and blew out the candle. The room was still lit by the golden sky. It was likely the fire in the village. He hoped it did as much damage as possible.

When she finally scooted down and turned to him, he could gaze at her face, cheeks glazed by the faraway light. 'You came for me,' she said, eyes glittering.

'At first I thought you'd stolen the sword and run.'

She sat up. 'The sword is stolen? Is that what Carantok was whinging over?'

'Yes.'

'But I didn't take it.'

'I know.'

'How did you know where I'd been taken?'

'Strangely, Sir Regis informed me.'

'By the saints . . .'

'Yes.'

She eased back down where he could gaze at her again.

He reached forward to touch one of those flushed cheeks. It was soft under his fingertips. 'I'm glad I saved you, too.'

'We are a pair, aren't we?' She sighed.

'Two of a kind, in a way.'

She studied him in the gloom. He wondered what exactly it was she saw.

'Crispin, may I ask you something?'

'Of course.'

Kat touched her finger gently to his forehead to pull a strand of hair from his brow. 'Why were you so angry at the sword? At . . . Excalibur, if I may call it so. You seemed . . . incensed at it.'

Crispin looked away, not truly seeing the cobwebs in the corner rafters, or the moth fluttering at the dingy window. 'I wasn't exactly angry at it. I was . . .' He sighed. 'I was angry that I was undeserving of it. That I had *made* myself undeserving. It never occurred to me to keep it. I never would have done that. But when I held it . . . it seemed almost to speak to me. To tell me . . .'

She adjusted herself on the pillows, lightly stroking his hair, fingers threading through it. 'What did it say?' she whispered.

Her fingers in his hair, their quiet murmuring talk, almost seemed to make the memory of how Excalibur felt in his hand – for he knew without a shadow of a doubt that it was truly Excalibur – almost made the memory something otherworldly, as if it had happened to another. But it hadn't happened to another. It had happened to him. And that single instance when it spoke to him was also his alone. 'That . . . I was forgiven.'

Her lips parted just that much. He wanted to kiss them. But her gaze was intent, and just the softest breath of a sad sigh escaped them. 'And you wouldn't believe it?'

'I can't.'

'Oh, Crispin. If there was anyone who deserved forgiveness . . .'

'Do you know,' he said, shifting, lying back, trying to favor the sore shoulder. 'Do you know that King Richard forgave me?'

'What?'

He liked the arch of her brows as they rose over her widened eyes. He decided to touch them, trace them with his fingertips. 'Yes. He forgave me. He loved me, so he said. Didn't want me to die. I never knew that. I never even thought about him and the consequences had I succeeded. He'd have been killed, you know. You cannot leave an extra prince about, around whom supporters could rally. He'd have been killed if Lancaster had been put on the throne. And I never even gave it a thought. A ten-year-old boy.' His eyes captured hers. 'Do I truly deserve forgiveness?'

'You do. That was your younger self.'

'As if that makes a difference.'

'But it does! Look at you now. Look how much good you have done. Would you ever have become this Tracker, this righter of wrongs, if you had been in a Lancaster court?'

He stared up at the rafters again. 'I don't know.'

'Yes, you do. You wouldn't have. Your entire course has been changed.'

'Are you calling it fate?'

'I don't know what you call it. God, chance. But harken to me. So many people would have died, would have hanged without you to stop it. So much justice would have gone undone.'

Again, he turned to her and smiled. 'And you, my pretty little thief, would have hanged, no doubt.'

'No doubt.'

He leaned in to kiss her this time, those soft lips. And when he lay back again, still smiling, he touched her face, that blushing cheek, that pert chin. 'I am surrounded by Tuckers at home in London. And yet I am lonely. What would you say to coming back with me? I am not a pauper these days. We live a comfortable life, as much as anyone can in London. Why don't you come back . . . and marry me?'

Her face froze. She had been listening lazily, lids drooping as he caressed, a small smile tilting up the edge of her mouth. But that easy expression faded. 'You don't mean it.'

'I do. I'm tired of being a bachelor, Kat. We like each other, you and I. We understand each other. Marry me.'

'Crispin,' she breathed.

'It won't be dull.'

She let out a breathy chuckle, but it hadn't reached her eyes.

'Are you worried that we would starve? That we wouldn't have enough to live on? We do. Jack and I get by, and with some to spare should you need the occasional indulgence . . . as I know you do.'

'It isn't that,' she said in a small and unfamiliar voice. She leaned incrementally away, so that his caressing hand could no longer reach her. He let it flop to the bed.

'Then what?'

Her face was like the light of a flickering flame; quickly changing from one emotion to the next. At one point her eyes seemed to gloss. He sat up. 'What is it? Have I shocked you?'

'Yes, you have.' She brought her hands to her cheeks that seemed flushed and pink. 'You don't love me.'

'In time . . . I could. Just as you could love me . . . in time.'

Another chuckle filled with breath and she threw back her head, elongating an already long neck. 'I could be selfish and marry you,' she seemed to be saying to herself. 'I think . . . I think I want to be. Oh, Crispin. It is so very tempting.' For a moment, her face was lit with the possibility. But just as quickly, the light – the glow on her face – faded into the gloom. She looked down at her lap. 'Alas, I don't think I can do that to you.'

'Do what to me?'

She seemed to gird herself to face him squarely. She was devastatingly beautiful in that instance. The fireglow lit her generously, her hair hid her breasts just that much. He was tempted to take her in his arms and forget about the sadness that suddenly seemed to permeate her expression and tilt her shoulders, bring her down to his chest, and kiss and pet it all away.

But she kept just enough distance between them that told him not to try.

'Someone told me I'm not fit for you.'

He frowned, suspecting just who.

'But they're right, of course. I'm a thief. And . . . yes, a whore at times. I couldn't do that to you.'

'Kat . . .'

'You have a reputation in London. How could you uphold it married to me?'

He shook his head. 'I'd . . . I'd . . .'

'You'd overlook it? No one else would. No one cares about Jack's past. But they'd care about mine.' She seemed on the verge of tears before she shook out her hair, and suddenly raised her knees and clasped them over the blanket. 'And anyway, I'd just grow bored with married life. Did you expect me to bear your children? Me? I'd never want to be so tied down. I'd want to roam. To go places. To have the nice things I occasionally have, to be fawned over. I am not for you.'

He wanted to protest. But deep in his heart, he knew she was right. And it made him all the sadder. But he did sit up, edge toward her and put his good arm around her. Kissing the top of her head, he sighed. 'Well, it was a nice thought.'

She patted one of his hands. 'Yes, it was. And I thank you with all my heart for asking it.'

He leaned back on the pillows with her, and her tense body soon relaxed. They lay like that till she fell asleep in his arms. And he wondered, fleetingly, what it might have been like if they could have done that for the rest of their lives.

In the morning, dressed, with an arm stiff with aches and the occasional spike of pain, Crispin, accompanied by Kat and Jack, met Teague, who was already down in the great hall.

Jack found bread and cheese in the kitchens and brought it out to them, along with a jug of ale.

'Well, Master Crispin,' said Jack, slicing off a piece of the crusty bread. 'Have you any idea where we can look for Excalibur?' He shook his head. 'I can't believe I just said that.'

'Nor can I,' admitted Crispin. He chewed thoughtfully on his piece. 'Who could possibly have known it was there?'

'Someone might have seen us steal it into the hall,' said Kat. 'Someone on the battlements who we didn't notice.'

'Shipley?' suggested Crispin. He rolled the thought over in his mind. 'No, I can't see Shipley being particularly stealthy or clever.'

'It has to be him. Or . . . I suppose,' said Kat, 'it might be one of the men-at-arms. Sir Stephen, or Sir Arno. Who's left?'

'Who indeed?' Crispin rose. 'I'm only going for a walk. To think,' he said to the two of them, who rose halfway to their feet when Crispin did.

He hated to be treated like a weakling. This was only a scratch. He had plenty of them.

He passed under the front entry and walked along the courtyard till he came to a place he could climb the battlements. Once he'd reached the top, he had a wide view of the endless sea, of the land and the sprawling village of Treknow. Beyond that, he saw the forest, still intact, but there was smoke coming from where Prasgwig lay, black smoke. The village was paying its due and he hoped the county sheriff would put a stop to them completely. That village was done, and he felt satisfied with that.

But where was Excalibur? For whatever it truly was, he could think of it in no other way. He couldn't help but recall his

conversation with Kat last night, how the sword had made him feel
. . . But in the light of day, *had* the sword made him feel? That
would imply it had special powers.

'God's blood,' he breathed. Hadn't he dealt with enough objects
that made him feel in one way or another? What of Saint Modwena's
relic in the red cow? Or the bones of Saint Thomas Becket? He
laid his hand absently on his scrip. Or the Crown of Thorns?

Running a hand over his face, he looked out over the naked sea,
watched the blue green like a blanket with a restless sleeper beneath.

'It makes a man think, doesn't it?'

He refused to be startled by Marzhin Gwyls's sudden appearance.
He should have been used to the caretaker's ways. But he had jerked
just that much, cursed himself, and turned to the man. 'I should
have known you'd turn up eventually.'

'Of course. I'm a caretaker.'

'And to what extent are you beholden to your duties?'

The old man stood at the crenellation beside Crispin, leaning on
one hand while clutching his staff with the other. 'Very beholden,
my friend.'

'I wonder what exactly those duties are, sir. Do they involve
stealing the relics of the past?'

'Stealing? Can one steal what belongs to them?'

Crispin straightened. 'Do not prevaricate with me. You stole what
Carantok Teague was storing under his bed.'

'Well now. I'm a man who doesn't like to lie. And so I will tell
you true. I didn't steal anything. But I did take what lay beneath
Master Teague's bed.'

'Master Gwyls—'

'Crispin, may I tell you a story?'

'I don't think—'

'Hush, young man,' he said, raising a finger. For some reason,
Crispin didn't wish to speak at just that moment. 'I'm telling you
a story. You see, it was long ago. Isn't that how they start stories?
It was long, long ago. When this castle was young. And the halls
were filled with people and light and festivities and food and laughter.
Oh, there was laughter and gaiety, and much music. And then a
child was born. It is something to be celebrated in most households,
but in this one, that child was promised to a stranger. A *strange*
stranger. He did not harm the child, but instead had him raised
elsewhere, and, on occasion, he visited him as he grew to manhood.

And as with all men born to noble households, there came a time when that boy needed a sword. And the strange stranger provided it. The boy merely had to pull it from . . . a stone.'

Crispin snorted, about to speak, when Gwyls raised a finger again, and Crispin sighed and leaned back against the battlement.

Gwyls smiled and leaned further on the crenellation, rubbing his chin and its beard as he looked out to sea. 'That boy . . . well, I suppose that *man* did great things with that sword. But there also came a time when he grew old, and tired. And that sword had to be put away, for the man had had no faithful heir. And the strange stranger took that sword and hid it away so no one could find it. In fact, he moved it many times to make certain of it. Finally, he brought it back home where that child was born on that long-ago day, and he put it in what he believed was a very safe place.' He glanced at Crispin with a startlingly blue eye. 'And then that place was found.'

Crispin sighed. 'And you are trying to tell me that you are that strange stranger and not a greedy man who wishes to sell a valuable object?'

'I am saying nothing of the kind. That's absurd, of course. All I am saying is that I am a caretaker and this object you are looking for came from Tintagel and must stay at Tintagel. You mustn't worry over it more.'

'I'm very much afraid I must worry. For it belongs to my employer.'

The old man chuckled. 'No, it doesn't belong to him. Not to treasure seekers. The treasures found here should be kept here. After all, if they wanted to travel, then they *would* have. The dead need their belongings, Master Guest. This is their resting place, and the things they held dear belong here as well. Besides, only the worthy may find Excalibur.'

'Were we talking of Excalibur?'

Gwyls smiled as he looked out to sea again. 'Are we?'

'Look, I will say nothing. If you return it forthwith, I will not tell anyone that it was you. Fair enough?'

'As I said, Crispin – may I call you so? Only the worthy may find Excalibur. And definitely only the worthy may keep it. Or so the tales say. Are *you* worthy?'

'I didn't find it. My apprentice and my employer did.'

'A minor matter. *Petitio principii.* You had it in your possession. Are you worthy?'

Crispin remembered the glory and the pain of holding it. He

swallowed a lump in his throat. 'Alas, no, Master Gwyls. I am far from worthy. I *was* a knight but I have no right to sit with the others at the Round Table. Arthur's own words would condemn me. For I have betrayed my king.'

'Ah yes. But did not Arthur's greatest knight and fast friend betray *his* king?'

'I am no Launcelot either, I'm afraid.'

'We all have our own paths. If you had kept the sword, what would you have done with it?'

'I didn't keep it. I surrendered it to my employer as I was hired to do.'

'But if circumstances had changed, and *you* possessed it, then what?'

He shook his head. 'I don't know. I should never have sold it, that much I know. Vanity? Keep it for vanity's sake? I don't know that either. In any case, do *you* know where it is?'

'Here. Tintagel.'

'Come now, sir. If you have it, you must return it. It is not your property.'

'And neither is it Carantok Teague's.'

'Nevertheless, he is now the owner and I demand you return it.'

Gwyls leaned out over the battlements again. 'I'm certain he will be adequately compensated.'

'That isn't what I asked.'

'Crispin, let us not leave each other under these circumstances. I'd much rather be your friend than your enemy.'

With a sigh, Crispin joined him again and leaned beside him. 'As would I, sir.'

'Good, good. Then go back into the hall, and tell Master Teague that all will be well.'

'You'll return it, then?'

'All will be well, Master Guest.' He smiled and turned back toward the sea.

He hesitated. But in the end, Crispin had no choice but to climb back down and face Teague. He wasn't about to manhandle the old man. If Gwyls had the sword, he wasn't going to sell it or trade it. He seemed genuinely concerned that it should stay hidden and part of the unearthed treasures of Tintagel. And, frankly, Crispin could see nothing wrong with that. He couldn't stand the notion that some fat merchant might display it in his hall.

He came to the constable's lodgings again, and the others looked up as he entered.

'Well?' asked Jack. 'Do we go searching now? Where do we begin?'

'About that. Master Teague, I think that the sword is well and truly lost this time.'

'What! But . . . I hired you to help me find it.'

'And find it you did. And possessed it for nearly half a night.'

Teague trembled in his anger. 'Master Guest, you very well know that this is not good enough.'

'And you must very well know, that this is all you can expect.'

'This is a conspiracy. You've plotted to steal the sword with some associate here.'

Before Crispin could speak, Jack had cornered Teague and backed him up to the wall. 'You had better apologize for that insult, Master Teague, or I will see that you suffer for it.'

'What?'

'I wouldn't argue with Master Tucker, Carantok,' said Kat, scrupulously studying her nails. 'He's terribly protective of Master Guest. As am I.'

'But . . . I . . . I *had* it . . .' he whinged.

'And now you don't.' She offered him a condoling smile. 'It happens to the best of us. But this might make you feel a little better.' She tossed him something which he caught. When he opened his hand, it was the brooch.

Crispin stared at her. 'How the devil did you get that?'

'It's witchcraft, is what it is,' said Jack.

'Don't be ridiculous,' she said.

Crispin wasn't so sure.

'This is not compensation,' said Teague, turning over the little bauble, his eyes gleaming just that much.

'At this point, Teague,' said Crispin, 'I truly don't care. Take it up with the caretaker.'

'He's the one who's got my sword? That Palliser fellow?'

'It's not your sword,' said Crispin, with surprising vehemence. He calmed himself enough to say, 'No, not Palliser. The other caretaker.'

Teague looked at him strangely. 'Other caretaker? There is no other caretaker.'

'Oh, come now. I've talked to him several times. I just now left him on the battlements.'

'Master Guest, I have been here a number of times, and I tell you there is only one caretaker, John Palliser.'

'Master Crispin,' Jack began. 'Who are you talking about, sir? I've seen no one else here but the porter, the chaplain, and the men-at-arms.'

'Not you too. It's that man who seems to linger everywhere we go, with his many questions and puzzling statements.'

'Who?'

'Confound it, Tucker. I mean Marzhin Gwyls.'

'I don't know that name, sir. I've not heard the others mention him.'

'Surely you've seen him. He wears a long beard, carries a staff, long gown. A Cornish man.'

They all looked at Teague, who had suddenly burst out laughing. 'Someone is pulling your leg, Master Guest. And a good jest it is, if that man has my . . . has the sword.'

Impatient, Crispin put his hands on his hips. 'And why do you say that?' Had he been fooled by a beguiling old man? He was beginning to have his regrets about *not* manhandling him.

'Well . . . that's a Cornish name, right enough. It means . . . Myrddin the Wild. A very old name for . . . Merlin.'

They packed up their things. Teague decided that he would stay on to try to recoup his losses, now that Crispin had convinced him – mad man or no – that he wasn't getting the sword back. He counted out the rest of their pay and seemed grudgingly cheerful again. 'Master Guest, I suppose you were right. It wasn't nearly as exciting owning the thing as searching for it. I must admit . . .' He laughed, shaking his head. 'I haven't had such a good time in a long while. This will make a fine story to tell, I'll wager.'

'That it will, sir. But if you aren't returning to London, what shall we do with the horses?' asked Crispin. 'Sell them, and send the money to you here?'

'Nonsense!' He took Crispin's hands in both his own. 'I tell you what you shall do, Master Guest. You keep them. As further payment to you.'

Crispin jerked back in surprise. 'Master Teague! You don't mean it. That is . . . that is much too generous.'

'I've got my baubles, Master Guest. Oh, more than I expected.'

He tossed the brooch in the air and caught it, closing his hand into a fist. 'This is worth more than a couple of horses.'

'But—'

'Master Guest.' He seemed abashed all of a sudden, and brought up a solemn expression. 'Consider it the pay you deserve. You and your man Jack achieved much. You found a murderer and brought him to justice. And I owe you more. Take the horses. A man like you should have horses.'

Humbled, Crispin thanked the man again and a shocked Jack did likewise. Horses! Never in a thousand years did he imagine he'd ever own horses again. Immediately, he began to ponder if they could build a covering for Tobias and Seb in the back garden beside the chicken coop, for they could not afford to board them.

Proud that Tobias was his – and he patted the horse's neck in true affection – Crispin looked back over the crumbling battlements, the sorry gatehouse, searching for that strange, lone man. Merlin, indeed! Had he been a mere invention of Crispin's imagination? Surely not. He'd talked to him several times. He seemed as solid as the rock Tintagel was built upon. Though . . . even as he watched, he witnessed more rocks let loose from the land-bridge and tumble into the sea.

He said nothing more about it as he and Kat rode on the back of Crispin's mount to Treknow. The village was abuzz with the tidings that Prasgwig had gone up in smoke, and its people scattered. No one knew how it had caught fire or where the people had disappeared to.

Crispin wanted Kat to at least return to London with them but she declined. She climbed off the horse and stood beside it, resting her hand on Crispin's leg and looked up at him. 'I thank you for offering – *all* that you offered,' she said softly, 'but I think I will stay with the players for a while. Besides, I think I have another tale to tell them that we might perform.'

'Jezebel?' said Jack, but his smile said he meant it as a jest.

She scrunched her nose at him. 'No. A tale of a gallant knight, who saved a fair maiden. Along with his squire, of course.'

Jack bowed.

'Just don't use my name,' said Crispin.

'Oh, I wouldn't dream of it. Farewell, dear, dear Crispin. God keep you.'

'And you too . . . fair maiden.'

She blew him a kiss and he smiled, watching her skip across the green toward the colorfully painted wagon.

'I was surprised she wouldn't come with us,' said Jack.

'I was surprised too,' said Crispin. He turned his mount, and headed toward London.

It took less than a fortnight, but they finally returned to the Shambles with more gold in their pockets than they had ever had before. Isabel was overjoyed to see Jack again, and kissed and kissed him. The children, too, were happy to see their father, but Crispin was most surprised to find that they were even happier to see *him* again, climbing all over him, pleading to be picked up.

And they all fairly glowed at the prospect of the two horses. The children gathered around them as if they'd owned them all their lives, leading them to the back garden and petting and cooing to them. Crispin realized those horses would be the most spoiled beasts in all of London.

It was good to be home, he decided, and later, that night, lying in his bed and thinking about Kat, Gyb jumped up onto the mattress and made his way to Crispin, standing on his chest. 'Did you miss me, too, you old tom?'

The aging black and white cat settled in, fluffing into a mound atop him. Crispin didn't mind. He felt the deep purr as he stroked the beast. 'I'm afraid it's just you and me, Gyb. I tried to get you a mistress. But . . . alas. I suppose in the end she was right. I couldn't very well take to wife a known thief. She was looking out for my best interests. But . . . dammit.' He hadn't realized how lonely he had become until the last chance to get a wife – a woman who would truly understand him – slipped through his fingers.

The cat rose, walked off his chest and curled into a bun, nestled up against his side. The coals glowed in the hearth, and the night descended around them like a velvet mantle.

But Crispin didn't sleep.

AFTERWORD

I s there a real Arthur? Where to begin! Historians have been chasing their tails on this for centuries. Welsh and Irish folklore are full of the kind of fantastic tales that begged to be folded into something like the Arthur legend. In the Welsh tales, Arthur was a pagan who moved through a magical realm. In later Welsh and Irish mythology, Arthur seems to be a semi-divine figure that easily transitions to the later medieval chivalric romances where the Knights of the Round Table could slip easily into the story.

A ninth-century Welsh cleric called Nennius was the first to wrestle the varying Arthur stories into one narrative, though he cheated a bit by wedging Arthur into the history between the end of Roman Britain and his own time period. Nennius's Arthur was not a king but a Christian warrior, waging war against the pagans.

But with the popularity of Tristan and Isolde, in Cornwall the focus was on King Mark rather than King Arthur. The court of Tristan and Isolde was said to be at Tintagel.

In the 1100s, Geoffrey of Monmouth, who lived near Wales and no doubt heard these tales, began his *History of the Kings of Britain*. And he built up Arthur as the King of British Kings.

The history of Arthur, from the French, Irish, Welsh, Cornish, and Breton tales, combined him with an amalgamation of the mythological characters of gods, nymphs – even wizards – and perhaps a fluttering of real people. To keep Crispin up to date in the fourteenth century, he only knew of Arthur through Geoffrey of Monmouth. What *we* know about Arthur generally comes from Thomas Mallory's *Le Morte d'Arthur* (on which the musical *Camelot* was based) from 1470, well after Crispin's time. And Tennyson's *Idylls of the Kings* is even later. So put yourself in the fourteenth century, when these stories were actual histories to the medieval mind, not fairy tales. The 'real' Arthur – one single man – likely never existed, but we may never know.

Tintagel is a real place. Some sort of fortress has been there since 700 CE. It was true that Prince Edward – the Black Prince as we know him – attempted to restore it, but no one knows quite why it was never brought back to its former glory. It had a complement of a caretaker, a few men-at-arms, a porter, a chaplain, and a constable. All that is true.

And as for treasure hunters, we need to say a few words about that. It was illegal in England to dig up barrows or even look for treasure in those days. In Germany, the thirteenth-century law book *Schwabenspiegel* was a little more liberal when it came to treasure hunting. Three-quarters of the find should go to the owner of the land on which it was found and a quarter to the actual finder. The king was not entitled to any of it, unless it was found on a public highway, which belonged to the crown.

But according to the English laws on troves since Edward the Confessor's time, all gold belonged to the king, full stop. If it was silver and found on Church property, it was divided up equally between Church and crown. By 1276, investigating treasure troves fell under the jurisdiction of the coroner. It was forbidden to be in active searches for treasure. So Carantok's charter was extremely generous.

By Henry VIII's time, they seemed to have gotten more concerned with the practice of witchcraft to find treasure, specifically with the help of demons (where's a helpful demon when you need one?). Harsh penalties were executed on: '*dyvers and sundrie personnes [who] unlawfully have devised and practiced Invocacons and conjuracons of Sprites, pretending by such meanes to understand and get Knowledge for their own lucre in what place treasure of golde and Silver shulde or might be founde or had in the earthe or other secrete places.*'

As for the chapel, it is indeed there on the island but the altar is, uh, unaltered, with no bump-outs in the back of it. My fiction.

And what about druids? Crispin and his contemporaries only knew what Julius Caesar wrote about people he called the *druidae* (always plural). The word druid or *druw* in Cornish means "oak knower," which I find wonderfully lyrical. Caesar observed that they were most notably in charge of public events, as priests were in most cultures of the time, and presided over sacrifices. And these sacrifices were often human. They seemed to prefer criminals, though the occasional innocent would do in a pinch. They created wicker mannikins to enclose them and burned them. We only have Caesar's word for it, since the early people of Britain had no written records.

Crispin is coming soon to the end of his tale. Sad, I know, but all good things must come to an end. I always had in mind that his story would have an end point, and we are almost there. I'd like to thank my agent, Joshua Bilmes, for standing up for Crispin all these years. I think he'll be sorry to see him go as well.

The next book is the penultimate, *Spiteful Bones*. A skeleton is found in the wall of a lawyer's house and is believed to be a missing servant from twenty years prior. But is the heinous crime of so long ago only a precursor of what is to come?

If you liked this book, please review it. See more about the Crispin series and other historical novels at JeriWesterson.com.